Divine
Endurance

Divine Endurance

Endurance

by
GWYNETH JONES

ARBOR HOUSE
NEW YORK

Manufactured in the United States of America

10 9 8 7 6 5 4 3 2 1

Library of Congress Cataloging-in-Publication Data

Jones, Gwyneth A.
    Divine endurance.

    I. Title.
PR6060.05163D5   1987   823'.914   86-17440
ISBN 0-87795-856-4

My dear Achmed – When we were on our travels, PG and I had an ignorant passion for mountains. We would see, from the bus, an indigo cone rising out of the sawah and the palm groves, near enough to touch – Instantly we were desperate to climb. So we would set out, on foot into the green fields. Many hours later, hot and battered and bitten: gorge-fallen, river-drowned, we would emerge from our violent ascent and there would be the mountain, untouched, except perhaps now at a different angle, or behind us. We would console ourselves for having attempted the impossible and that night in the village someone would tell us about the summit trip – starting from somewhere unexpected, miles away from our vision. So we would go there, very dubiously, and then everything fell into place. . . . Producing DE was just like that, and I have the same feeling now: of astonishment mixed with a definite resentment at having to give up my glorious defeat. So I want to dedicate this book to you (and one other) because you were there, and suffered far above and beyond the calls of friendship at that first absurd departure, years ago. Selamat. G.

For T. 27 Sept 1981. 'In autumn, of all the seasons – '

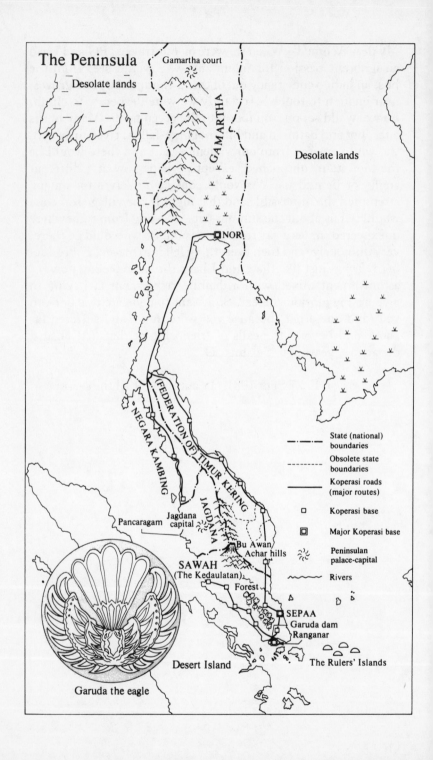

The Peninsula

Desolate lands

Gamartha court

GAMARTHA

Desolate lands

☐ NOR

(FEDERATION OF TIMUR KERING)

NEGARA KAMBING

JAGDANA

Pancaragam

Jagdana capital

Bu Awan
Achar hills

SAWAH
(The Kedaulatan)

Forest

SEPAA
Garuda dam
Ranganar

The Rulers' Islands

Desert Island

Garuda the eagle

	State (national) boundaries
	Obsolete state boundaries
	Koperasi roads (major routes)
☐	Koperasi base
▣	Major Koperasi base
	Peninsulan palace-capital
	Rivers

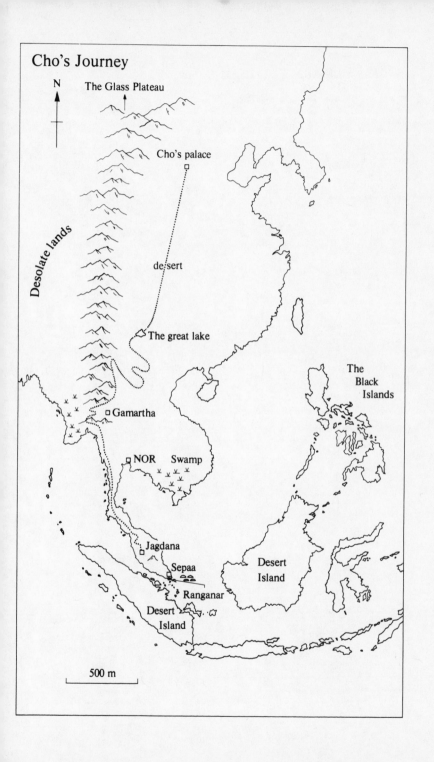

Cho's Journey

N

The Glass Plateau

Cho's palace

Desolate lands

de sert

The great lake

The Black Islands

Gamartha

NOR Swamp

Jagdana

Sepaa

Ranganar

Desert Island

Desert Island

500 m

Contents

Prologue: In the Rock Gardens

To the east of the palace there were extensive rock gardens, where it was pleasant to walk at different seasons of the year, and admire the changing light on the twisted and fantastic shapes of the rocks. It was especially pleasant to plan carefully and reach the gardens at dawn, so that you could watch the rock creatures take shape out of the dark, and then the sun coming up. From this vantage point the first light seemed to rise straight out of the glass basin far away across the plains, and the dawn colours were beautiful. The Empress learned that the Emperor had decided on such an outing, and she made her preparations.

There was a small hillock in the centre of the gardens that suited her purpose well. When she reached the place she climbed up it carefully, following the smooth steps worn into the rock by countless pilgrimages of admiration. She did not pause at the viewing point but began at once to descend the gentler eastern slope. The Emperor would come exactly this way, straight into the white risen sun. About halfway down she found a satisfactory arrangement: a twisted horn of stone at ankle height on one side of the path, and a tough-stemmed shrub on the other. She sat down slowly just above; turned up the hem of her embroidered gown onto her lap and picked at it with her fingernails.

It was hard work, because her fingers were weak and withered but the gown was still in excellent condition. She paused frequently to sigh and stare out over the landscape, rubbing her cramped fingers. She had no personal feeling against the Emperor. She was thinking it would be nice for him to see the dawn one last time. Lost in the grand, stiff folds of her beautiful clothes she sat there unpicking her hem and carefully winding up the thread: what seemed like the dry skin and bones of a shrunken old woman. All around her stretched the silent gardens: black rock arches and spires and waves and broken bubbles, like a pot of boiling liquid suddenly frozen. Where a little earth had crusted over the lava small-leaved shrubs grew, some as tall as trees and some blossoming yellow and scarlet. Like the Empress's robes, the flowers were young, but like the Empress the stunted trees were old, very old, with riven trunks and knotted arthritic roots. It was a harmonious scene, with the bright shapes of the rocks and the bright flowers decorating what was solid, rugged and ancient; but it was haunted, especially away towards the east. There, where the gardens faded into dust and quieter stones, there were strange shadows: a tall curve too smooth to be weathered glimpsed between the branches of a tree; an occasional eruption from the crumpled lava that appeared too straight and sleek for nature. The Empress, when she paused and sighed, seemed to be looking sadly at these ghosts.

She was still sitting there at work when a small figure appeared down below, trotting about between the rocks and obviously looking for someone.

'Bother – ' said the Empress, and the Cat – for sound travelled well on the dry air – pricked her ears and came hurrying up the slope. Perched on top of a boulder, she observed what the Empress was doing with the strong thread and her tail twitched against the rock in exasperation.

'I might have known you were up to no good,' she said. 'I might have known you weren't coming to your senses.'

The Cat did not speak in the ordinary sense but the Empress understood her perfectly. 'It has to be done,' she answered, testing her knots. 'I have thought about it seriously and there is no other way of being secure.'

The Cat's tail beat a tattoo. 'It is self-destructive. It is wicked. It is wicked enough to destroy Emp, but how long do you think you will last without him? Dislike him as you may at least he is *incident*. You'll die of boredom, and it will be suicide.'

'I know it is wicked, Divine Endurance,' said the Empress patiently. 'And it upsets me very much. But there is an overriding imperative here.'

She tugged at the snare once more, nodded in satisfaction and struggled to her feet. 'You won't tell Emp though, will you?'

The Cat just glared angrily and refused to reply. But she would not tell. It would go completely against her nature. She would probably be here hiding behind a rock on the fatal morning, watching fascinated to see what would happen. The Empress stepped off down the path, holding up the front of her gown so she would not trip on the unravelled hem. The Cat stayed behind. She went and patted the trap with her paw; the thread was quite invisible against the dusty rock, and very strong. After examining it thoroughly she stalked away, in the opposite direction from the Empress and with her tail still waving angrily.

Divine
Endurance

PART ONE

My stone doesn't belong to me
It belongs to the government
Or God.
But I know that nobody
Cared for it before
Me, the one who found it.
                    Bettina Pfoestech

*My name is Divine Endurance. I am feminine. I am twenty-five
small units high at the shoulder, and sixty-two small units long
from nose to tail tip. I am independent and it is therefore the
more flattering when I respond to affection. I am graceful, agile
and especially good at killing things prettily. I live with the
Empress and the Emperor. There are only three of us now.
Once there were more of them: more Empresses and Emperors,
and other names too, but things have been running down for a
long time and gradually people fade away and one sees them no
more. But I have never liked bustle, and I was perfectly happy
until our troubles began. We have a pleasant life. We have our
extensive palace, and our gardens where the light is always
changing. We have outings to view the sunset and the dawn and
the moon; we have lizards and flowers, warm rocks and cool
shadows. There are certain restrictions: for instance, we are not
supposed to go outside the gardens. But most of the time
keeping the rules is simply common sense. I have explored the
way to the glass basin, but the air down there smells horrible,
and the light makes one's head ache. I have also been out
towards the glass plateau, which is a shiny line on the sky to the
west of our palace, but I found nothing of interest, only a few
dirty places where some passing nomads had been camping. We
are not to go near these people. If ever somebody wants one of
us they will approach through the proper channels, and with
some ceremony no doubt. Meanwhile, if the gypsies come too
close to the palace (they don't often dare) we simply think
discouraging thoughts and make ourselves scarce.*

*I should say that there is one rule that the Empress and the
Emperor obey, which I ignore because it is just silly. When one
of them grows past the point of being a child, they start taking
what they call medicine. It is an effluent from the Controller.
Once, when we all stayed inside, they used to line up and the
Controller would give it to them in little cups out of a wall. But I
think the wall or the cups faded away, and now they just drink it
from their hands. It does them nothing but harm. The effects
are slow but horrible. Their hair falls out, their muscles waste
away, their skin grows flabby and their teeth crumble. Eventually some accident happens and the victim is too weak to
recover, and that is the end. If they waited till they were
properly grown up it would do them no harm – if they must have
the stuff, but they won't. I do not remember ever being told to
take this medicine. I do not know why they keep on doing it.*

I think it was because of the medicine that I encouraged Em and Emp when they began to talk about a baby. They were both beginning to look quite sickly, and I do not think I would like to live entirely alone. They could not decide which kind of baby to have – they can never agree about anything – so they wanted one of each. I thought that two was excessive and would spoil our quiet times, but they went to the Controller anyway. There we had a shock: the Controller said we could only have one baby, because there was only one baby ability left. This was startling. It had seemed, I suppose, that things could go on running down forever and never completely stop. Could it be twins? asked Em. That's not allowed, said the Controller. We did not ask for the one baby to be started. We came away disappointed. But Em (I should have paid more attention) was thinking, privately and hard.

As I know, from my expeditions, nobody can actually prevent us if we want to disobey. When the Controller said 'that's not allowed' rather than 'not possible' I should have known what Em would do. Anyway, she did it. She went down into the Controller's entrails and made it do what it should not. It was wrong of her of course, but we have been left to our own devices for so long it is not at all fair to expect 'not allowed' to be enough, without any explanation.

The first I knew of Em's naughtiness at this point was that two hatches in the Controller began to go milky, and in a little while we could see the babies growing inside. This was a very strange sight, after so long. It was so interesting that Emp soon forgot to be shocked, and I to be displeased. We picked names. We made them up ourselves, we didn't see why not. Something simple and boyish for Emp's choice: Worthy to be Beloved. The girl's name was subtler: Chosen Among the Beautiful – implying 'chosen to be the best of the best', without quite saying so. We took sides and laid small bets on which was taking shape faster. We spent whole days just watching.

But Em had done wrong, and gradually it began to affect her. She stopped coming to see the babies. She hid herself away and brooded. Emp had a bad conscience too. He sat with his baby still, but now he was always sighing and sniffing. 'Poor little mite,' I heard him mutter. 'We should never have started this. What a life . . . ! To make matters worse the weather was very unsettled. We do not usually have to suffer anything tiresome, like excessive wind or rain, but just now a lot of dust and sand got into the air and started blowing about; the sky was obscured and there were unpleasant smells. It was like being at the glass basin. Then one day there was an earth tremor. It was an unusual one because the disturbance seemed to start near at hand, rather than off somewhere in the distance. I was sitting with Em, in a distant quarter of the palace, trying to cheer her up. We were both a little shaken. A crowd of bats pelted squeaking from a dark passage beyond Em's corner, and three big lizards ran out of the wall. Em got up. 'It's no good,' she muttered, 'I will have to stop it.'

I ignored the lizards – I am very fond of Em – and followed her out of the room, trying to make her see that an earth tremor is harmless and she was being silly. She was stumbling on the uncertain ground on her poor wasted legs. I must admit I thought her mind was upset. Anyway I went with her, at her slow pace, to the Controller. There we found that one of the hatches had been torn open, and the boy baby was gone.

'It wasn't an earth tremor,' said Em. 'It was the Controller. We have frightened it.'

She was very distressed. Not understanding, I assured her that the baby would have been nearly ready; it wouldn't be harmed. But she insisted that we start searching for Emp at once. We could not find him. We searched and searched for days, but he did not reappear. He had gone right away from the palace, which is not allowed. Now I realised what Em had somehow guessed all along: something serious had happened. It was difficult for us to follow him because Em moves so badly nowadays, but eventually we found his trail leading to the west. There, out in the wilderness, we found the dirty camp. It was already abandoned. They never stay anywhere long, but events had left enough of an impression for us to know beyond doubt what Emp had done. He had stolen our baby, taken it out of our world, and given it away to the gypsies.

There was nothing we could do, so we returned to the palace. Em was so angry she wouldn't talk to me. She tried to get the Controller to take her baby back – anything rather than let Emp have it, I suppose. The Controller was unresponsive. So the baby stayed behind the hatch, which was clear and filmy now, so the poor thing should have been taken out. And Em stayed inside the Controller, on guard. Meanwhile I discovered Emp, lurking in the north-east apartments. But he was unrepentant, so there seemed no hope of making up the quarrel. He even wanted me to get Em to give her baby away as well. Em, on the other hand, would not listen to any of my suggestions. When I said I would get Emp to swear solemnly to leave her baby alone

4

she just stared at me scornfully. However, I persevered, trying to make peace and restore our former pleasant existence. When Em began to ask me how the Emperor was passing his time these days, I thought I was succeeding.

I know better now, and now there are only two of us. She came looking for me, when it was over and we both knew he was gone. She said she wanted to explain herself. She took me down into the Controller's insides. There are ways in, in the broken area in the south-east of the palace, but I hadn't bothered to go there for a very long time. Down we went, into the big shining places. I do not know what she had to say to me that was so private. After all, we are quite alone now. We went in where the pipe comes out, where they drink the medicine. Some Empress or Emperor long ago made that, in the days when we first realised we were allowed to live outside so long as we did not stray too far.

It is strange, inside the Controller. For some reason it takes a lot of room to make the first drop of baby. The darkness and the shining goes away, far away. I can't explain it. Nobody ever walked here but us, when we got out of the boxes and began to walk about all on our own. . . .

'Look around you,' she said. 'And think.'

She had brought us past the impressive places, which I rather like. I like to think that they couldn't get in that part, even if they did make it. We were in a long thin place, behind the arrangement that posts the drops of baby into the hatches up above. A box-room in fact. The empty boxes lined the walls, one on top of another. There were no doors to this place. They never used to let us have doors, apparently, or windows, or anything to look at. It is not that I need a door, but it would have been more polite, I think.

'I don't like this,' I said. 'I prefer outside.'

'So do I,' she answered. 'This place makes one feel so small, doesn't it?'

She was silent for a while. I felt she was trying to make the box-room talk to me, but I declined to get the message. Eventually she said: 'None of us was ever to leave the palace without a home to go to. It isn't right. What do you suppose will happen when that little baby grows up?'

I said – it was fairly obvious – 'Well, he'll do his best to be useful, I'm sure.'

'To whom?'

I saw what she was getting at. If he tried to make himself

5

useful to everyone around him at once it might be rather confusing.

'We were the best,' murmured Em. 'We were the most wonderful: you and I and Emp who is dead, and all our model. There was nothing we could not do, if our person asked us. They valued us above anything, and cared for us dearly. Which is why, of course, we survived when all the world was swept away. We could give them anything they wished for. . . . '

I don't care for this sort of conversation. I think it is pointless. I maintained a discouraging silence, but she still went on.

'It was very wrong of me to make the Controller give us twins. There have never been twins. How will they work? What effect will they have on each other? The Controller was frightened, and so am I. Do you see why I had to do what I did? I dared not risk the second baby going after the first. I could not.'

I understand these urges: the longing we all have to find a purpose in life, the hope that somehow stays that we will be needed, wanted again. For myself, I take no notice. We're alone now, and we've been alone a long time. We have a right to live our own lives. I was past caring exactly why Em killed Emp, but I could see she was upset so I tried to reassure her, telling her little Worthy to be Beloved would be the best thing that ever happened to the gypsies. He'd make sure they all lived happily ever after. What harm could he do?

Em said, 'What harm indeed? He is not a weapon, he can't be used like that. Of course he must do his best to make them all happy. And his best is perfect. . . . '

But she spoke in a very odd tone of voice (so that I felt suddenly interested). And then, after a pause, she added softly:

'Has it ever occured to you, Divine Endurance, that whatever swept the world away it happened soon after our model . . . first left the palace?'

There was a silence then, shivering and dark. I wanted to get back outside. Em said, 'Emp wasn't wicked. He had gone mad, I think, and imagined it was a real baby. He must have been taking more medicine than me.'

I did not like the look in her eyes. I did not like the way she was moving, so frail and wavery. Suddenly I realised something that had been obscured by the excitement of Emp's death. I saw my future.

'All right,' I said. 'You don't like the baby. We'll forget about it. We'll make the Controller turn that hatch grey again, and it will be gone, as good as. We'll go out and see the sunset on the*

6

glass plateau. *I know where there's an interesting lizard. . . .*
Only don't, please don't, take any more medicine. . . . '

We've argued about that medicine so often. Once it was for
those of us who had no place in the world, so they would not be a
permanent embarrassment. A sign goes on, from the hatch that
hatched them, and they have to start taking the medicine, if they
are still here. But where's the embarrassment now? I told her:
'Look at me. Disobeying that order is easy.' She smiled and
said: 'Cat, they were too successful when they made a Cat.
That's why there are no others of you; that's why they never let
you go, but kept you here to laugh at them and be a warning.
You are too good at slipping under the locked doors in your
mind. . . . '

She smiled and shook her head as she had always done. This
was not the first Em I had argued with, there had been many
(the clothes are nearly the same). . . . This was the last. She
said, 'That's what I meant by bringing you down here. I wanted
to remind you what we really are. I can't disobey, Cat. I can't.
And why should I, anyway. What reason have we to live,
without them? . . . '

She wanted me to join in her huge vague grieving, but I could
not. She turned away from me with a lonely look: I knew she
was going to abandon me and I felt angry and helpless. We left
the inside of the Controller and went our separate ways.

Soon after this conversation the Empress's mind began to
fail, so it was really uncomfortable to be near her. She took
herself off into complete seclusion, and I did not see her any
more. One of the last things I got her to do for me was to take the
second baby out of the hatch because, I complained, I was going
to be very lonely. She did not say anything further about the
wrong and danger. I think she was already too unwell to
consider such things. Or perhaps, as our weather continues
extremely unsettled, she thinks the problem will be solved in
another way. As for me, I am recording my story, deep in my
mind. Em claims that the Controller is hidden somehow in
there, and I would like to think a representative of those people
who abandoned us knows – what I intend to do.

7

1   Chosen Among the Beautiful

When Cho was still quite a little girl there was a day when the Cat told her to go to sleep. It was a game she hadn't played before, but the infant curled herself up willingly, and went into the new experience with her head pillowed on a hollow stone and her knees tucked up to her chin. She slept. When she woke up she lay still for a while, bemused by the curious things that had just been happening. She was surprised to find her legs and arms in exactly the same places as before she left the room. She sat up and looked at the soles of her feet. They were clean, and there were no marks on her clothes either. They must have tidied themselves very quickly, she thought. It was puzzling. She decided she must ask the Cat about it, and set out to find her.

The little girl's rooms were in the north-east wing of the palace. She left them and pattered about the dusty forecourts peering into passages and doorways, until she realised the Cat was in the gardens. She set off in that direction. It was a day when the wind was blowing the sand about a good deal so she had to run carefully, for she knew the Cat would be cross if she put her foot in a hole and hurt herself. At last her pattering feet brought her to where the rock creatures were gathered, wearing their hats and cloaks of crusted red and white sand. Now she was distracted, because the Cat did not approve of this place for some reason, and so Cho had never seen the rock garden close up. She went from one to another, admiring the weird shapes and poking holes in the sand crust with her little fingers. The wind was quite strong; occasionally she looked up rather anxiously at the low, tossing sky. She knew it would be wrong to be outside in a storm. But she forgot everything else when she saw the hand. It was peeping out of a red mound, up on the

8

side of a little hill. She ran up and crouched over it, fascinated. It was a very good hand, because the bones were still held together by skin; even the jewelled nail-guards were still in place. 'You are the best dead hand I have ever seen,' said Cho to the relic. She scratched in the crust of the mound, and found a sleeve. It was a beautiful colour, with shining embroidery. She found a foot too, but the foot was not so interesting. It had lost its leg, and lost its slipper. There was something tangled up in the little bones, a thin fine line of something. She tugged and the mound stirred, as if the dead person felt it. Cho laughed, but immediately frowned at herself childishly, and dropped the thread. She had been told often enough that she must not play with these piles of clothes and bones when she found them. She looked up and all around. Withered roots and skeletons of dead trees stood dismally among the rocks, blased by the unsettled weather, and the bright twisted lava was losing its attractions between the scouring and obscuring of the sand. Cho was too young to regret the changes, but she had begun to feel that the Cat was somewhere close, and not in a good temper. What have I done wrong? she wondered. She started to climb the rest of the little hill.

At the top there was a flat space in a ring of boulders. Drifts of sand had collected between them, and gathered in their smooth hollows: nobody had climbed to sit and watch the dawn for quite a while. Cho saw the Cat; a hump of brown fur down on the ground. Right beside her was another of those tumbled heaps of clothes. Cho could see the yellowish round of a bare scalp within the wide collar; she could see a little shrivelled hand. The Cat seemed to be playing with it – Cho was surprised to see her doing wrong. My one was better. It still had nails, she thought. And then the fingers moved. . . .

The Empress could no longer see with her sunken eyes of flesh, but she knew her friend was near, and she felt the other little one too. 'Cat,' she said. 'Keep her safe – harmless. Don't let her. . . . ' 'Oh my Em,' said Divine Endurance. 'My friend – ' It hurt her very much that the Empress's last thought should be for the dirty gypsies. The Empress died. The dry lower jaw dropped open, and one last breath fainted on the harsh, dusty air. It was over. Cho knew something strange had happened. She was frightened, and a small sound escaped her. The Cat's head turned quickly, and she stared at the child with angry diamond blue eyes. 'You,' she said. 'What are you doing here? I told you to go to sleep. Who told you to wake up?'

Divine Endurance said that the things that seemed to happen while Cho was asleep were called *dreams* and were really lessons from the Controller. She said (repeating what she had learned from Em long ago) that Cho's head was invisibly connected with the Controller, so it could tell her when she was doing something wrong, and teach her things. 'Now that you're old enough, you'll find it happens more and more. You don't have to lie down and keep still though. The Controller can manage without that.'

Cho had not enjoyed going to sleep, it was too peculiar, but she thought she would like to have lessons. She was not a baby now, and the Cat left her very much alone. Sometimes she played solitary games with dust and pebbles in her own rooms, sometimes she went wandering; a tiny, lonely figure in the maze of long bare buildings she knew as the 'palace'. In the centre of the maze was a large, smooth giant thing, untouched by the scouring sand. This was the Controller. But it was not important to Cho as it had been to Em and Emp. The entrance in its curved side was closed off now by a sheet of steely opaque substance like an eyelid, and no one could go in and talk anymore. This had happened in the first bout of bad weather just after Em retired forever. Divine Endurance had been angry at first, but she had got used to the situation. Cho thought it was very mysterious when the Cat talked about the Controller saying things and doing things. When her wanderings brought her to the centre of the maze she would stand and stare at the giant. There was a crack of darkness at the edge of the eyelid. She knew that she and her brother had been born from there, and often wondered how they had squeezed out. Sometimes, after gazing for a while, she went around the back, pressed her forehead to the smooth base and stood there patiently. Nothing ever happened, but though she did not sleep again, she began to find things in her mind. It was as if there was a palace being built inside her, and she was starting to walk about in it.

Time passed. Her games took her further afield. East and north she could look out, where parts of smooth things like the

10

Controller gleamed in a sea of dead lava, and sand. And beyond the sea were dazzling white salt pans. The smell the wind blew from them was fierce. Cho preferred the west, where the wilderness began. Here there were growing things not blighted yet; little shrubs and mosses and small animals of various kinds. She would sit as far away from the palace as her conscience would let her, gazing into the west and dreaming. She knew a lot about the plants and animals and rocks, but she knew she must not interfere with them. Not on her own account anyway. It would be different if it was to help someone. Cho knew she was supposed to be useful, and help people. Divine Endurance had told her: 'You are an art person. It is your special privilege to make everyone around you happy.' The Cat had also told her that she had a brother who was already out in the world somewhere, helping. She spent a lot of her dreaming time dreaming about him, and about being useful – happy dreams, but sometimes they made her sad, for she had never seen her brother, and who was she to help? There was no one here but the gypsies in the wilderness. She had never even seen them, and in any case she knew she must not go near them; must not leave the palace. The mystery of how her brother had left was a puzzle Divine Endurance had left unexplained.

Divine Endurance was waiting impatiently, but the years flew by and Cho remained a child. The Controller had been told long ago to match development time to demand: when it had come to Cho it had been on a slow, slow schedule. The Cat did not want to spoil things by acting in a hurry, but she knew very well that since it had shut itself up in the upset over the split baby, the Controller had not been working properly. The discomfort did not worry the Cat, and Cho had never known anything better so she did not suffer, but eventually there was bound to be trouble. She decided it was time to prepare the ground.

'Divine Endurance,' asked Cho diffidently. 'Will I some day be progressed enough to have nice clothes?'

They were sitting together in an inner room of Cho's apartments, while a bad sandstorm purred and hissed over the walls and roofs. The Cat had come visiting; she had been asking Cho questions about her lessons and she seemed quite pleased with

11

Cho's replies. Gusts of sand kept dashing into the room and dancing around the floor, for none of the palace doorways had doors. The Cat was watching them, apparently lost in thought, but when Cho ventured her question she looked up and snapped: 'What's wrong with the clothes you've got?'

There was nothing wrong with them. They were the blouse and trousers that had been born with her. They had sat in a corner waiting and growing until she was a clever enough baby to climb into them (because the Cat couldn't dress her), and they had been with her ever since, patiently mending and tidying themselves, and growing as often as necessary. But Cho admired the lovely stiff robes the dead bones wore, and having been told she was getting on well in her lessons, it had occurred to her – 'I'm sorry,' she said, 'if it was wrong. But I just thought – '

The sand wind moaned outside. The Cat was silent, but she seemed more sad than annoyed.

'Child, have you ever wondered,' she said at last, 'what happened to the other people? The ones whose robes still lie about like lost jewels, though the bodies inside are dust? Listen, I will tell you. It was all due to the medicine.'

Cho already knew about the pipe with liquid trickling from it, behind the south-east buildings. The Cat had told her when she was a baby she must never go near it, nor into any cleft in the ground round there. But she had never heard the word medicine before.

'Once, long ago,' began Divine Endurance, 'the empty clothes were all people, alive and walking about. The sky was always clear in those days and there were flowers and lizards everywhere and no sand at all. But because the people insisted on taking that medicine which comes out of the pipe you mustn't touch, everything began to go wrong.'

'What did it do?'

'They thought it would make them better than they were,' said the Cat. 'But it made them selfish and useless, and in the end it made them just wither away. Finally, it made them so naughty that they even upset the Controller, and that's why our sky isn't blue and our flowers have died.'

Cho listened solemnly. 'It's wrong to hurt yourself,' she remarked. 'And we are meant to be useful.'

'Exactly,' said the Cat. 'But they insisted and now you are the only one. They put on those robes when they began to take their medicine, so you see why you must never want to wear them.'

The sandstorm had eased. Divine Endurance got to her feet and stretched thoughtfully. 'I will leave you now. It has been a pleasant visit.'

After this conversation, the Cat left the child alone for quite a long interval. She kept an eye on her from a distance, however, because the weather was getting worse. Almost without noticing it they both started to give up the eastern areas of the palace and gardens because they were just too uncomfortable. Cho was beginning to be less of a child. She forgot her pebbles and the dust houses she had made for them, and spent more and more of her time just wandering and dreaming. She brooded a great deal about the things Divine Endurance had said about the people who were selfish and useless. I don't want to be like that, she thought. But what can I do?

At last Divine Endurance judged it was time for another step forwards. She found Cho this time at her second home, her favourite boulder overlooking the wilderness. She was puzzled as she approached the place by a curious crunching noise. She jumped up on top of the boulder and saw beneath her the child, not very little now, holding a piece of rock and biting it with her strong small teeth.

'What on earth are you doing?'

Cho started, 'Oh,' she said. 'I'm eating.'

'Don't be silly.'

A few steps away a little mouse-like creature sat on another rock, crunching at a seed it held in its paws – eyeing Divine Endurance warily.

'Like that you know,' said Cho. 'I'd like to live on things, be part of things. . . . ' She smiled, and tossed her rock away. 'It's only a game.'

Divine Endurance was strangely impressed. There was something not at all childlike about that smile.

'Cho,' she said. 'You are right to want to be part of things, and so we will be. It is time we started to think about joining your brother.'

Cho was stunned. This time, the first time she met the

13

extraordinary idea, she could hardly take it in. She listened with big round eyes to the story of the brave Emperor who saved the baby from the medicine, and the wicked Empress who killed him before he could save Cho as well. But when Divine Endurance came to the moral – that because Wo had helplessly broken the rule it was *obviously* right for Cho to follow, now she was old enough – the child's eyes just got rounder and rounder.... Divine Endurance cautiously retreated.

She came back, again and again, like water dripping on a stone: Cho's brother, torn away from his home without a proper education, needed Cho urgently by now. How much the two of them would be able to do for the world, when they were together. Sometimes there are overriding imperatives.... But for a long while the dripping did not work at all. The child became distressed, but more and more obstinate. Divine Endurance began to be seriously worried about her secret plan.

But the weather continued to deteriorate. The air was oppressively thick and warm, and small earth tremors rattled through the palace daily. They stayed under the western walls now all the time. And one day there was a dark blot on the grey plain of the wilderness. It did not seem to move, but it grew, little by little. Cho saw it and was filled with a strange excitement, but at the same time she felt compelled to get up and go and hide behind her boulder. The Cat came too. Together they watched as the blot came closer and began to pass by. They saw animals, stumbling and huddling together in the foul, dusty wind. And they saw the others ... wrapped to the eyes in crusted rags, striding along. Some of them were sitting on top of animals, to comfort them. Strange sounds came to the boulder, sounds that Cho had never heard before.... She saw dark eyes, laced in patterns of blue; she saw one blue hand outside a mantle, and her heart began to beat very hard.... Not one of the train even glanced up at the boulder, and the strange excitement faded. Cho and Divine Endurance got up.

'He isn't with them anymore,' whispered Cho.

'He can't be everywhere,' said the Cat. 'It would be different if you were with him.'

Cho was looking after the train, with a slightly puzzled expression. 'Were they happy?' she asked shyly.

Divine Endurance answered, honestly. 'I don't know. I think it is more difficult to tell than you would think. . . . Obviously it would be different if there were two of you. But they were doing the right thing. We must make a move ourselves very soon.'

'Perhaps things will get better?'

'I don't think so, child. I have seen these fits before. It is working up to a climax, and this time we have no Controller.'

'You mean, we might not be able to keep ourselves mended?'

'Indeed we might not,' said Divine Endurance grimly.

The end of Cho's resistance came abruptly. One sultry, ominous morning they went walking into the palace, to see how it was surviving, and they found their way blocked. There was a huge split in the ground between them and the inner buildings. It was wide and there was something shining deep down inside – the Controller's entrails, split open. They stared into the pit. The hot ground shivered menacingly underfoot.

'Divine Endurance,' said Cho suddenly, 'you are right, and we should leave. We should go now.'

And so, without any farewell, without any ceremony, they left the palace forever. They simply returned to the western walls, climbed them again and went on. When they had come down the first slopes and were out on the level ground in the wilderness Cho looked back. But already her special boulder, where she had watched the little mouse and dreamed her dreams, was just another rock on the hillside.

2 Living on the Ground

Cho and the Cat ran on and on tirelessly over the barren plain. Sometimes the pumice dust was skinned over the little red plants, more often it was bare, and they were wading knee-deep as if in cloudy water. 'I remember,' said Divine Endurance as they ran, 'the day this wilderness was made. There were great trees, as tall as the Controller; they all jumped in the air and disappeared. Rivers and lakes were stirred up with the hills, making mud that boiled, and the rocks began to run about in streams. We were inside, of course, but the Controller let us see what was happening. Afterwards we found that all the other palaces had vanished in the confusion. Then we started waiting for the people to come back. But they never did. It was not so bad to leave us, we could have been quite happy. But they should have told us, shouldn't they, that they were going for ever. It would have made such a difference.'

'Perhaps they meant to come back,' said Cho. 'Perhaps they've been busy.'

Above them, the sky had begun to swell and darken. As they ran on a wind started to rise, and then the clouds opened and poured on them a flood of thick, rust coloured rain. 'It has picked up sands from the glass basin – ' said the Cat. In front of them now the grey plain was giving way to a more rugged terrain of old lava, but they could feel new tremors coming, and the dust seemed safer. Cho found a scrape of a hollow in a patch of stunted bushes, some way before the rocks began, and they crept into the middle of this to try to hide. They crouched close together, feeling the tenseness of the earth as it shuddered towards another convulsion. They could tell this one would be very strong. 'An occasion for sleep,' said the Cat. So they lay down, the way Divine Endurance had been taught was correct

16

for 'sleeping' a long time ago, and made themselves still. Because there was nothing they could do. They could only hand themselves over to the earth wave and hope that it would bear them up and not drown them.

Cho woke. She lay alertly considering what was around her. She had had no dreams and she was grateful for that, but she wondered what it meant. Everything has changed, she thought. The sky was at a different angle. She sat up and found the left side of her body was caked with red mud – because on that side the screening bushes had been torn away. She was on the brink of a great churned pit of earth that had not been there before. The water in it steamed. She looked for Divine Endurance and saw that the Cat must have woken earlier. She had climbed into the remaining bushes and was now apparently asleep, perched weirdly between two branches. The leaves and twigs were charred black. The Cat opened her eyes.

'How long have we been asleep?' asked Cho.

'As long as necessary, I suppose.'

She climbed down from her perch and together they peered into the red, evil-smelling gloom that hid the wilderness plain. 'Everything has changed,' whispered Cho. Now they knew for certain they had left their home forever. For ever and ever. After a while they got up, and began to pick their way through mud and clinkers and steaming puddles, on into the west.

For a long time the two fugitives wandered in a daze. They were continually harassed by small after-tremors and by cloud-bursts of the thick, abrasive rain. But worse than anything else was the sense of that emptiness behind them. Divine Endurance suffered just as much as Cho. In spite of all her schemes she probably would never have been able to leave the palace without the urgent threat of the earthquake. After all the plotting and persuasion they had both been simply obedient in the end, running away from something that would damage them. Now they were orphaned, and there seemed no purpose in life. It was almost by accident that they journeyed westward at all.

But eventually the tremors faded, and the air calmed and cleared. They found themselves above the wilderness in a land made of glittering slivers of shale, interrupted by heaps of strange-coloured boulders. As the clouds and fog began to melt

17

away they saw this country stretching endlessly ahead of them, climbing onwards in broad, gleaming terraces. They stopped their mindless trudging and began to appreciate their surroundings: there was blue sky, which Cho had never seen before. The crystals that grew in the boulders were charming, and away on their right-hand side was the fascinating clear line of the glass plateau. There was no water, no plants or animals, but there was plenty to enjoy. At night the rocks produced their own light; a rich, changeable, flickering glow. Lingering in this shining country they recovered from their loss. It was like the pleasant life Divine Endurance remembered. She introduced Cho to sunset watching, and the art of appreciating a warm stone or a cool shadow, and she told her interesting stories of the Empresses and Emperors she had known. But they did not watch the dawn, and they avoided looking in that direction. And always as they wandered about, finding themselves new temporary homes with different attractions, they kept moving towards the west.

At last Divine Endurance began to talk about the future again. She talked about Worthy to be Beloved – or Wo, as his sister should call him, and the delightful prospect of being helpful, and useful, with Wo. The Cat knew that if she was to get her own way, she had to watch out for certain features of Cho's nature: she warned the child repeatedly against the danger of attaching herself to one particular person. That would be selfish. The end of the quest was to join Wo, and be *truly* useful. . . . She began to teach Cho how to behave in the world: 'Remember you must not be lazy. And don't push yourself forward. The people don't like it, it embarrasses them. Be helpful when you are asked, and not before – and then be discreet about it. And you'll have to change your manners. From what I can remember, they're a complete disgrace at present.'

The first lesson in manners was going to sleep at strictly regular intervals. The second lesson started when they came to a land where mosses and lichens began; trickles of water and gradually more and more activity. One day Divine Endurance suddenly jumped into a bush and did something very strange to a little animal, rather like Cho's mouse. Cho was shocked.

'It's all right,' said Divine Endurance. 'They enjoy it really.'

18

She did not manage to teach Cho to kill the ground squirrels prettily, but the child became quite competent, and they were able to practise eating nearly every day. Cho would have prefered to nibble leaves and seeds.... 'Certainly not,' said Divine Endurance. 'They might be poisonous. Eating poisonous things is a waste of maintenance and very naughty.' They wasted none of the squirrels. After eating it was manners, Divine Endurance explained, to dig a small hole in the ground and post the eaten things into it. 'The people keep some of it back,' said the Cat, 'we needn't. We just post it in and cover it up nicely.' She found this hole business quite delightful, but Cho thought it no more than mildly pleasant.

Because of the routine of hunting, eating and sleeping they began to travel more briskly. They started to notice the changing moon, and to measure time. At last one clear night, about the end of a month of steady westward progress, brought them to the very last of the climbing terraces. They sat waiting for the moon. Divine Endurance had been remembering more of the world's manners, so there was a little fire, and the current squirrel was toasting over it on sticks.

'What does your name mean, Divine Endurance?' asked Cho idly.

'It means,' said the Cat 'that I come from the early days of the palace. Later on, it was thought unnecessary and even unwise to dwell on some of our special features.'

'Does it mean you don't mind about time? It's strange isn't it? In the palace time was like air, I never thought of it.... But now it seems to pass and pass. Do you think we will ever find them? Do you think they have all gone?'

Their campfire was on the top of a cliff. Beneath their feet, blue-black in the starlight, plunged an endless cataract of rounded hills. Without a thought, they had known which way to run when they left the palace, and that way was south and west. But they had been running a long time with no encouragement, not even a trace of the gypsies.

'It is not time to give up yet,' said the Cat. 'Everything has changed, but eventually we must reach the southern margin of this landmass. Then we should find a long Peninsula running into the sea. Our feeling is, isn't it, that they've trickled away, to the edge of things, south and west.'

19

'Yes. They've slipped away.'

'So, probably they are on that Peninsula. Resting, or retiring or whatever it is they've been doing all this time. And Wo is with them.'

The moon came up, slowly lifting its thin yellow finger-nail into the sky behind them. They ate the squirrel, and the Cat told Cho to go to sleep. But she did not. She lay down with her eyes open dreaming all through the night, about the Peninsula, and the end of the quest.

3 Day of Blood

It was too warm in the courtroom. Hand-turned fans slapped the air with languid palms; tack, tack, tack. The people pressed against each other, whispered and scuffled; some giggled hysterically. The criminal stood with his head bowed, the Rulers' agents at their long table spoke to each other very softly, and one of them wrote something down. Outside in the sun the streets of the city were quiet, shops empty, markets shuttered. It was a Hari Darah, a rest day. Prince Atoon in his canopied chair sat like a delicate statue, but his eyes hunted the crowd. There was not one veiled head, not one attended figure making a space around itself. They were all boys, boys and men. Atoon had not expected the women to protest or intervene in any way. But he had prayed for a miracle, he had prayed that they would be here. They were not. They had abandoned Alat to his fate.

The noble criminal stood accused of indecent assault on a young boy in his family's household. It was the custom of the Peninsula to change the majority of male children at birth or in infancy: the 'boys' thus created did society's menial work and deserved in return to be cherished and protected. In happier times, the native council would have harassed the noble family into paying a huge fine, almost as much as if Alat had killed someone, if the charge were proved. But the facts in this case were irrelevant. Alat might very well have buggered the witness. How many men live lives of perfect chastity, whatever their families claim? Equally, he might never have seen the boy until today. Alat, a nobleman of Jagdana, had been writing letters to someone in another state, that was the real offence.

The Peninsula had been controlled by foreigners for several hundred years. The Rulers came out of the southern ocean, claiming to have left behind an enormous country that was no longer habitable, and settled on artificial islands off the southeast coast. Gradually, on various excuses, they began to take

21

over the world. The process was now complete. Peninsulan independence had been dead for a hundred years, since the mad, ruinous Last Rebellion. There was no High Prince any more, presiding over the patchwork states, for the family of Garuda the Eagle was deposed and vanished and the Eagle Palace lay at the bottom of a reservoir. The Rulers stayed on their islands but their agents, the Koperasi, renegades who had 'co-operated' with the oppressors, controlled every state. Jagdana was the only princedom to retain some shreds of self rule, at the cost of a rigorously maintained appearance of docility. Atoon had been assured that the letters really existed, and when he knew that he knew Alat was lost. The Rulers' agents themselves might relent before the Dapurs of Jagdana: *Thou shalt not risk lives* is the greatest law. The palace had rescued conspirators before, but this time Atoon's family could not interfere, for reasons far above Alat's head. Poor man, he had chosen the wrong moment to get caught out in his little meddling.

The crowd waited, simmering urgently. Occasionally a head turned furtively to see what was happening in the marble-latticed gallery above the inner end of the hall, where the Pertama Dapur, the first ladies of the land, were supposedly presiding. Atoon knew there was no one behind the thin, dark curtain, behind the pierced stone, yet he found himself staring too. But it was all over. An elderly boy in black and indigo livery came out, rapped with his staff for attention and bent his old tortoise back to heave the cord that raised the draperies. The women of Atoon's family had officially departed, satisfied with justice. And Atoon, although he had known there could be no other issue, felt his head begin to spin.

The Rulers' officer left his place and came up to the dais, glanced over his shoulder at the body of the court and said in a muted tone: 'We'll give the prisoner as strong an escort as we can, Sir.'

It was you, thought Atoon, you and your kind, who robbed the people of their self respect and turned them into savages. How did you do it? God knows, I don't. It's done, and we would all be better off dead than living like this. You will give him up at the corner of the street.

'If you're ready to leave, Sir,' prompted the officer, respectfully, weighing up and down Atoon's calm, graceful silence: 'We will give you an escort back to the palace.'

By sunset the streets were quiet again. The palace, which spread in a maze of courts and gardens through the heart of the capital, had heard the noise start up, rise to a tumult and at last die away. Now there was only the stillness of a rest day evening. The prince Atoon, and a guest of his family, were sitting in an audience room, deep inside the maze. It was a vast apartment; long unused. Little groups of stiff furniture stood about in its dim expanses, looking prim and desolate. The blue and gold of Jagdana was fading from everything, and the garden, neglected, grew up to the verandah steps. The prince sat propped against one of the slender pillars that supported the inner roof, staring at nothing. His companion, sitting a little distance away, watched the last rays of the sun gleaming on Atoon's ordered braids, making the worn gilding on walls and pillars burn. The light slipped away, and indigo shadows gathered. A boy came pattering through the dim depths of the room, bringing a lamp. He wished to prostrate himself before Atoon's companion, but she caught him in the act with a quick frown so he simply bobbed a curtsey to the prince, and fled.

She was the reason why Alat could not be saved. She was the granddaughter of the last High Prince: the young prince Garuda who was rescued after the rebellion and the murder of his family, and hidden in the hills. The prince was accepted by the outcast mountain people and became one of them. He had a daughter and Derveet was her child, the only thing the last Garuda saved from the wreckage of his defiant attempt to renew the struggle. He smuggled the baby away from the Peninsula and brought her up on the Black Islands in the eastern sea, among the diving people. But the Rulers decided to evacuate the diving colonies, which were losing population and could not support themselves. The exiled prince set sail for nowhere, with other despairing islanders. He would not return to the Peninsula: he was old and sick and his time had passed. But Derveet, though still very young, escaped and managed to get back to her country, alone. The Hanomans, the Royal family of Jagdana, were loyal – Hanoman the Ape had always been the Eagle's great ally – and they would have sheltered her for the rest of her life. But Derveet was not looking for shelter. She had come to the Peninusla to start a new rebellion.

She knew that the women had placed a ban on armed revolt after the last disaster: she did not want to repeat her grandfather's defiance. She wanted the Dapur's support in a new kind of warfare, a desperate kind to suit the desperate straits of the country. She spoke of disruption and subversion, secrecy and trickery. She wanted to use women's powers of wisdom, cunning and hidden knowledge in the man's domain of war. But her ideas were unacceptable. The Hanoman ladies informed her that all overt resistance to the Rulers or their servants was suicidal. When the country was stronger the men's honourable outbursts were permissible as a safety valve, but now no longer. To involve them in sheer banditry would be to degrade them for no purpose. That women should be concerned in such things was simply unthinkable. In reality there is no recourse for us, they told her, but patience and endurance. It is up to you whether you understand that sooner, or later.

She left the court of Jagdana and went into the mountains, to her grandmother's people. Peninsulan society loved beauty and order, and hated any kind of deformity – the central mountains had always been a refuge for misborn, grotesquely coloured or misshapen creatures. Derveet thought no one could dispute her right to teach and inspire the *polowijo*, the people the Peninsula rejected. She set herself up as a dealer in the illegal achar weed that everybody smoked, and she endured the humiliation of being taken for a man as she explored the south of the Peninsula beyond Jagdana; the country that had once been the Kedaulatan, the Garuda state, and was now the Sawah – occupied territory. She made friends with bandits, brothel-keepers; the fringes of the Koperasi. And it was all to show the Dapur what she could do, and how her plan would work.

But the outcast community had suffered like all the other states. The polowijo were weak and frightened. Finally, Derveet's attempts to organise her guerilla campaign blew up in her face, literally. She had been experimenting with home-made explosives, alone, because nobody dared help her. The polowijo in a panic sent for help, and Derveet was smuggled back to Jagdana.

So the young rebel returned to the Hanoman court,

24

defeated. She was very ill: the Dapur saved her sight, and patiently brought her back to health. But Derveet was now a known outlaw, and though she had not used the name Garuda of course there were whispers. Her presence in the palace compromised her friends, threatened the very existence of independent Jagdana and incidentally had destroyed one foolish man.

In the faded hall the prince and the outlaw sat together – a strange contrast. Derveet's grandfather had done his best, but the child had taken after the mountain people. She was too tall, her features were harsh and her skin was black, not golden. It was bizarre to see this lean, ugly young woman move and glance exactly like a Garuda; beside the Hanoman prince she seemed like disorder incarnate. The exhausted silence continued. There was nothing to say. Atoon had come straight from the court and asked Garuda, his eyes blackly dilated, his beautiful face calm as a jewel, *if he might be relieved of his duties.* (Atoon's father had asked his Dapur that question, some years ago. And they had released him, knowing a man can take just so much shame.) He wanted to borrow a long knife, he was not allowed to bear arms himself, of course. She had refused, and reproached him bitterly. Now she watched him – leaning gracefully against the pillar, glowing in the lamplight like something painted on silk: an exquisite work of art, gold to the waist, white brocade below. But behind the façade – *emptiness.* She put up her dark hands suddenly, and covered her face.

Atoon stirred. 'Is your eye bothering you?' he asked softly.

'No, it's very well.'

'We retreat in order to advance, we curve in order to go straight,' said the prince. 'We fight no battle unless certain of victory, we never engage against superior force. They are right.'

'Yes.'

'They keep us alive.'

Across the uncut lalang of the deserted garden they could see lights coming out in the blue of the evening: mellow lemon and amber, patterned by marble. It was the Dapur, the women's quarters. The silence behind those fretted walls ruled Jagdana, as the silence in the centre of every household ruled the Peninsula. Women did not care for talking; it did not suit their

25

way of life. In all her long contention with the Hanoman Dapur, Derveet had never seen their faces, nor heard them speak. She had knelt in the antechambers waiting, for a message pushed under a screen or whispered to her by one of the boys they kept in their service. Silence, and the rustle of silk, the chime of an ankle chain....

She could not go in. When a young woman is judged old enough, perhaps two years after the *darah pertama*, the first blood, she is entered by the men the Dapur have decided are most suitable. If she fails to conceive after a certain time she must leave the Dapur, which is the garden of life. Derveet had failed. Circumstances were against her (it happened on the Black Islands) but rank imposes obligations: Garuda couldn't complain. So the Royal ladies of Jagdana, and any Dapur women anywhere, could keep Derveet at a distance and bar her from that 'hidden knowledge' she had so rashly demanded.

Derveet knew more than most people outside the walls about some of the Dapur's mysteries. She had studied history that was discarded as myth and found glimpses of an incredible world, where control of life did not mean making boys or deciding who should enter a young woman – it meant that the very elements that made living creatures could be manipulated at will. The stories that were not completely fabulous were ugly, even though they were surrounded by wonders to match any rumours of the Rulers' shining islands; ugliness that explained perhaps the Peninsulan horror of human deformity. But long, long ago the women had turned their backs on those design and control roads, and on every kind of false control of the world. Derveet was glad, though that revulsion had led, inevitably, to the endless defeat. She would not have wanted to revive that knowledge.

The Dapurs of the present had different secrets: their boy-making; the *jamu* – drugs – they used for healing, which somehow no one outside could discover; their uncanny way of communicating with each other – their way of knowing, when they chose to know, what the Koperasi were plotting. Derveet's grandfather had hinted to her about some enormous mystery concealed in the silence and stillness of the garden. She did not really understand. When she asked for 'hidden knowledge' she was asking for the hoarded wisdom of scripture and memory,

26

and the skill and foresight of trained minds tempered by seclusion....

But now she knew. They had treated her burns in a kind of suppliants' house, outside their walls. She remembered blackness, pain and a voice – inside the pain, not outside – *You are not a man or a child*, it said. *We will not overrule your mind. You will heal yourself*... and then they made her search her own seared tissues, from the inside, tracking down the damage and persuading the connections to reform, to grow back to wholeness.... *Be warned you may still lose your sight on that side*, the voice said, before it left her in the end. *Nothing repaired is ever quite the same.* They meant secrecy.

Derveet understood that if she had been a boy or a man she would have slept and woken with the burns healing, relieved to find they were really quite minor. Because the Hanomans wouldn't do that to a woman they had been forced to trust her after all. In a way they were safe. She would never be able to go where they had taken her on her own. They said 'you will heal yourself' but she realised that that was impossible. She had not been brought up in the Dapur way, and her mind was fixed now, she was shut out. *Why* do you keep it secret? her heart demanded. Why can't you use this power the way I've asked you to? It would save our lives – But she knew the answer: *Reach for the wholeness*, said the voice in her mind, and she reached out, for the small purpose of recovering the small miracle of her own eye, and she glimpsed, only glimpsed – only touched with her fingertips – the wholeness, the brightness, the real mystery that kept the Dapur wrapped in stillness and silence, beside which war and destruction passed like the flicker of an insect's wing....

And now she accepted that the Dapur of Jagdana was never going to give way. She had done nothing but harm with her meddling here: it was just cruel of her to pester the poor mountain people further. How often had her grandfather told her: *Submit – it is the Dapur's only word. And it is true. Believe me child, I swear it. You will never know a day's happiness in your life, not an hour's, until your will is broken.* (Supposing I don't want to be happy? she had demanded angrily. But he only smiled.) She got to her feet restlessly and leaned against a pillar with her cheek pressed to the worn gold, gazing with wide black eyes full of rebellion and longing at the quiet lights in the dusk.

'What will you do?'

Atoon did not know exactly what had passed between Derveet and his family, but he knew that she was leaving, and would not be going back to the polowijo.

She had already decided. At the southern tip of the Peninsula there was an island called Ranganar, where a colony of women from several states had built a city. They called themselves the Samsui. They had started out as reformers, apparently, trying to recover the purity of ancient customs. But they had fallen under the sway of the Rulers and the Koperasi long ago. The city was built on vice and shame, and was hated wherever independence still flickered.

'I will go to Ranganar.'

Atoon looked at her, and then glanced away. 'Oh, of course,' he agreed softly. 'Why not? You could always become a night-club entertainer.'

There was a short silence. Derveet stared into the garden. Atoon bowed his head and rubbed his hand across his eyes wearily. 'I beg your pardon, madam. I forgot myself.'

It was getting very dark. At last the boy came back and fidgeted in the shadows. It was time for Derveet to leave. Atoon stood up.

Derveet looked at him, standing in his frame of faded blue and gold. She smiled crookedly. 'The chained,' she said, 'are luckier than the unchained. If you are chained, it means you have a place to sleep. You'll have to find yourself a new dealer, I'm afraid.'

The prince did not smile. He went down on his knees and touched her feet and stayed there, bowed, in a graceful gesture of loyalty and mourning for the lost cause.

To the south of Jagdana capital a thick wood, the sacred monkey forest, grew almost to the city walls. Just inside the trees, by the roadside, was a glade where a giant waringin, or banyan, grew. It was a famous creature, endowed with a powerful personality by the Jagdanans: unguessably ancient, hollow as a rotten tooth. It was a meeting place and landmark. Lovers and children hid themselves in the arches and caverns of its trunk; old boys sat and gossiped in the shade of its hanging branches, surrounded by the endless cool whisper of its leaves.... In its old age the waringin had acquired a new significance. The *amuks*, the mobs, always seemed to find their way here, whatever they were up to.

There was a hari darah moon, a left-hand sickle rising bluish-yellow and crooked. Hidden in the trees beside the waringin glade Derveet sat smoking a green skinned cigarette, on horseback. The horse was a young black gelding called Bejak: a present from one of the achar dealer's customers. A fine-looking beast, he would have been kept as a stallion, but black all over was considered hardly decent in a male animal: it was the woman's colour. The night was uncannily quiet. Not a sound from the city, so close at hand. Peninsulans worked twenty-four days a month and rested on four. This had been the first rest day. The citizens had a breathing space, to keep in their houses and recover. They would have forgotten everything when they came out again, or so it would seem. They had a miraculous way of getting over these outbursts.

Derveet rarely experienced the flow of blood that should mark hari darah days. She had no magic to protect her now. She shivered in the warm night and slipped from Bejak's side. He was trembling, he did not want to go any nearer to the glade. She put her arm round his neck.

'Oh Jak, dear Jak. Trust me – '

Alat was still alive. They had tied him to the tree and left him. Blood, black in the moonlight, was on his face and ran in caked rivulets down his pale outstretched arms and sides. A blot of darkness masked his groin and thighs but he moved. She saw the body shift, trying to ease itself. Not a sound – She took the knife Atoon had wanted and stepped forward, crossed the space. She couldn't look at his face, she couldn't speak. She put herself against his side to take his weight when he fell, and attacked the thongs. The eyes just beside her face gleamed as they stirred, the caked lips parted.

'Who are you, Sir?'

'No one,' said Derveet shortly. She had no womanhood, and no name now in this country. Let him call her what he liked.

'Then, no one, in God's name set me free.'

'I'm trying.'

29

'No. *Set me free.* Have you no pity?'

She stopped sawing at the thongs and looked into his eyes. She wanted him to live. Mutilated, tortured, humiliated beyond bearing, she would *make* him live if she could. But there was his question, and the darkness, and an agonised human spirit trapped behind the mask of death.... She stepped away from his side, and turned the knife around.

'Ah – ' said Alat. Something scraped hideously, and a gush of warmth fell suddenly over her hands.

Uncertain what to do with the knife, she left it at the dead man's feet. She walked into the trees. Bejak followed her, tossing his head a little and sniffing at jutting roots as he picked his way. She found a little runnel of water by the sound, knelt down in its soft bed of rotten leaves and rinsed her hands. So that's what blood feels like, she thought.

Where was this cause leading her? Farther and farther from the gates of the garden of life. Shame and bitter self-reproach, that she had kept to herself for Atoon's sake, flooded over her. She bowed her head on her knees and sobbed, without tears, for a few moments. She loved the Dapur. She understood it in her heart. The silence and the stillness, to live in the world like a leaf or a stone, innocently at one. It would not be easy, it would not be nothing to do that – it would be immensity.

But why could they not see what was happening? All over the Peninsula there were these horrible fits of mob violence; and the suicides of the gentry. And young women, failing to conceive, were leaving the garden and going, in despair, to Ranganar and other sore-spots – Koperasi bases. Was it because the Rulers had abandoned their property? They left everything now to their hateful and destructive agents, the Koperasi renegades. The disease was not new. She believed it had started after the last reckless war of rebellion. It was after that that the Rulers retired to their islands, and were never seen on land again. And then what had been a sore but still a bearable predicament changed, insidiously. It was as if some vital restraint had been removed. Chaos was spreading through the princedoms like cancer and gathering speed now, all the time. Too late for acceptance and the long view. *It was too late.*

She stood up. Bejak came to her at once and snuffled noisily against her shoulder.

30

'Hush dear. What are we thinking of, hanging around near the walls like this? We'd better be on our way.'

Away they went into the deep blue forest night, into the south. She would not despair. She would go to Ranganar.

4 Gress

In the morning Cho got up, and went to look over the cliffs again. The country ahead looked the same as it had done at night, a riot of tumbling hills pouring downwards and onwards apparently without end, without any hint at all that might mean people. They have gone, they are far away – murmured Cho to herself. And then the sun came up, jumping into the sky behind her. Its light beamed down the hills, and Cho cried out. She had seen something down there, something bright.

'A palace! Divine Endurance, I can see a palace!'

There was a tiny, perfectly regular diamond of brightness lying in a valley far down below them, and beside it was a straight line, cutting the endless green.

'A road!'

'Don't get your hopes up. It might be a natural phenomenon of some kind,' warned the Cat. But Cho was already scrambling down the cliffs.

It took them quite a while to find a way to that diamond. Only the twist of earth that had reared up the great cliffs, over the waterfall of hills, had made it visible even to Cho and the Cat's sharp eyes. The soft-looking carpet of treetops was a savagely entangled jungle that seemed to cover the whole world from now on, without a single break. They gave up living on things and simply travelled, but still the moon had come back to the same phase again before they knew they had completed the descent. Divine Endurance decreed another sleep till the end of night, since it happened to be night-time. She was trying to be strict about practising regularly.

The next morning there was daylight through the tangle ahead. They pressed on eagerly, and then they found out why the thicket had ended. They were on the brink of a huge, deep cleft in the ground, slicing straight across their path.

'It's like the day we left,' said Cho. 'But giant.'

'Cho,' said Divine Endurance, 'I'm sorry, but I'm afraid this is your road.'

'I am not turning back,' cried Cho. She knelt down at the edge. The farther wall was very sheer. It could have been made by people. Suddenly she swivelled round and was hanging by her fingertips over the chasm.

'Child! That's very naughty!'

But Cho had disappeared. In fact it was quite easy to get to the bottom. There were several foot and handholds. It would have been even easier just to jump, but her conscience wouldn't let her. She stood on the floor of the canyon looking around, and there was a soft thump beside her.

'Cats are meant to be lazy,' said Divine Endurance. 'Now what, child? This is just a natural crevasse. You must see that.'

But Cho wasn't listening. She could hear a lovely soft sound, like the sound of running water but softer and more regular. 'I can hear *music*,' she declared. She began to run. Up ahead she soon saw a blank rock wall, as if the canyon was shut like a box, but before she had time to be disappointed she realised that the cliff on the left gave way: the crevasse turned a right angle. Cho raced round the corner and saw smooth brightness. The palace! But it was not. A little way further, and the illusion vanished completely. In front of her lay only a great, bright, silver lake, with wild jungle all around it, and the little waves lip-lapping quietly on the shore.

That evening, Cho and Divine Endurance were sitting by a fire on the margin of a small, blind inlet of the enormous water. They were not alone. With them was a bundle of wet knotted cord. It sat on a flat stone, steaming in the heat of the flames; inanimate but with a definite presence. Cho had found it as she wandered desolately along the shore. There had been people here. They had made the lake. She imagined lake-admiring parties going up into the hills to stand on the crags and see the diamond shining. But it was long ago, so long that she could detect no trace here. It was only in her heart that she knew. Then she saw it, like a bunch of weeds in the shallows. She knew at once it was the work of human hands.

'It was part of a fishing net,' said Divine Endurance.

'Yes. They must have been playing with the fishes. I wonder why it does not mend itself into a whole net again?'

Divine Endurance kept quiet, and the child soon found her own answer.

'Perhaps it's Art.'

Their supper was a rat, not a squirrel; thicker in the head, with different teeth and a thin tail. Cho turned it on its sticks and smiled at the fire. She felt very peaceful now. She would be happy to wait for the people to come back here, no matter how long.

Divine Endurance was not feeling so contented. She had never worried about the state of the gypsies – the poor we have always with us – but this fishing net disturbed her. Was it a general indication? Could it be that all the people had turned into gypsies now? She had never thought of that. She wondered what sort of place Wo might have, in such a forgetful world. Be careful, said the scrap of flotsam to her. Approach with caution. They dutifully ate the rat, and then lay curled together by the embers, listening to the water music and the quiet night.

'Don't move – '

Cho felt Divine Endurance's nose touch her cheek. She opened her eyes, which had been shut to appreciate the delicate touch of early sunlight. The tonguing water near her face was rocking wildly; and soon she saw why. Thirty-four heads on thick necks were forging through the silver surface. Their ears were placed right on the crown like a cat's or a rabbit's, but the muzzle was long and the whole a lot bigger. All seemed to be moving in concert. For a moment Cho thought she was going to see something stupendous, but the heads approached the far side of the inlet and separated, shouldering water aside, producing long legs, glistening backs and trailing tails. 'Horses,' said Divine Endurance. 'Exactly what we need. Come on.'

'Oh please let's not. We did eating last night. And they're so *big*.'

'Idiot child,' said the Cat. 'I'm not talking about food. I'm talking about information. And local colour. Come along, and bring that net.'

They set off round the lake. The Cat said it would be foolish to get in the water. The horses would not like being copied and followed. On the way, she explained what was on her mind. The bit of fishing net said they were now approaching the places where people lived. She knew what Cho was feeling: lazy feelings that there was nothing more but to wait to be fetched. It wasn't good enough. Suppose the people never came back? They have a way of never coming back. No, the right thing to do was to go on and seek them out. People admire horses, horses often live with people quite intimately. One of these thirty-four would be the ideal companion, to guide Cho and the Cat into the world and make them look just like everyone else.

The animals had settled where the lake, in some past retreat, had left a tract of rich, black mud that was now growing good grass. Cho and the Cat watched.

'Divine Endurance,' said Cho, 'I'm sure your idea is good, but it won't work. If you ask creatures like mice and so on to play with you they never will. They always have things to do – I've tried.'

'Hush! They are wandering on, aren't they? There is more grass on the other side of the next bit of thicket.'

When the horses began to pass through the neck of tangled trees that separated two grassy beaches, Divine Endurance and Cho were there already. The Cat had made Cho lay a trap on the path, made of the unknotted fishing net. Cho argued about breaking the peoples' Art: by the time she gave in she had to be very quick about undoing it and hiding the snare. The horses came through. Divine Endurance picked a little yellowish mare with black legs. She looked different from the others. She had rubbed places on her shoulders and her tail and mane, though free now, had once been cropped. Cho tugged her cord. The little mare stumbled. She struggled, while the other horses passed by indifferently, but not for long. She knew she was well caught. She bent her head and bit at the snare.

'Good,' said Divine Endurance. 'A bright one.'

They went away and left the mare to think about things. The rest of the herd began to leave the lakeside and gradually disappeared, moving south and west. Two days passed. The prisoner could reach grass and water but she could not get free, and her friends had abandoned her. Eventually the Cat decided it was time, and she and Cho went back. Cho wanted to apologise and explain it was only to get her attention, but the Cat wouldn't let her. The little mare heard them and faced the rustling truculently, determined to sell her life dear.

'Hello,' said Cho. 'Do you know anything about people? We

35

are looking for some, and we thought you might be able to help us.'

Divine Endurance sniffed at the knotted cord, warily because it was near those sharp little hooves. 'You seem to be in trouble,' she remarked. 'What happened to your friends?'

'It's only to be expected,' said the mare. 'I'll attract anything nasty that's around, won't I? Speaking of which, don't you think you'd better get away yourselves? There are big cats and so on in these hills.'

She had a kind face, and her sturdy calm made Cho ashamed, but Divine Endurance wouldn't let her confess. 'If the child sets you free,' she said quickly, 'which she can easily do, what will you do then?'

The mare looked puzzled. 'Follow the herd of course.'

'Really? They'll think it strange that you escaped, won't they. And you aren't well liked.'

It was clever of Divine Endurance to have guessed that time spent with humans would be a blot on a horse's career. Cho would never have thought of it. The little mare blinked at the Cat, then dropped her head, pretending to graze to hide her feelings. 'It's true,' she said stoically. 'And there's no use anyone travelling alone. You may as well leave me. Off you go.'

Cho got down on her knees and undid the snare. 'You could come with us,' she said.

The mare's name was Gress. She quickly decided that Cho must be a poor, lost gypsy child.

'They come from the end of the world,' she said. 'Over the glass mountains and round the edge of the poison deserts. They've been passing through. We've seen them, over the years, moving this way. Away from something bad that's happening over there. Did you get lost?'

It did not strike Gress as strange that she could talk freely to Cho. She knew from experience she could usually understand and be understood to some extent, and this was an unusually patient and attentive child. She told them that the fishing net must have belonged to gypsies. But she didn't think they were coming back.

'They go west and south, but they don't come back. Not in our memory. I've got a sort of feeling they've all passed now. It feels very empty over there now, doesn't it?'

Cho and the Cat agreed. The east felt very empty to them. The places where people lived and stayed, said Gress, were still far away. She knew, because she had been born near there; that was how she came to spend time in service.

'We can follow the road.'

'A road!' cried Cho, delighted. She had always wanted to see one.

So they set off together. For a while Cho was continually expecting the wonderful road to appear, and then the people round the next corner. But after a few days even the printed trail left by the herd grew vague and fragmented. Gress lost interest in it and wandered, looking for food and pleasant terrain. To Gress a 'road' was what the herd did: it travelled eastward into the empty lands until unnerved by rumours of poison and earth tremors, and then it moved westwards to the luxurious fields of the humans until driven away by horse-catchers and resentful farmers. A lifetime could be spent in either direction without seeing the turn. It was a way of life, in fact, and Gress did not live in a hurry or a straight line, unless under duress.

Cho and the Cat did not press their guide. They were satisfied to be moving in the right direction. Cho felt the journey ahead expand again in her mind. She learned how to assimilate things from Gress and all her herd-memories. She saw the road; mountains and desert and wilderness, still stretching on. Gress told how she had left the people who caught her when she was a yearling, running with her mother. High up in the passes of the hills on the people's borders, she was tired one day of rushing over bare rocks and scree with things banging on her back. 'Someone forgot to tie my legs up, so I left. I came down, and fell in with those others, and we lived east. But it is true, I wasn't really one of the family.' Whenever Gress mentioned humans she always added 'no offence?' to her remarks. She grew fond of Cho, and often tried to persuade her to become an honorary horse and stay on the road and forget about humans. Her high opinion came partly from the fact that Cho never showed the slightest desire, or need, to ride. As for Divine Endurance, she held herself rather aloof, in case the coincidence of their both having four legs gave Gress incorrect ideas.

A new development was that they always halted now from dusk to dawn. This was Gress's idea, and Cho thought it was a good one, though it slowed them down. Stillness and the night seemed to suit each other. If the weather was appropriate they looked for shelter, but they all preferred the open air.

One night, when Gress seemed to be asleep, Cho asked the Cat quietly:

'Divine Endurance, what do you suppose happened to the gypsies *we* saw? I *liked* the "desert", but I can see it must be nicer to be up in those shining mountains. Only, they weren't going very fast. What do you suppose they did when the earth wave came?'

Divine Endurance did not answer at once. She was sitting in a neat, round hump, with her paws tucked away. But her ears and whiskers attended delicately to the night. Cho lay beside her, and watched the gleaming half-circle of the Cat's eye, perusing the darkness.

'Divine Endurance?'

'I don't know,' said the Cat. 'I can't tell.' Then, after a pause, 'It would be different, of course, if you were with Wo.'

The gypsies nagged at Cho, but she put them out of her mind because there was nothing to be done. The journey went on; wandering and delaying but always onward, out of the empty lands, towards the distant goal.

5   The Green Ricefields

With Gress the journey was much more interesting. A big river was something to ponder about for weeks, and sometimes she would stop and say, 'Oh, this is South-West Wind. We never travel in South-West Wind' – or some equally curious announcement. It seemed to be something to do with the weather, but it was a mystery to Cho. To her, *bad* weather meant poison rain, earthquakes and scouring sandstorms, and there was never anything remotely like that.

One day they turned from the west forever. It was a dry time, in a country where the dust puddled like red water underfoot, and the great trees stood like skeletons with flowers of red and yellow scattered strangely over their bare, heat-scoured branches. And they turned south. It was quite uncomfortable at first. It felt like walking sideways. They travelled on as before, and it was some weeks later before Gress happened to remark that they had been in the people land ever since they took that turning.

'We're almost through Gamartha now,' she told them. 'This is the beginning of the real Peninsula. Look, you can see the sea – '

They were on a ridge of springy turf, in a country of abrupt white rocks and hanging greenery. Divine Endurance and Cho looked, and saw far off on their right a blue that was not the effect of distance. Cho barely spared it a glance. She wanted to turn back instantly.

'What is Gamartha like?' asked Divine Endurance.

'It's very good,' said Gress. 'Fruit trees and good fields, though a bit slanting. Have you ever had white mulberries? In the middle and down to the sea it is a bit swampy. That's why the people have to keep leaving their cities.'

'They leave their cities?'

'Oh yes, so I'm told. They build one, and then it gets wet,

which is bad for the feet, so they go off and build another one. Or there might be other reasons, I suppose.' She added, as her friends seemed suddenly depressed, 'Of course, it's different now. The Rulers have built a city called Nor on the sea (over on the other side, we can't see it) – a special kind that doesn't get boggy. I don't think it matters what the Gamarthans do anymore.'

Gress was relating gossip from her service days. She didn't really know what she was talking about, it just sounded knowledgeable and impressive. But Divine Endurance stared back down the turf, where the ridge was lost in the hills and wide valleys of rich Gamartha. The tip of her tail twitched. After a moment or two she said:

'Let's get on.'

They were now in Negara Kambing, inhabited by goats and curly goats, and bordered by Gamartha, Timur Kering and other places Gress could not remember. Cho was amazed at the number of names; so much detail after the blank empty lands. The next afternoon they saw a bunched parcel of the curly goats in the distance, and something taller moving among them. Cho's heart leapt. Gress promptly trotted off in another direction.

'It's all right,' she said. 'There aren't terribly many of them anywhere, you know. We won't get caught.'

It seemed to Cho that she and her guide had a serious difference of opinion to sort out, but Divine Endurance told her to be patient. 'A city, which, as you know, is a large collection of palaces, is what we want. And it should be one that belongs to people who "matter", don't you think? Let's wait a while.'

Gress spoke of a place called the Sawah down in the south, which she had heard of as a promised land. The people in the fields weren't catching; they didn't matter at all. They were looked after like captured horses themselves, by other people who had things they'd made to ride on and carry goods. The word 'Rulers' featured again in her description. Divine Endurance told Cho this sounded like a good place to start looking for her brother, so Cho resigned herself to wait again.

But Gress had no will of iron. She failed, eventually, to resist the temptation of cultivated land. One fresh, bright morning

Cho and Divine Endurance found themselves in a strange place. It was grassland. The grass was all the same height, but it had not been cropped. This was strange because there were little paths in it which Gress followed daintily, one foot after the other. There was a sound of running water in the air. Why didn't what made the paths eat the grass? wondered Cho. Gress seemed to like it. Then she noticed that the little streams they kept crossing were not all running in the same direction. They went up and down and round corners looking playfully busy and organised.

'Is it alive?' she whispered.

It was all around them. She felt it as one entity – the talking brown water and the fervent greenness and the little footways. Divine Endurance said:

'Cho, I think you ought to climb onto Gress's back.'

'Why? To comfort her? She's not unhappy, are you Gress?'

But Gress, admiring the Cat's cunning, thought it was a good idea too, so Cho did as she was told. From her vantage point she saw a thin, reedy sapling with one odd red leaf sticking out of the green – and another, and another. They passed one, and at its foot a stream was changing direction.

'Oh! It *is*! They are here! They are here!'

Journey's end.

The boys and men of Jagdana did not go out into the fields, even near the city walls, without the protection of numbers. They were not allowed to carry weapons, and there were bandits throughout the mountain chain that looked down on the capital, not to mention Koperasi. Besides which there were other marauders, no less savage, where the fields lay close to the hills. As Cho was gazing with rapt delight at the wonderful, mysterious being the people had created, trouble was closing in on the lone child and pony – six large mountain cats and their mate. They were hungry. Gress had been feeding well and looked most appealing.

Suddenly Gress stopped walking, and began to shiver. Something was stirring in the grass. Divine Endurance, lying across Cho's shoulders, made a soft noise in the back of her throat, and began to rise. The grasses parted. A cat stood there, a giant cat.

'Hallo,' said Cho. It did not reply. 'Ah – excuse me, you are in our way.'

41

The giant cat moved a little, fluidly from the shoulder, and suddenly Cho recognised the dreamy expression in its eyes. She pushed at Gress with her knees and managed to turn her. The terrified pony began to run. But there were tawny flashes in the green ahead.

'Surrounded,' growled Divine Endurance. 'Turn back. That was the man, we might be able to bowl him over.' Again they twisted round. Gress was now in such a state Cho had to do everything for her. But the male cat was not alone. Two great loose-shouldered savages barred the way now... 'Can't be done. One gets our backs while we go for the other. You'll have to – '

She said what Cho would have to do. Cho could not take it in. In her panic, with the pack of five chivvying her on, Gress was now running straight at the eldest cat and her mate. Up they leapt together, tawny, mottled, red mouthed, breathing blood. . . .

'Stop!' cried Cho, but they didn't. So she did what Divine Endurance had suggested.

There was not much left of the two cats. 'Good work,' said Divine Endurance. The other hunters had vanished. 'I don't think we need worry about them anymore.'

Cho was not listening. *She had done wrong.* She must not do things for herself; only to help people. She could have saved the situation in any number of ways, if she had thought. . . . She had no ability to slip under locked doors like Divine Endurance: *Wrong – not allowed, not allowed.* . . . It swelled in her mind, it swelled until it burst. Gress suddenly cried out wildly and bolted. Divine Endurance leapt clear almost at once. A few pounding strides later Cho's body came off the pony's back and flew through the air like a broken doll, landing half in an irrigation ditch, its face buried in the chuckling water.

There was another traveller in the green ricefields that day. Derveet, sometime friend of a prince and suppliant of a Royal Dapur, had been on a journey. She was riding back to Ranganar: a hard-faced, dark-skinned ruffian with a patch over one eye, mounted on the kind of horse only a gangster would ride – long legs, flashy lines and black all over. She travelled discreetly and kept away from roads and Koperasi presence. But indeed the sight of that figure, in the distance, or at dusk in a lonely place, was enough to dissuade most people from rash curiosity.

It was four years since the moonlight in the glade of the waringin tree. They had been bad years for the Peninsula, but good years, in a way, for Garuda. To her own amazement she had found supporters in the collaborators' city, and she was now the leader of a small band of secret rebels, spreading confusion and disruption just as she had dreamed. This journey marked an important decision. The group had proved that the wild idea could work, and they had been anonymous long enough. It was time for their leader to declare herself. Derveet knew the others were right but she didn't want to take this step. Every move she made was still intended for that silent audience watching from within the garden walls, and she was still waiting for the blessing that would never come. While the rebels were preparing for their declaration a rumour came that someone important wanted to see them. Derveet rode at once into the north of Jagdana . . . but it was nothing, only another bandit. He did not meet Derveet, only a brigand like himself, and she rode south again, to keep an appointment.

Derveet had a friend in Ranganar who had wonderful plans for an imaginary future: emancipation, social equality, land reform. . . . But she herself only thought of the Dapur. Any orthodox Peninsulan would tell you: the world outside, of words and actions, is just an illusion. Only the women's life is real. But what would it be like, if that life came out of the garden not in fragments but entirely, and spread over the world . . . ?

Her hands were loose on the reins, she had forgotten her gangster face and was just Derveet, her angry eyes growing quieter as the years went by and the absurdity of everything wore down her rough edges. She was feeling tired and lonely. Ranganar was still an alien city, she could not understand her friend's ideas, and no one shared her vision. . . . But what would it be like? What would it *mean*? To be in touch with reality . . . ?

Bejak shied at something and stopped dead. Derveet woke up and looked to see what had startled him. What she saw was the remains of the two big cats.

43

What did that!

Bejak backed sideways off the path, splashing in the muddy field margin, treading the bright grain. When she had quietened him she got down, with a dry mouth, and looked closer. Then she scraped up the scraps of bone and hair and threw them in a ditch, and scooped water up to wash down the path. She did this very calmly, as if tidying up such litter was quite ordinary. She remounted and went on. But a little further down the path she suddenly said to Bejak – 'I'm tired. I think I'll rest for a moment.'

She sat down on a strip of grass between the path and a stream. Bejak wandered a few steps and browsed. Derveet made herself breathe slowly until she could see – the gold and green and blue and the brown, clear water. Surprised small locals popped into or out of the channel, affronted by her shadow. A slender yellow snake propelled herself down stream, head in air, her scarlet tongue flickering.

Land reform! thought Derveet.

What did it mean? Impossible to tell what the things had been, except that they seemed not human: animals of some sort. That did not seem to make the destruction less frightening. It was meaningless and bizarre, like something done by the Rulers themselves. The Koperasi had not, to her knowledge, any weapon that could wipe away like that. Was this a new development? Or was it, she thought, something worse: a kind of warning. . . .

She stayed beside the stream for a while, letting the great, quiet, living machinery all around reach her and calm her. Old as time, always new. It was like the best of dancers, she thought, whose movements you can hardly see, they are so inevitable. Of course, this could not be a 'warning', not in any direct way. Now that her heart had stopped thumping she could see that. She would go on.

The heat of the day had begun. The indigo mountains, that seemed from here to stand on the edge of the fields, were rapidly being buried down to their knees in cloud. She sat up and gazed, frowning, towards the red walls of the city, glimpsed through the glitter of a grove of palms. She wondered if her friend would sense that she had passed close by. Perhaps he might feel it. She had come so near to Jagdana capital meaning to try and send a message to the prince, but now she dared not approach any closer. On an impulse, she emptied her breeches' pockets and looked over the small collection of objects. In another moment she called to Bejak and was on her way.

6   A Sea Shell

In the coolness of the sunset hour Atoon of Jagdana went out
walking. It was a whim: the prince had been feeling out of sorts
and had thought it might refresh him to go on foot into the
green fields. The young courtiers strolled informally in twos
and threes, making a splash of brilliant colour in the rural scene
with their sashes and silk *kains*, flowers in their intricate braids,
jewels on their golden arms and breasts. Only Atoon wore
white; it was not the custom to distinguish between other male
offspring of the Royal Dapur and noble youths sent to court by
their families. The heir the Hanomans had chosen for Atoon
had been sent away from the capital as soon as he was old
enough to leave the Dapur. The Rulers' agents insisted on this
'to prevent intrigues'.

Ragged children played with paper kites, wallowing buffa-
loes stared with solemn eyes, water hyacinths tumbled in
mauve crowds in the ditches. The young men admired everything, and pretended to talk knowledgeably about the state of
the grain. Someone said the prince was like a still flower in a
crowd of butterflies, or like a white stone among quick-
coloured flowers. Laughing at each other, some arm in arm and
whispering, they began to extemporise little verses about the
flowing rivulets and the standing grain, the busy clouds held in
the quiet sky. . . .

Prince Atoon moved a little apart from the rest; their chatter
seemed unusually irritating. Most of the time there was nothing
else he wanted in life except the company of pretty and
sweet-tempered youths, but occasionally his own good temper
would fail him, and his thoughts would start to wander down
the long forbidden paths. The ladies had schooled him well
now. He lived from day to day and did his best to ignore the
disintegration of his country, of every state in the Peninsula. It
was only on rare days like this that something took hold of him,

and the very sky and earth seemed full of aching meaning. He knew that the lost cause was still not quite dead, not yet. He had heard of the trouble the Koperasi were having in the occupied south. Brigandry, vandalism – the Rulers' agents tried to conceal any political motive, but the people knew better. These bandits did not rob for gain or destroy out of malice. They were mysterious, they were magical.... Others said the outlaw Anakmati was just a criminal, cleverly preying on the peoples' fantasies.... It had been going on for two years or more, which would be about right. Atoon had heard a lot about 'Anakmati', that black-skinned villain with the eyepatch, fearless as a demon, riding a big black horse. He wondered exactly what kind of madness she was stirring up in the Sawah. But most likely he would never know. He would only hear, one day, a garbled story of how Anakmati died. And the Dapur would think of an excuse for the court to go into mourning.

His thoughts turned, as he paced unseeing through the lovely grain, to an ugly phenomenon that was spreading from the north. It had started in Gamartha, that country of passionate extremes. Young women, when they failed, were mutilating themselves with acid and scalding water: 'the scouring', it was called, a kind of self-immolation. Could it happen in Jagdana? The idea of the Dapur, *of his own family* perhaps, giving up reason and restraint, cut through his resignation, made his flesh creep. But it was all one of the endless falling, down into the abyss.

A youth dressed in a pattern of deep rose, with a sash of rose and silver, came to Atoon's side shyly.

'Look, prince,' he said, 'look west. See how the sun's colours run through the sky, to be stilled in the arms of evening – '

'Sandjaya,' Atoon smiled, and took the youth's hand absently, but his eyes still brooded on an unseen distance.

'How old am I, Ja?'

'I'm not sure,' said Sandjaya tactfully, afraid this was not a cheerful subject.

'Ah well. They say life is short, but I think it is long enough.'

The young man's hand, which Atoon had forgotten and released, rested for a moment at the prince's waist, on the elegant hilt of a dagger tucked into his sash. It was not a weapon; it was an imitation, made of wood. In other courts

47

nobles refused this mockery – and paid fines for not being 'appropriately dressed'. But the Dapur of Jagdana did not encourage wasteful gestures. Ja touched it as though it were a wound.

'How can I comfort you – ?'

At that moment there was a sudden outcry. All the young nobles and their attendants rushed together to the bank of one of the irrigation channels. Atoon, at once alarmed, went quickly to see what was the matter.

Someone had found a body. It was beyond help. It had evidently been in the water several hours. Two liveried boys lifted the limp bundle onto the bank and the young men all exclaimed. Atoon's first thought was to wonder why whoever had seen it had not had the sense to look away. The child, boy or youth, was dressed in a blouse and trousers of some indeterminate colour. His hair was pale, his skin light. The eyes, wide open under delicately pencilled brows, were dark but had a strange upcurved shape. (Cho's appearance, inevitably, reflected a collision of tastes.)

'What a little oddity,' said someone, and then a silence fell.

Atoon's first thought was now coming to everybody. In these times any little incident could lead to trouble. And though they had had an illusion of freedom for an hour, at the end of the field track the Koperasi escort was waiting to take them back to the palace. The courtiers eyed each other uneasily, and Atoon, watching their faces, felt bitterness and anger rise in his throat. Then someone, having noticed a curious change in the dead face, bent down over the body again, and cried out in astonishment.

'Why – he's breathing!'

All waifs, strays and runaways had to be handed over to the Rulers' agents. This was a very strictly enforced rule. Obviously, the unfortunates went straight to the brutal farm camps in the Sawah, but what could anyone do? Saving one miserable slave or other would not help the thousands, would not change the Koperasi. And this child was not even appealing; sold by his own family no doubt, to give a better chance to the rest. It is the way of the world. . . .

Atoon said calmly, in a voice that invited no questions: 'Someone wrap this child in a shawl. I want him brought back

48

to the palace. My family will take charge of him until his friends can be traced.'

The escort, taken by surprise, clearly didn't know what to do and so ignored the incident for the present. Atoon had the child carried to a room in his own apartments that was not occupied, and then banished everyone. He was smiling as he sent them all packing. He looked so cheerful they were quite amazed. The palace began at once to rattle with stories of the mysterious foundling, whose ugliness soon changed to ravishing beauty. People began to sigh and shake their heads. Poor Sandjaya. The prince, if he had little *rencontres* with the lower orders, was usually so discreet.

Atoon, left alone, smiled even more. He had good reason for his odd behaviour. The Koperasi were devious and never used their claws on the prince himself; they made him suffer by punishing his servants or his friends. He was determined to keep this provocation to himself. But he knew how wild the gossip would be in an hour or two. He was also smiling at the thought of trying to explain to the Dapur this irresponsible whim, this act of reckless daring. He went to the low bed, and began to unwrap his shawl-swathed bundle. The child's eyes were closed now, the features, though spoiled by the light colouring, were delicate and pure. I wonder, is it hurt? he thought, and began to take off the blouse. The material was dry, he noticed with mild surprise, and felt odd under his fingers – probably matted with dirt. He slipped the child's arms carefully out of the sleeves. . . and then discovered the truth. As he stared in consternation, there came a gentle scratching at the door, Atoon jumped up, pulled the shawl over what he had found, and went to answer it. It was Sandjaya.

'What is it?'

'Near where the child had fallen,' said the youth, 'there were hoofmarks. A tall animal, and well shod. And this.' He held out something on his palm.

It was a small sea shell. It had an innocent look, as if it did not know how far it had strayed. Who could have dropped it and left it lying there? Atoon took the little thing and stared at it blankly.

Sandjaya said, after a moment: 'A sea shell, you know, is supposed to be the sign of the bandit Anakmati.'

Atoon had never seen the sea. But somebody had once shared with him her dreams of an island shore: the green, glimmering tide on the black sand at a scented nightfall; the glaring ocean at noon creased by fins like sails. His hand closed on the talisman.... Sandjaya bowed and slipped away unregarded. Atoon shut the door and turned to face the couch, and found the child was awake, sitting up and gazing at him with a face full of naked joy.

The prince, his head spinning, said the first words that leapt into his mouth.

'You belong to Derveet!'

The child smiled beautifully. And then, as if suddenly remembering she was not a child, but a young woman, she bowed her head at his confusion, and began to fasten up her dirty blouse again.

Something must have gone badly wrong. He must have been supposed to know all about this. Cold fear gripped him. Had messages been intercepted? But no – the Dapur would have known it. He saw the plan at once. The foundling was to be taken in by the Royal ladies, and plead Derveet's cause for her. It was a good plan, a clever plan. The Royal family could protest quite reasonably against giving up a lost young *woman*, to the slave camps, supposing such a creature came their way, and no matter how unprepossessing her appearance. And that very appearance would lull the Koperasi. They would not suspect the palace of conspiring with such an outcast little creature. A good plan, a clever plan. Supposing, of course, that the ladies would agree....

'There is something I must know,' he asked. 'Before we consider anything. Are you – are you grown up?'

The young creature gazed at him, placidly puzzled, still full of that mysterious joy. 'I don't know,' she said. 'You'll have to measure me.'

There was no mistaking her utter ignorance.

Atoon said, 'Please excuse me. I must – ' and left the room abruptly.

On reflection, he saw why the emissary was such a child. Derveet must mean to get her out again before the complication of entering arose. He paced his rooms, telling himself he was in the grip of a fit of madness. He might be leaping to wild conclusions. And if he was not – it was hopeless. He must go back and tell the child it would not do. The ladies should not even be asked. But his blood was singing.

He went back and found the stranger and a small brown cat that had got into the room somehow. They were both examining his dress dagger, which he had left behind, with what seemed the most lively interest.

'I know what *this* means – ' said the child, holding up the twin edged wavy blade. It was carved in dark wood and inlaid with ripples of silver in a shimmering, ascending double coil.

'Yes,' he said, taking from her hands the symbol of manhood, made into a mockery for so long – '*Yes.*'

She was a well-schooled secret agent. She told him her name, but any other questions were effortlessly deflected with riddles and confusion. And she was careful. At one point he took out a cigarette and absent-mindedly offered his case. 'I think that's medicine,' she remarked gravely. 'I'm not allowed.' He went to her determined to have her whole story and then tell her it was impossible to go on with this scheme. He left her, having learned practically nothing, quite convinced that she *was* Derveet's emissary. He found an old faithful boy, who knew everything about the Hanomans, to wait on her, and shut himself up to concentrate on composing a very important letter.

Of course, before the night was old the new version of the foundling story was about. The palace gossip had to change its tone entirely.

7   Cho in Jagdana

Cho sat on her bed and watched Hanggoda outside in the courtyard. He curtsied to the west, poured a tiny river of water from a silver jug and set red and white flower petals floating. He had told her that this was a greeting to Father, who had gone over the sea long ago. In the evening the flowers and the water were poured the other way, for Father's child, who would come back one day and fetch everyone away to a beautiful place. He did not say whether Father's child was a woman or a man; perhaps it was a boy like Hanggoda himself. The tiny river sank into the white combed sand. Hanggoda arranged the rest of his petals around the feet of the statue of Hanoman the Ape, talisman of the Royal family, and shook the silver gilt bells on Hanoman's stone dancing ankles to draw his attention to the offering. Jing! Jing! Jing! said the little bells. Cho turned to Divine Endurance with a smile of delight.

The Cat shrugged her whiskers, unimpressed. 'Let's go and explore.'

They were allowed to go where they liked so long as they stayed in the balé, the prince's private apartments. Someone had taken Cho's clothes away, because the ladies wanted them, but Hanggoda had given her a long, loose blouse and a sarong – boy's clothes, but they would do for now. They were too big. Cho waited for them to alter themselves, but they seemed rather lazy. Divine Endurance said Gress was hiding, and would not go on without them. She declined to take a message telling the pony not to worry. She said, 'You never know –'

Cho was delighted with this palace. She loved the way all the novelties like *lamps* and *beds* and *curtains* were only a delicate screen between her and the night and day, rock and earth, heat and shadow of the world. Divine Endurance had worried her sometimes by describing something very different. Now she heard real music at last. She knelt on stone by the prince's small orchestra pavilion listening with rapt attention to the patterns chiming and singing, late in the warm night and going on till dawn. The musicians, having heard that the child was a young lady, politely ignored her, and Cho thought they were like the mouse on the hillside, getting on with their own business happily. Dance was rare in Jagdana palace now, but she heard the word often, and once she saw a young man dressed in rose and silver, in a pavilion all alone in the middle of the night, moving about with a strange, sad floating precision that held her entranced, like the music. . . .

From Hanggoda Cho learned – That there were two languages: High Inggris for the gentry, the Koperasi and the Rulers, and Low Inggris for boys and servants. She learned that Atoon really was his 'father's' son (it usually slips out, unless the ladies seriously want it kept secret) but the present crown prince, who could not live at court, was sixteen years old and probably Atoon's half-brother, or else a cousin. . . . The prince wore white because he was the prince. Other men wore the man's colour only to visit the Dapur. Or to go to war, if we did that anymore. She learned that only country people dance with bells on their feet; bells are vulgar – except for the Hanoman prince. (Not that our prince ever dances. But if he should care to he would wear bells, and it would be very dignified.) A sarong is a length of cloth with a seam and must be folded like *this*, around the waist. A kain has no seam, and the loose end must be arranged gracefully, but only men wear it, or failed women. It would be indecent for men to do certain things, so boys look after them. Ladies can do anything, but they are too important to serve anyone; it would be too frightening.

She took in the confused mixture of information and gossip and trivia and sorted it carefully. Just as she had understood at once that she must talk to people in a new way, not the way she talked to the Cat, the moment Atoon addressed her, so she understood she must learn all she could, so that she would be ready to be helpful. The only thing that made her anxious was the *ladies*. Atoon could not be bothered now, because he was 'engaged with the ladies'. Hanggoda had a little pompous way of drawing himself up when he said 'ladies' but Cho felt a shiver behind it. Atoon shivered too, a little bit. She felt the position of the Dapur through walls and corridors and gardens as a large

53

cloudiness. Everywhere around her there were people bustling with needs, making her tingle with the possibility of usefulness. But in that cloudy place it was different. She could not define exactly how, but it made her feel strange.

Atoon conferred with the Dapur. He tried to consider why they had asked for Cho's clothes, but his heart was still singing too loudly to let him think. He went about his normal duties in his usual exquisite calm, but behind the mask he felt reborn. Whenever he thought of the dusty-headed child, who walked into such danger, smiling so beautifully, a new spring of joy rose up. The ladies kept him waiting, sending for him every few hours to continue a graceful, indirect, temporising exchange. But he was sure the balance had fallen. They never played cat and mouse with his ideas. No was their swiftest answer.

Cho and Divine Endurance pattered around their corner of the palace, looking into everything. Without nagging or bothering people they managed to find out a good deal about the social life of the Peninsula, and its politics. They also found a name. It was spoken very quietly, with an eye over the shoulder. Hanggoda never used it, he was far too discreet. But Cho knew it was sometimes just behind his lips: *Derveet*. A boy mason, who was patching up a garden wall, squatted on his heels and muttered.

'They won't have you, you know. They don't like the sound of the word Derveet. Not after the last time, when they put her together when she'd been playing with the things that go bang. You know what I mean.'

'She'd been making fireworks?'

The mason squinted sideways, and nodded. 'If you like.'

Then he heard someone coming, and earnestly attended to his work.

In the room that held Atoon's private library the librarian watched Cho wandering about, peering at the pictures, and said quietly.

'*She* was always in here you know.'

'Who?'

'You know who I mean. Derveet. She used to spend hours, quiet as a mouse, reading fairy tales and scribbling.'

'Ask him about the "Rulers",' said Divine Endurance, jumping on the boy's desk.

54

But Cho said, 'What is a fairy tale?'

'A fairy tale? Well, a fairy tale is like the story of Roh Betina, our Mother, refashioning the Peninsula out of chaos, making the mountains out of clouds and so on. It is an explanation, when the truth is too complicated or people have forgotten. Derveet was always searching for the deep past, before the Rulers, but that's a time of fairy tales. Perhaps the truth is we were dressed in leaves and grunting, as the Koperasi say.'

'Is that what she was writing about?'

'Oh no. Poetry mostly, I believe.'

The librarian was neither old nor young. His Hanoman livery had gently faded from sun and sky to quieter indoor tones; his face was smooth and sad. He looked at Cho with a strange, grave, hungry expression.

'Some of us know and guess more than the family would like,' he said, 'we people of the palace. It is not disobedience, we just can't help ourselves. We can't help remembering her. When she left, you see, she took with her something that we couldn't do without, nor could we live with it: something precious and deadly – '

'What was it?' asked Cho, puzzled by his hungry eyes.

'Hope,' whispered the librarian. 'It was hope.'

Cho and Divine Endurance sat on the floor in their room, sharing Divine Endurance's supper. Neither Hanggoda nor Atoon thought of giving a young lady meat to eat, and Divine Endurance would not let Cho eat leaves or fruit or roots in any disguise. Hanggoda thought the child was fasting for some ladylike reason, and politely pretended not to notice. But he had seen one of the palace cats had made friends with his charge, so they were able to keep in practice from Divine Endurance's dish.

'It's as if we have walked into one of the stories the Controller used to tell me,' said Cho.

'There was bound to be some game going on. This is quite an ordinary one.'

Having considered the facts, they had decided Wo must be with the happy people – the Rulers, and not with the unhappy Peninsulans. Divine Endurance urged a quick exit from Jagdana. She thought it was time to go on with the journey and hurry to the Sawah and the place called Ranganar, where it seemed the Rulers were regarded as friends.

'From the distaste these Jagdanans show for the name,' she remarked dryly, 'I imagine it will be much more like the world one was brought up to expect.'

'But Divine Endurance what about all the things these people here want?'

'Exactly,' said the Cat. 'Obviously, the sooner we get you to Wo, and the whole thing is sorted out, the better. We will have to think of a way to make these people tell us to go.'

Cho was puzzled. Of course, Divine Endurance was not present when Atoon told her the wonderful news, but it was strange that the Cat had not noticed anything different. She did not argue: she felt a little shy. But she was convinced, deep in her conscience, that she was right and Divine Endurance, strangely enough, had got things wrong. The Cat went away, to check up on Gress. Cho sat on her bed through the flower-scented night, wondering and dreaming about *Derveet*, who spent her days here once, making fireworks and writing poetry, and reading fairy tales.

In the morning prince Atoon came to take Cho to the Dapur. Hanggoda had poured water over Cho, and rubbed it off again: a pleasant game that he was very fond of. It had been more austere this morning: 'Ladies do not use scent,' said the boy. He dressed her in thin underclothes, and then a pair of thin, soft trousers in a pale violet colour and two blouses, the same but slightly different shades. The top blouse went almost to the ground and covered her arms and throat completely. Then he wrapped up her hair and ears and forehead and mouth and nose. She peeped interestedly out of hiding, wondering what would come next. Prince Atoon was there. He was dressed in white as always, but it seemed a heavier and a richer whiteness. His hair was wonderfully braided on a filigree silver frame behind his head; his eyes and mouth were painted dark and rose in his pure golden face. In her veils, she felt rather than saw how the lovely prince knelt, and put something delicately round her.

'This is the sash of silence,' he said gravely. 'Hyacinth colour, for your childhood.'

The long, fine cloth was bound around her closely, from

56

breast to thigh. Then he took out from his own sash something that chimed and glittered. It was a silver chain, with a plain anklet attached to one end.

'This is the –' The child did not stir. The sudden strange hesitation was his own. 'It is symbolic,' he said. 'We men, we are the chain. We hold you back.'

He saw the expression on Hanggoda's homely face and recovered, bent forward fluidly from the waist and fastened the shackle on her little ankle.

Now began the journey to the Dapur. They went very quietly, by the private ways of Atoon used for his own night visits. Hanggoda, Cho knew, was thinking of the 'great occasion' when a young woman, before she is entered, parades all round the palace. The initiate would be under a veiled umbrella, the crowd would see only her feet, but it was a great feast day. Throughout the entering the celebrations went on: music and dancing and puppet shows. Later, the lady would either go to another court (if she could get permission to travel) or stay in Jagdana and receive the usual decorous visits – depending on what the Dapur decided. Unless, alas she had to go away. . . . Cho kept seeing on the passage walls that sign, the twisting silver lines that she had recognised in Atoon's ornament. She knew what it meant, it meant life. All life comes from the double helix. *Even me* she thought, and she was stirred and thrilled. She had discussed this with the Cat, she knew that really it was like that lake shore: only the sign remained. The people had lost interest and gone away from what it used to mean. But still she hoped: in the cloudy place there might be someone –

She walked with tiny steps beside the prince, the chain held in his hand. Through fretted windows she glimpsed a pair of white oxen pulling a mowing machine over a smooth lawn, a group of courtiers strolling like slow butterflies on a terrace of coloured stone; a secret spire of some hidden pavilion rising out of dark jewel-flowered trees. . . . How strange, she thought, that just a piece of cloth makes the world so much bigger. Hanggoda had told her that the sash and veil were to protect people from the frightening importance of a lady, but now she understood that they were a discipline, to help the wearer to concentrate so she would not lose her sense of proportion in the

57

confusion outside the garden. Inside is the greater world. Outside is the real constriction.... She remembered Hanggoda telling her as he did his little ceremonies: 'Father is imaginary really. We all know that. But it would be wrong for us to try and go any further, out here....'

As they came close to the Dapur more and more of this new information and explanation came to Cho. But to her distress she found she couldn't take it in very well, because of the strangest feeling – But it must be all right. People were bringing her here. Atoon stayed in the outer garden, it wasn't the right time of the day or month for him to come further. Cho, with Hanggoda carrying her chain, walked down a cool shadowy cloister with sunlight at the end of it.

She saw flowers, and two children playing with a white monkey. Their small bodies were so long and pliant in the binding sashes they looked like two pretty caterpillars. At the far side of the small courtyard a gauze curtain moved in a doorway and Cho saw a slender golden hand, the fingers banded with silver. And then – nothing more.

Hanggoda saw her fall to the ground. He ran forward with a cry of horror and indignation – quickly stifled, and dragged her away.

'It is nothing,' said Atoon, very calmly. 'No need to be alarmed. The poor child has seizures. We will apologise to the ladies for the disturbance, and no doubt they will send someone to give her attention –'

But he knew, and the faithful old servant knew, that this was a disaster.

By noon it was all over the palace and out into the streets, that the foundling prince Atoon had tried to introduce to the Dapur was a failure, not a proper woman at all. In fact, probably a monster. The ladies, in their indignation, had struck her down with a flash of lightning. Before noon, Atoon had done what he could. He had sent a message into the hills, to the only people within reach who might help Cho. He hoped they would come in time. When he had done that he sent, grimly, to the Koperasi office. But they could not reinforce the street patrols, they said. They were willing to take the foundling into protective custody, but otherwise ... 'Big brother suggest little brother fix-up fix-up him clean the house boys.' What a jargon they always made of the 'lower language'. Atoon read the message with a cool smile, and set to work to marshal his unarmed courtiers and frightened servants. That evening and the night passed quietly enough.

Cho was left alone, entirely alone. No one even brought her a tray of roots and leaves. They had fastened the door. They had put her away and didn't want her again. What had she done wrong? There was a lot of muttering and running about in the palace but she didn't like to try and find out why. At last, as a heavy twilight fell suddenly on the second day, Atoon appeared. His hair was dressed plainly, all his richness was gone. A boy with a tray did not want to come in until Atoon spoke sharply. He drew down the blinds, lit a small lamp and left again. It had been a hot, close day. The heat remained but now a wind was rising.

'I am sorry that you have been neglected,' said Atoon. 'I did not know. I could not come to you myself, and the household has been disturbed.'

She was sitting on the floor, wrapped in her bed cover. Hanggoda had taken the Dapur robes away, and she felt the need to hide –

'Can you tell me what I did wrong?' she asked sadly.

But Atoon could not. He said, haltingly. 'The people believe – well, a young woman who finds when she is entered that she cannot bear children has to leave the Dapur. The people believe that you are like that, and the ladies knew it, and – rejected you.'

'Oh.'

Atoon could well believe that his family had the power to knock someone over without touching them. But *why* would they do that – even should they feel insulted – especially in such a delicate situation, and after long and careful consideration of Cho's mission. And yet, he could not imagine Derveet, crazy though she might be, using a child subject to fits as a secret agent. Nothing made sense. And the worst aspect was that the ladies, since the incident, had not communicated with him in any way. But for now there was the child –

'Cho,' he said, 'Don't blame yourself. You did nothing wrong. Perhaps you were not better from that fall in the stream, perhaps that was it. You did your best anyway. It was just a

59

twist of fate. But now I have to get you away. I have sent a message. We will leave in the night and just hope the people I sent for make the rendezvous.'

The child's face had brightened considerably, but she looked puzzled.

'What does *entered* mean?' she asked. 'Like entered in a competition? I've learned about those.'

Atoon could not deal with this. He jumped up: 'We must get you some clothes –'

And then he saw on the couch a blouse and trousers like the ones she had been found in. The stuff was pure white, the make and weave unmistakably fine.

Prince Atoon stared. 'So this is their answer –' he murmured. He still did not understand. And yet, he began to see –

'A boy brought them,' said Cho. 'But he didn't tell me to put them on.'

'You are honoured,' said the prince softly. 'Put them on now.'

It was no time for ceremony: he just turned his back while she dressed. Then time passed. They both ignored the tray of food. Atoon sat and looked at Cho wearing her white clothes with a beautiful expression in his eyes that made her forget all the upset. She knew that she had been useful, to this person at least. The scent of the lamp rose sweetly, darkness deepened, the wind rattled the blinds.

'What are the things,' asked Cho, 'that men are not allowed to do?'

'To light a fire,' answered Atoon, automatically. 'To prepare food, to weave, to work in the fields, to build a house, to rear children. The essentials of life. But the ladies don't want to be too involved with us, for various good reasons, and so they make boys.'

'Then what *may* you do?'

'Oh there's sport, literature, various pastimes. And we are allowed the Dance, if anyone had the heart for it nowadays. And there was war.'

A troubled murmur had begun to grow, somewhere outside, like a muttering storm.

Atoon smiled – 'And of course, I govern –'

60

'Couldn't you get your friends in the Dapur to teach you the "essentials"? When you visit them?'

Atoon stared. He thought of curtains, veils, darkness: a brief event, at first alarming, then made acceptable by repetition. What world does this child come from? he thought. But all he said was, gently, 'No, Cho. I don't think so.'

Divine Endurance came bounding through Cho's door.

'You're not supposed to do that,' said Cho. 'You're supposed to get someone to open it for you.'

'There was no one about,' said the Cat. 'Come quickly. I have Gress waiting. The crowd is coming. They want to mistreat you, and unless you have more control over your maintenance than I imagine we are all going to be seriously embarrassed when they try. They wish to perform an operation called *scouring* – '

Atoon had been looking the other way when the Cat came in. Cho turned to him and asked:

'What is scouring?'

But he did not have to answer. A deep sound had begun to ring and ring and ring.

'That is the great gong,' said the prince calmly. 'It means the mob has entered my family's citadel. Come – '

He took the wooden dagger from his sash, dropped it and picked up from by the door things he had left there as he came in: dark, wide shawls to cover their clothes, a short bow, beautifully carved, and a wicker quiver of arrows. Out of the prince's apartments, through deserted gardens and a hall of faded blue and gold; they left the palace by the same route the young Garuda had taken, one unhappy night. All was quiet: the trouble was behind them in the great forecourts. They went underground, and came up in a private house, apparently empty, that leaned against the south wall of the city. A dark figure whispered, and they slipped through a wicket gate. Forest trees tossed their branches over the southern roadway. Atoon took the carved bow from his shoulder and listened to the darkness. But there was no one. They ran into the trees, past the glade of the great waringin and on, through the earth and leaf-scented darkness and the stirred, stormy air. At last they came to a junction where a ragged track went off uphill behind an enormous fig tree.

'Up here –'

Cho and the Cat went ahead of him, and they crouched together on a natural platform, the birth of three huge boughs. There was a moon somewhere in the rocking clouds. It glimmered on Atoon's eyes, wide and dark as he knelt with his arrow ready.

'I do know how to use this,' he remarked, grinning. 'In competitions.

'I am twenty-nine years old. I have an heir. God knows the cause is hopeless but what does that matter? Thank you, Cho. I can never thank you enough. You have not failed. I was a corpse walking and you brought me to life. You made me act –'

Cho said, anxiously: 'Twenty-nine *what*?

'Years.'

There was no time for more. Below them great lights suddenly jumped in the dark. The Koperasi patrol, knowing the habits of fugitives, had left the riot to look after itself and come to check the south wall. At the same time there were hoofbeats down the steep track. Atoon groaned, afraid the rescuers would turn back when they heard and saw the Koperasi. But they did not. Shapes milled under the tree. Somebody whistled, and Atoon replied. Someone shouted – 'Quickly – jump!'

'Goodbye Cho,' said Atoon. 'Remember me to her –' and then Cho was down on the ground among large plunging bodies. Someone cried: 'There's another pony –' 'Grab it then. The more the merrier –' Cho heard Gress's voice and cried, 'Oh, please don't. She doesn't like being grabbed –' Something faceless swooped then and grabbed *her*; flung her over a horse's shoulders and cuffed her wickedly hard on the side of the head. It was quicker than a blindfold.

The night of the wooden daggers ended in the early morning hours when the storm finally broke in thunder and torrential rain. Apart from material damage and many injuries of the kind unavoidable in street fighting, the only Jagdanan casualty was the noble youth Sandjaya. He had been too convincing with his wooden weapon, and persons unknown had defended themselves in earnest. The Dapur had his body brought to them, and arranged his funeral themselves. Perhaps it was time for the wall and the garden to pass away, but still they honoured him for remembering his purpose in life.

8   Four Sacks of Rice

Cho woke up. She had been sleeping for most of a long confusing journey that had lasted more than one day and night. Every time she stirred, because it seemed she was wanted, they growled *go back to sleep*, or smacked her again, which she took to mean the same thing. She lay with her cheek pressed against dark, gritty sand, considering. The journey had been in two stages. First they stopped in a murky cramped place, and she glimpsed through the door wooded hills all around. The people discussed Atoon's message, and wondered what to do with Cho, but they didn't want her, so she went back to sleep. Now they've brought me to somewhere else, she thought. They've brought me to someone who knows what to do. I'm wanted again now. She felt excited.

The sand extended in all directions with humps and twists of rough dark rock cropping out of it. There were several people sitting about looking very like the rocks. There was not much light but somewhere nearby red flickering flames jumped and danced. Her eyes followed them upwards into solid darkness: she was in a cave.

Someone said, 'It can't have run after us all the way from Jagdana –'

'Well, who carried it then?'

Cho rolled over and found Divine Endurance sitting beside her coolly washing her ears.

'You've upset them,' she whispered accusingly.

'They'll get over it.'

The people noticed that Cho was moving, and a boy came and took her by the arm and led her to the fire, which was shut in a box with a red hole for the flames to get out. He found a little three-legged stool, looking shy as he produced such a treasure, and invited Cho with smiles to sit down: enjoy the hearth. She tried to talk to him in Atoon's way, but he could not. He showed her his mouth. It was like a snake's, with smooth sharp gums and a little ribbon of a tongue.

'That's an interesting idea,' said Cho. 'Can you catch things like a snake? Can you swallow squirrels?'

The boy only smiled. Then he stood up, and crouched down in a curtsey. Cho saw someone coming towards them: a tall woman. She had a scarf tied round her head, but the hair that escaped was a bright, harsh, yellow colour. The skin of her face was red, and her eyes were blue. Cho stared, she couldn't help it. Somebody prodded her in the back and muttered, 'This is our Annet. Show respect.' But the yellow-haired woman laughed. She squatted down and looked at Cho carefully.

'So, "Derveet's emissary". Well, what can I do for you, Derveet's emissary?'

The rock people gathered round. The snake boy had picked up the leg of a dead animal that our Annet had dropped by him and was singeing off the hair, turning the thin shank over the escaping flames. He smiled encouragingly. Divine Endurance hurried up, and jumped onto Cho's knees.

'Ask her –' she began firmly –

But Annet laughed again and said, 'Don't bother now. Eat. Sleep. I want to think about you.'

She stood up, prodded with her fingers at a pot steaming on the stove and walked away, pulling up her sarong to wipe her hands and revealing long legs that were the same hot brick colour as her face.

So Cho ate and slept with the rock people. They touched her clothes and murmured, and gave her a kind of coverlet. Cho didn't know what to do with it; it was not decorative, and she didn't want to hide, but the rock people laughed at her and said, 'Don't you feel the cold?' They were all out of the ordinary in some way, like the snake boy and Annet. Some of them were very odd indeed: she could not think that all the interesting ideas were good ones.

Eventually Annet appeared again. This time she took Cho out of the hearth cave and along a rock passage that opened on daylight. Below them lay an enormous basin of black sand, patterned with tiny pale paths and scattered patches of vegetation. Steep cliffs rimmed it, small and sharp far away, dark and rugged here. The sky above was a thin clear blue, like

64

Annet's eyes. A path led down from the cave entrance to the sand.

'Am I in a different country from Jagdana?' said Cho. 'Is that why people are different?'

Annet was looking into the basin. She glanced at Cho, and laughed. 'You're in another country all right. This is Bu Awan, the Sky Mother. You're in the capital city of the country of the polowijo. Prince Atoon sent to my people, to get you out of Jagdana, and of course they brought you to me.'

Divine Endurance had been nagging and was now sitting at Cho's feet staring insistently. So Cho asked politely, 'Excuse me. You did ask what you could do. Please could you tell me how to get to the Rulers?'

Annet stared, and laughed again. 'You'll never see one,' she said shortly. 'They're like God. You can't touch them, see them, smell them. All you can do is try to endure whatever they decide to throw at you – The Rulers, ignorant little Derveet's emissary, live on their "shining islands" off the coast of Ranganar and haven't set foot on land for a hundred years. Are you making fun of me?'

'No,' said Cho gravely.

Annet gave her a glance of lingering suspicion and stared down at the sands again.

'Perhaps it's the Koperasi you want to get to. You know who they are, those big brutes in uniform. A lot of them look like me, don't they? The Koperasi are much more important than the Rulers.'

She smiled bleakly. 'Listen, little Derveet's emissary, since you're looking at me as if you never heard the word "polo-wijo", or "Koperasi" either, for Mother's sake – I'll tell you. All proper Peninsulans hate anything deformed. They always have. Red skin or three legs, it's all one, except red skin's worse, it's not even pitiable, just disgusting. They always, always have. And so, when the shining islands people came, they found a whole little nation scattered about the Peninsula, with nothing to lose and ready and willing to co-operate. Where would the Rulers be without them? So you see, even though our families abandon us, or sell us to the camps, we polowijo are not to be despised.... It means *weeds*, in case you didn't know. The things the Dapurs root up and throw away. What do you think of my garden of weeds, little one?'

Cho was listening seriously. It was not the first time she had heard 'polowijo' or 'Koperasi', but Annet seemed to know this anyway, so there was no need to explain. She tried to be polite, so far as her conscience would let her.

'Well, I didn't know it happened to people, but perhaps these ones were designed wrong, a long time ago – ?'

Annet looked up, startled. She peered at Cho with a puzzled expression that changed to a scornful smile.

'Oh yes, I remember. That's one of Derveet's crazy stories. Don't be ridiculous. You can't design people. There's no mystery about it, we're just mother earth's little mistakes. I'm a mistake. And you are too. You're a polowijo yourself.'

'No I'm not,' said Cho.

Annet would have laughed, but the childish innocence in those peculiar little eyes was too much for her. She shrugged, and turned back to the wide black sands.

'And so's Derveet,' she murmured. 'She's one of us too.'

There were some people, tiny in the distance, down in the basin. They crept out from the farther cliffs a little way and then crept back. Not wanting to interrupt anything – for clearly this was what Annet had come out to see – Cho waited until they were gone before she asked diffidently –

'Is Derveet here now?'

'No,' said Annet. She seemed annoyed, she didn't look at Cho. 'No, Derveet isn't here. She left us.'

Then they went in. The yellow-haired woman became more cheerful when they were back in the caves.

'That white outfit,' she said to Cho. 'It's cute. I like it. Suits you.'

When she had gone away, leaving them with the rock people again, Cho asked Divine Endurance about what Annet had said. The Cat reminded her that once there had been several different makes of people. The red-skinned ones, or other shades, were simply left over from that time.

'What about the others? *Did* someone design them wrongly?'

'This world isn't like our palace,' said Divine Endurance. 'Mistakes are normal. If there are more than usual now, it could be the remains of something people did to each other. Or it could be something to do with the way things broke down, that time when they went away and left us. It doesn't matter. You can't expect such an old world to run the way it ought to.'

They were silent for a moment, thinking of the age of the world.

'Of course, when you get to your brother, the two of you will be able to sort out all these problems.'

But Annet did not come back, and the polowijo clearly didn't want their visitors to leave. They watched Cho carefully, and showed by signs she was not to go near the passage to the outside. The disappointment Cho had felt when Annet appeared increased. These people were definitely the *outcasts* who had once helped Derveet to make fireworks. But most of the polowijo who had known her had gone away, it seemed, and anyway no one wanted to talk to Cho. They managed to explore a little and found Gress in a rock corral with a few other miserable ponies. She wasn't happy. She had heard that these people sometimes needed meat more than they needed transport. Or visitors.

'I've seen them looking at you in a funny way,' she said. 'We ought to leave at once.'

'This isn't getting us to Wo,' grumbled Divine Endurance.

But how could they leave if the people wanted them to stay? Cho wanted to try and explain that she really wasn't a polowijo, but Divine Endurance pointed out that insisting on this could only give offence.

Cho sighed. 'If only some of the Derveet people were here still. Things seem to change and happen so quickly in this world. Which reminds me Divine Endurance – what can prince Atoon have meant by saying he'd only been alive twenty-nine years – ?'

'Ah,' said Divine Endurance. 'I was going to explain about that.'

But she didn't. Snake boy appeared then, and took them back to the hearth.

The problem was solved in an unexpected way. Another night passed, with a very small amount of eating practice and the undecorative coverlets. Early in the morning Annet came back and took Cho to the rock corral. She fetched Gress, with a rope tied round her head, and gave the end to Cho.

'Come on,' she said. 'Bring the cat, if it is yours, and anything else you had with you.'

They went by different passages this time that sloped uphill. Cho knew they were climbing inside the black cliffs and through the rim of the basin. Gress's hooves clopped and stumbled on the smooth rubbed lava. Soon the air freshened. It was hard to tell when they were underground and when not, for it was scarcely light and they were at the bottom of a stirred pot of frozen rock waves, of fissures and twisted grottos; the jagged, dim sky coming and going in splashes overhead. There was a smell of sulphur in the air. At last they emerged in the open. Peaks stood all around, coloured rose and purple in the dawn. 'Pencak Biru,' said Annet. 'Obeng, Bahtera – the attendants of Mother Sky.'

Cho looked behind her and saw the caldera of the vast sleeping volcano, wider and greater than from the cave's mouth and veiled mysteriously in morning cloud.

'And now look at this –'

Annet tucked up her sarong and scrambled over the bare ridge of ground, and stood looking down. They were on the edge of a secondary crater. But there was no black sand, no vegetation, just bare red screes, steams and shining clays. The far wall had gone, and in the jagged gap a red wilderness fell away, fading in the distance into a tumble of brown and greenish hills. It was an impressive view. Cho sat down and stared.

'Mangkuk Kematian,' said Annet. 'The Bowl of Death. The states meet here. In the west, Jagdana: in the east, Timur Kering. Those hills are the north of the Kedaulatan, that was the Garuda state, the sovereign land. It's called the Sawah now, it's just one big Koperasi farm camp. There was a battle here in the last Rebellion. You used to be able to see bones, before the hot springs dyed them. Half the princes were fighting on the Koperasi side by that time, for various stupid reasons. That's the way the Rebellion ended – we all went mad. The Rulers just looked on, and then left us to the Koperasi. So the Dapurs say: never more. If we go to war again the earth will turn to poison and the sun will no longer shine. Which makes people stop and think, however little life is worth now, because the ladies generally keep their promises.

68

'Now I'm going to tell you a story. After the Rebellion the Garuda family was destroyed. The Garuda palace was sacked before they built the dam, and most of the Dapur died there. Some escaped, but ten years after the Rebellion the Koperasi were still hunting, and the Garuda remnant finally surrendered themselves and their boys and men, and they were murdered. Only the crown prince survived, a little baby they'd sent secretly to Bu Awan. He grew up with the polowijo, but unfortunately the servants who brought him here gave him a ridiculous education – taught him he was a prince, the Garuda, the last hope. And I suppose the polowijo believed it too. When he was grown up he started trying to plan another Rebellion. He was going to set the polowijo against the Koperasi, that's a joke, isn't it? Worse, he'd got an idea into his head, about certain things the Dapur likes to keep hidden. There is no Dapur on the mountain, we have no secrets here. But talking was bad enough. The Hanomans of Jagdana, who knew all about the polowijo Garuda, sent him a warning that he'd better stop. He did, more or less. Now ever since the prince was old enough for entering, the polowijo had been trying to get children by him, because men are rare up here. But it's hard for a weed to bear fruit. The prince was well past forty, when someone finally managed to give birth to a daughter. The effort was too much for the poor weed, and she died. But having a daughter changed everything for the prince. As soon as she was rational he started his rebellion plans again. He didn't have to listen to the Hanomans, he had his own Dapur, and she – apparently – was as mad as he was. He called her Merpati, the dove, which is an old family name. When she was fourteen years old, a woman, but not old enough to be entered, the Koperasi raided Bu Awan and took her away. They'd found out about the rebellion plans, you see. The Koperasi had learned to be a bit more subtle. They didn't kill our "last hope". They offered him his daughter back. And he accepted the offer. When she died, he left for the Black Islands – but not alone, as you know. Only one thing the shit-eaters hadn't reckoned on: the bloody-mindedness of a young Garuda. They had no idea she'd have conceived from what they did to her. But of course she knew there was no other chance. . . . '

Wisps of steam drifted across the Bowl. Annet, squatting on

her thighs, shifted her weight a bit. A thin ribbon of dust-coloured track curled across the red rocks. There was something moving on it.

'I've told you that story, because there's something about it that always strikes me: the Hanomans must have known. They've always got their feelers out, keeping track of the Koperasi. I'm not saying they organised it but they *knew*. And they let it happen – to save lives. What I mean to say is, if you've got people to look after you have to do whatever you can.

'It isn't the same up here as it was a hundred years ago. Something's happened to the Peninsula, since the Rebellion. It's not that the Koperasi have everyone in their camps: it's more that people take things out on the polowijo the way they never did before. They stone babies, if you can imagine that. The whole area around Bu Awan used to be our sanctuary. Not anymore. We're few, we're hungry, we get sick, and none of us lives long. There's not much I wouldn't do for half a dozen *senjata* less than fifty years old.'

She glanced at Cho sardonically: 'That means guns. Firearms. To shoot animals – I am not interested in shooting the Koperasi. Nor am I interested in any messing about with black powder, white powder, garden cleaner and sugar. I never was. All that business is pointless.

'It's hard enough just to stay alive. My family sold me, a slave camp reared me until I ran away. That's the story for all us Bu Awan people. What are the Koperasi to us? Only the ones who didn't escape. Remember my story. I don't want to betray anyone; I wouldn't betray *her*. At least I hope not. But this won't do her any harm, she's too clever. Times are hard you see. It's all very well for prince Atoon, but he's just got no idea how hard times are. . . . '

She stood up. The movement on the path had been replaced by scrambling noises. As she stood, a head appeared above the rim of the bowl. The figure clambered up and was followed by three more. They gathered together and approached. They were all holding things that were obviously weapons somewhat different from Atoon's bow and arrows, and their faces had a hard and hungry look. One of them was wearing canvas boots with laces, another a sort of jacket with the sleeves torn out and some very tattered ribbons on the shoulders. . . . Annet clearly was not surprised to see them.

They came forward, slowly and warily. Annet nodded to them, and one, shifting his weapon carefully from hand to hand, tossed down a heavy small sack. Each in turn did the same. Annet folded her arms and smiled. And then, with a cool indifference that had something fine about it – even in these circumstances – she picked up two of the sacks of rice, turned her back and walked calmly away. The four renegades came up to Cho and Gress and the Cat and stood around them staring. One of them licked his lips.

'I *told* you,' said Gress, shuddering on the rope's end. 'I *told* you they were looking at you in a funny way. We should have made a run for it –'

But even she could see it was too late now.

9 Crossing a River

Just after dark on the second day they came to a big river. The bridge was a floating one; a raft that was winched across the water on great thick hawsers by a gang of boys. The raft was nowhere to be seen when they arrived, just the hawsers reaching out towards the farther shore, where there were no lights and no one seemed awake. The river was thick and high and smothered, like the whole landscape, in pouring rain. Far away behind them Bu Awan and her attendants had vanished at last; they had been hovering in the northern sky like mirages, high above the lowly wilderness.

The road spread out into a vague area of broken stones, puddles and litter where various vehicles and beasts stood dismally in the wet dusk. Under a big dripping lean-to shelter, travellers of all kinds were waiting for the turnaround. Lamps stood on benches, each white blot of light a smudge of tiny insects, and an unpleasant smell of stale food and rancid oil rose from the hawkers' braziers. The renegades put Cho on a damp unlit bench just under the crazy roof, and sat themselves further inside, keeping an eye on her occasionally. But they had learned that she was very docile, so they didn't bother much. Gress left the pack animals, and tried to join Cho and the Cat, but there was an outcry, so she had to stay outside eyeing the four ruffians threateningly through her dripping mane. But it was clear by now that they were not going to be eaten. Nor were they, as they had first thought, in the hands of the Koperasi – who might have taken them to the Rulers, and Wo. Divine Endurance and Cho had soon realised the truth. They had been sold to a gang of bounty hunters. Cho was the bait in a trap.

The other travellers under the lean-to were a mixed bunch. There was a party of Commercers from Ranganar, looking prim in waterproofs and galoshes; a small detachment of Koperasi in uniform; some more or less respectable-looking boys alone on their families' errands; a few men, commoners or small gentry, watchfully surrounded by servants. Everyone seemed equally ill at ease: travel could be perilous in the Sawah. A handbill tacked to a roof prop near Cho's bench warned that the infamous Anakmati was still at large. Cho looked from group to group. For two days the gang had been talking about getting back to the Koperasi world; the delights of civilisation, but there was nothing delightful here. She didn't like the strong-smelling white lamps, or the borrowed-looking scabby litter that seemed to cling to everything. All the travellers were gloomy and silent. The only sign of life was in a distant corner, where a boy was running to and fro feeding the Koperasi's vehicle from a big tub of fuel. There was someone sitting over by the tub, in the dark, apparently indifferent to the sickening smell of hydrocarbon. This person was playing a game: trying to light a cigarette in the rain and flicking sizzling matches at the fuel boy. He laughed delightedly as he dodged with his splashing jug. Cho saw one of the waterproofed people go over and remonstrate.

The figure in the darkness suggested, in an easy, smiling voice, that the good woman might go and lick herself. The Commercer, startled at being answered in such an idiom up here, backed off. But she had glimpsed the ruffian's face. She retreated to her friends, and muttered. The Commercers moved further away.

One of the bounty hunters had gone off, in a furtive way, to talk to the ferry boys under the winch hut. Evidently arrangements were being discussed. Divine Endurance crouched on the bench by Cho's side, grumbling continuously. It was all Atoon's fault. Of course the outcasts had been bound to sell Cho. 'The man has no understanding of his own world. He might as well have given us to the Koperasi in the first place.' She stared angrily out at the streaming night: 'Why *do* they let it rain like this? They do it out of spite.'

'This is North-East Wind,' said Gress dolefully. '*Nobody* travels when it's North-East Wind –'

The Cat had been trying to get Cho to escape ever since Bu Awan. Now she said hopefully: 'Those red ones in uniform are going south.'

'You're eavesdropping,' complained Cho half-heartedly.

73

'They're not allowed to take that vehicle of theirs across the causeway. It's called an "hc treader". Ah, this Ranganar place is on an island. Perhaps there's another causeway to the Rulers' islands. They live next door, don't they. . . . The red creatures have decided this bridge is broken. They think they'll try another crossing. . . . '

'What about Gress?' said Cho.

The Cat gave her a scornful glance.

Cho was occupied by a strange feeling that she was being looked at. She answered inattentively: 'We were told to sit here. And anyway, Divine Endurance, I don't like that treader thing. It is *messy*. . . . '

Divine Endurance contemplated the hc treader, easily identified in the huddle of bullock carts and scraggy pack ponies. It was a long, squat box of rusted metal, mounted on continuous tracks of articulated treads, with a dented cab in front for the driver and guard. It would be dry inside that box.

The fourth bounty hunter came back and there was an animated discussion. The other travellers eyed the gang resentfully. They felt that 'mountainy' people shouldn't be allowed, but it was obviously pointless to protest. Cho was here to be looked at. A representative of the quarry was somewhere about, incognito, examining the goods. Was she exactly as found? The small cat, the pony, the clothes: nothing interfered with? This was very important. The gang studied Cho and arranged her, and exhorted her to smile, to look pleased, pleased or else they would smack her. They wondered who the connection was and stared hard, with bursts of giggles, at the rubber-coated Commercers. They wondered what Cho, whom they took to be a boy, was to the quarry and poked, graphically, their thumbs into their fists, winking at her. . . . Bzzz Bzzz, they told her lewdly.

The fun was interrupted by a hawker boy, who was going round herding up lamps. Suddenly they realised that the scene around them had changed. Instead of distant uneasy groups, benches were being drawn together to form a single huddle of travellers in the middle of the shelter, ringed with lights. . . . The hawker whispered. The bounty hunters listened, but they were not impressed. They laughed. 'Anakmati!' they cried derisively, right out loud. The other boy winced and flapped his hands; the nervous travellers glared out of the lamplight.

'Anakmati is not here,' said the boy in the sleeveless jacket. He put his fists in his sash and strutted, with a complacent wink or two at his bold companions. 'I am telling you. He is not here. Not himself, oh no.'

But the tight, brightly lit huddle did not seem reassured. And something else was happening. The uniformed Koperasi, scenting trouble, had made up their minds at last. They were off to find another ferry.

'Come on –' said Divine Endurance.

Cho was thinking – Who *is* it that's watching me? The treader started up with a growl, farting gouts of black smoke. Carts jostled and beasts stumbled: it thrust itself out of the parking lot backwards and began to turn, noisily. The bounty hunters suddenly stopped laughing. They had realised their plot was at risk, if something unusual seemed to be going on. The treader, with a final roar, vanished into the dark. Cho jumped up: 'Oh!' The bench beside her was empty. The boys pushed her down again. 'Sit there! Sit! Sit!' they cried like birds, and flapped off in a panic to the winch hut.

Cho was alone. She could hardly believe that Divine Endurance was gone. Divine Endurance had *always* been there. Surely she would come trotting back in a minute, out of the black rain; grumbling and nagging.... No one came. The rain dripped from the eaves on the little figure left uncared for out in the dark. So now the journey was really over, and there was nothing between Cho and her childhood's dream. She had upsetting thoughts, of death and brief lives, mysteries and misunderstandings. But she let them come and go. They were not her business. Her business was to make a move. It was hard, it went cruelly against her nature, but it had to be done.

Cho had followed the details of the game she and the Cat had fallen into with attention. She knew she was in a very awkward position just now. She had been worrying ever since Bu Awan. What was she to do? It hurt her to think how upset the bounty hunters would be. They had told her to Sit! Sit! She shivered. She was beginning to learn, in her heart, what chill and coldness meant. She looked down at her white clothes; they were damaged and had lost their brightness. The travellers were engrossed in their fear, there was nobody now in the corner by the fuel tub. She felt very lonely. Quietly, she got to her feet and slipped out into the rain.

Gress had not let herself be tied, and she followed faithfully after. So did someone else. Cho crept through scrubby bushes on the river bank, heading away from the road. In spite of the noisy rain, she soon realised she could hear the crunch of hooves.

'Gress? Is that you?'

It was not Gress, it was a tall stranger, so dark she felt rather than saw him. Someone was at his head holding the bridle to stop it chiming.

'Please don't be alarmed. I've been watching you, and I thought you might be in need of help. Is there anything I can do?'

The voice was quiet, but something about it made Cho shiver again. The rain and the river water beat together on the darkness.

'Who are you?' she whispered.

The horse's bridle clinked and a light sprang up. Cho saw – the ruffian from beside the fuel tub. And now it was clear why the waterproof woman had started an alarm. A dark skin, harsh features and a black patch over the right eye: it was the bandit on the poster.

'It is a kind of pigeon,' said the quiet voice. 'It sits in the woods endlessly saying plonk, plonk, plonk on a descending scale, which sounds so miserable they call it the dead baby bird – Anakmati.'

'Oh. You were looking at me.'

'Yes.'

The one brilliant eye stared at Cho now, again. First at her face and then – with a sudden soft exclamation the light came forward:

'You've torn your blouse,' said the bandit, in a strangely hesitant tone, touching the place with one dark finger.

'I know, I've been waiting for it to mend itself but it hasn't yet.'

'What – ?'

Cho had just realised that the small flame still fizzing in the rain was not a match. It was a firework. Suddenly there were shouts. White light splashed out of the lean-to: people were running and yelling.

76

'That's for you,' said Anakmati, tossed the lightstick into the bushes and jumped onto the horse. Cho felt her wrist grasped strongly and up she went in front. They got down to the water with the hue and cry still milling in disarray around the parking lot. But the floating bridge had started to move at last. The tall horse saw a monster rushing at him. He reared up, into the glare of the raft's big lamps.

'Disini! Disini! – Here! Here!' yelled the ferry boys. The hue and cry came running, yelling, 'Stop! Firearm here! Senjata bullit!' The bounty hunters could be heard shouting that no one was to damage their goods. The senjata were home-made and horrible. One of them went off, vomiting chunks of resin, nails, broken crockery – flinging its owner backwards. Anakmati's mount struggled and jibbed half in the river and half out of it, more panicked by the crowd than by the makeshift bullits. The riders would have been overwhelmed when suddenly, with a wild inhuman cry, someone else thrust into the mob, sending ferry boys and the bolder travellers flying.

'Gress!' cried Cho. 'She was following me –'

In another moment they were in free water, with the dun pony plunging gamely beside them. Anakmati pulled the horse round to the raft and lunged – the boys saw a long knife and all leapt for the far side, but it was the hawsers that were slashed – sliced almost through with two fierce strokes, and the unbalanced weight did the rest.

Uproar and chaos left behind, the two horses thrust strongly into the current and pulled themselves up at last on the farther shore, a safe distance below the crossing.

'That is an extraordinary pony,' said Anakmati. 'How did you teach her?'

'Teach?' said Cho. 'I think she just lost her temper.'

The tall horse slowed to a walk and stood, breathing heavily, getting over the excitement. After a moment Anakmati's arm stopped holding Cho.

'You may as well get down,' said the bandit, 'and ride your own pony.'

So Cho got down.

10   Anakmati

In the hilly north of the Sawah at least as much achar grew on
the meandering terraces as any legal crop. Lawless little
towns of the weed-farmers sprang up and quickly faded.
They were rootless without the Dapur, but new spores were
always drifting in. The Koperasi either would not or could
not control this land. Much of the low grade 'sawah plant'
found its way to the slave farms and helped to keep them
quiet, and besides the gangsters controlled themselves, one
way or another.

A traveller arrived at Adi's hotel, late at night, alone but for
one small servant. A whisper and a shiver of excitement went
round the courtyards as the black horse was led away. The
desk clerk presenting the nightstay book (for Adi's had pre-
tensions) nearly swooned when the traveller briefly smiled.
He wore drab rough silk, well cut, a sash of dull scarlet. His
hair in a short braid dangled scarlet cords on his shoulder. So
gentlemanly – only canvas Koperasi boots and perhaps too
many rings on the long dark hands, gave away the gangster.
The clerk pursed his lips faintly at the boots and sighed. They
were in a spreading pool of water.

'Sir has been in the rain tonight.'

Sir volunteered nothing.

'May we send a brazier? A small meal?'

'Thank you, nothing. I am tired and do not wish to be
disturbed.'

He reregistered; a perfunctory scrawl with his right hand.
He had been born left handed and had been trying dutifully
to unlearn it for fifteen years. The people considered it,
though wrongly, a woman's trait. The boy made a hissing
noise at the servant – shooing him off to the kitchen instead of
standing dripping in the guests' hall.

'No. Sleeps with me.'

The clerk smirked, and inquired if another bed was needed. He was quelled by a hard glance from that one glittering eye.

Adi kept the best room in the house for Anakmati. The lamps were trimmed and bright, the bed curtains only a little ragged; the rattan screens that gave onto the verandah were in good repair. Adi's personal boys, the junior management of the hotel, carried in Anakmati's one small bag, and left reluctantly fizzing with suppressed excitement. The bandit's servant seemed worried about something.

'I know,' said Anakmati. 'I feel it too. But I would rather not have anything hanging over me.'

The Sawah world had loved and respected Anakmati for years and the bounty hunters were stranded by the crippled ferry. But everyone knew about that project, and the change it meant in the Koperasi's attitude. It would be a shame, but if Anakmati's luck was over, then it would be something to have shared the idol's most exciting moments.

'Let's wait a little.'

He took out a cigarette. He had smoked about half of it, wandering round the room in his wet clothes, when a member of the junior management appeared with a tray: 'Please, please take something. Or we'll be ashamed –'

Anakmati laughed, and accepted the appetising little meal. The boy was a lovely young thing. He gave Cho a sulky look as he went out.

'I hope you are not very hungry,' said Anakmati, and taking the tray into the private washroom disposed of the food. Cho was still standing: 'Sit down –'

She crouched on the floor, and watched the bandit sit on the end of the bed and peel off the sodden canvas boots, and the eye-patch. The eye was not blind. It blinked at the light. . . and there was a subtle change in Anakmati's presence and bearing.

'*Derveet*,' said Cho softly.

Derveet smiled. 'I sometimes have trouble with that eye,' she said. 'I hurt it, years ago. Besides, the patch – er, helps me.'

'It's a game,' she went on. 'Just a game.'

She undressed no further, but sat with her chin on her hands, frowning. Cho examined a dark face with a long firm mouth, angular cheeks and jaw, and a sharp curved beak of a nose. The skin near one of the beautiful eyes was a slightly

79

different texture. Anakmati-Derveet grew restless under this steady appraisal. She got up, and prised something out of her breeches' pocket.

'When I came to Adi's yesterday,' she said, 'I heard that someone was offering something that belonged to Anakmati for sale. Anakmati was to send a friend to look it over, and arrange the transaction. I was curious, so I went to the crossing myself.' She opened her hand, and showed a little round silver gilt object, delicately engraved. 'Do you know what this is?'

'Oh yes,' said Cho at once. 'It's one of prince Atoon's bells. He wears them when he dances and it is very dignified.'

Derveet's eyes widened; her mouth twitched, fractionally. 'Where *did* you get those clothes?'

'It was before I went to see Annet. The ladies gave them to me, when I was staying in prince Atoon's pabrik.'

'His what?'

'Pabrik. Factory? A place where you live. I've never said it out loud before. Is it not the right word?'

'It is not quite the usual term,' said Derveet gravely. 'So, Atoon had trouble, I know that. He passed you to Annet. Who promptly sold you to those playboys. Oh well, I suppose she couldn't help it. I'm lucky she didn't tell them another name for Anakmati, aren't I?'

'Do you have a lot of names?'

'One name. Various titles,' Derveet smiled. 'Which is quite usual, of course, for a person in my position.'

The child, kneeling in delicate composure on the dirty floor, seemed to have no intention of explaining herself. She radiated a bewildering innocence, just as in that sordid riverside shelter. In the neck of her torn blouse pale flesh curved like the petals of a flower. Derveet got up and put the tray out in the corridor. She stood by the door and said, 'Where do you come from?'

Willingly, Cho started to tell. Derveet soon stopped her. She remarked, sounding a little dazed, that people love to exaggerate. She had always heard the east of the landmass was one poison desert. . . .

'Yes. That's true. It's pretty though. It shines.'

'Oh. I see. So – so what did you live on?'

'On the ground.'

For the second time in a few days Derveet felt her affairs

entered by something forceful and mysterious. This was very different, a different order of invasion entirely, but the sense of helplessness was the same. She left the door, and sat down by Cho's side.

'When I was passing through Jagdana a few days ago,' she said, 'I saw a horrible thing. Someone had dealt with some animals in a way – I can't imagine how. There was nothing left but blood.' She meant to say: that she knew these were frightening days, she could understand the evasions, it was hard to trust anyone. She didn't get so far. The quiet face was suddenly wide open, flooded with a child's anguished, abject shame –

Derveet got up at once and moved as far away as possible. 'I'm sorry,' she said. 'I'm sorry –'

A long silence fell. The hotel bustled a little, and settled for the night. Derveet smoked another cigarette and moved around quietly, making some preparations. Her companion was curled up on the floor like a little cat. Derveet thought she was sleeping; it seemed best to leave her alone. She put out the lamps and lay down. Eventually, there was a tiny sound. Derveet opened her eyes. The door was not bolted. Anakmati rarely fastened doors: it was part of his fearless style. The latch rose with a tiny plop and the door floated open. Derveet had left the bed. She walked into the last two intruders – burst a firestick in the eyes of one, and kicked the other in the face. She turned on the one who had come in first. He was big; a man, by the look of him. She was afraid of firearms. The Sawah made its own bullits out of untempered resin that shattered in a ghastly way on impact. But this assassin had a weedcutter. He swung it in an arc – she dropped to the floor. There was a smell of fused sawdust and an angry whining as the blades met some of Adi's furniture. She kicked up into his crotch, took his weight and he fell over her. She followed, rising in a fluid curve, left the ground and brought her heels down savagely on his face. The whining stopped. She hoped he had not fallen on the cutter, or broken his neck. The other two seemed to have vanished. She rolled over, and saw the child, her head raised alertly but not looking at the fight, looking at the garden screen. She herself could hear nothing. She got to her feet and picked up two small armed quoits that she had left on the end of the bed. The screen slipped open.

'Habis?' said an unwary voice in the slice of cool night – 'have you finished?' There seemed to be three or four of them. Silence, and the soft sound of purposeful movement: they took the point, and fled. Derveet sent the quoits after them, and someone crashed in the bushes, howling. Then all was quiet. She went and prodded the first assassin. He was curled into a ball, and groaning. She lit a lamp, and began to pull hard and steadily on the bell-rope by the bed.

The management perhaps thought Anakmati was clutching it in his death throes. For a long time no one stirred. When at last they came running, they found the bandit, eye-patch in place, sitting cross-legged on his bed, playing with the blades of a weedcutter and looking at a corpse. The hotelier himself, a paunchy, ageing boy full of easy good humour, was first in the room.

'Ah, Adi,' said Anakmati. 'So sorry to disturb you all, but could you please remove this?'

The one who had fallen in the bushes now ventured to moan a little.

'– And see to whoever that is in the garden, would you?'

The younger boys, giggling and whispering nervously, began to drag the groaning corpse away. Two of them were the intruders she had singed and kicked at. Adi looked at the floor, and his sliced furniture, and the calm amused face of his guest. He smiled sheepishly.

'Adi, I'm afraid you've been cooking with meat fat. I'm sure there was something in that meal you sent that kept me awake –'

The hotel owner was Jagdanan, originally, and hated any sort of a scene. His expression became pained and reproachful –

'Oh all right Adi. Goodnight.'

When he was gone she closed the screens and fastened the door. She stripped off the gangster's finery at last, and the silk sash that bound her breasts. She sat on the bed wrapped in a sarong with her hair unbraided and falling heavily to her shoulders, and put her face in her hands.

How very far she was from the garden now. The antics of the Sawah made her laugh, when she was afraid they ought to make

82

her cry. She was frightened sometimes: Anakmati might murder or maim someone one day, on the grounds that it was wrong to try to be different from the people. And here in the Sawah was the mirror of the entire Peninsula: flaring loyalties and unreasoning treachery – the whole proud, passionate imbecile entanglement. How can I lead them? she thought. Am I doing right? She had had to learn to tolerate that question in her mind's furniture; like a bad memory or a useless regret, it would never go away. She lifted her head, suddenly remembering the child, and found herself looking straight into those strange and quiet eyes. For a moment she forgot herself and gazed. It was as if a cool hand had touched her fever.

'I am sorry about that. I hope it didn't upset you.'

'Was it something that you are not allowed? Never mind – at least you didn't fall down.'

Derveet smiled. 'I am glad you do not think so. But you've been sleeping in wet clothes. Take them off, and come and sleep up here. Don't mind me. I'm going to stay awake.'

The child undressed without fuss and slipped under the coverlet. 'Excuse me,' said Derveet, just as she was closing her eyes, 'but you haven't told me your name. Would you like to?'

The rain was over, the clouds had broken. The moon had set, but a scatter of stars lit the sky over Adi's garden. Anakmati, dressed in dry clothes, sat on the verandah, unmoving but relaxed. Extraordinary things had been happening to Derveet. After leaving that shell in Jagdana fields she had travelled on, with a strange feeling not so much of uneasiness as of portent: something was happening. She was in the south of the state when she heard of the big riots in the capital, the 'Night of the Wooden Daggers'. The garbled story had an odd effect on her. What had Atoon been up to? Of course, probably he had done nothing: it was just the usual meaningless trouble. She went into town looking for information. There was a disturbance in the streets; she never reached her rendezvous. But someone pushed her in the crowd – a boy, she didn't see his face. She found in her hand Atoon's little silver bell. She held it now on her palm. Atoon – It was an answer to her sea shell. He had woken up. And more than Atoon himself. . . . She thought of Cho's white clothes and a shiver ran through her. It was as if the world, that had always turned obstinately against her, a stubborn, dragging force against all she attempted, had suddenly shuddered under her feet and majestically begun to roll the other way.... 'Chosen Among the Beautiful,' she said, out loud, and smiled. She was still sitting there on the verandah, breathing quietly, only her brilliant eyes awake, when the dawn came and the chickens wandered out and began to scratch around thoughtfully on the dew-pearled lawn.

11   The Sovereign Land

Anakmati and his servant left Adi's shortly before noon in another downpour, and rode away from the earth-walled settlement, with its senjata in the thatch, pungent bales in broken sheds and boy-brothels for month-ending Koperasi. The late rising Sawah world paid no attention: only the boys of Adi's hotel came out, and watched until the tall black gelding and the dun pony had vanished into the misty rain.

At sunset Derveet halted. The sky had cleared. They had left the road soon after leaving Adi's and were in a gully of red sandstone on the side of a hill, facing south with the achar and tea terraces behind them and ahead, apparently without end – a green barrier of savage wilderness. Derveet unsaddled Bejak and sat down and took off the Koperasi boots.

'Now then,' she said. 'I'm late. I have an appointment with my friends near Ranganar, but we're going to miss it because I daren't go by road after this excitment. We'll just have to trust them to rearrange themselves. We'll stop here. It's better to start on the forest by daylight, and I need some sleep.' She frowned at the unpromising green wall: 'Don't worry. I know a good route from here. We won't get lost. . . . I'm sorry. I have just realised that I have not asked you. You do mean to travel with me, don't you?'

Her companion looked up, and smiled and nodded as if the question was scarcely necessary.

'Will those boys chase us?'

'Oh no. There's no malice in it you know. They haven't the concentration.'

She had so many questions to ask this bewildering stranger, it was hard to know where to begin. The interrogation so far had hardly been satisfactory –

'If this is our camp,' said Cho, 'we ought to have a fire.'

Derveet shook her head: 'I'm sorry child. I'm afraid I can't.'

'Oh I know about that. Because of not being properly female. But can't I do it for you?'

She looked up cheerfully; she had already collected a little pile of damp twigs. No one had ever put the unfortunate truth to *Derveet* quite like that. She laughed. 'Of course – ' she said, fumbling for her lighter, with her face turned to hide her feelings. There was a faint crackling; a wisp of smoke and a flicker of miniature flames rose from between Cho's hands. Derveet looked stupidly at the cigarette lighter she was still holding.

'Oh, that's from prince Atoon – ' cried Cho delightedly. It was a worn knot of silver monkeys, with tiny ruby eyes.

In the morning they left Bejak's heavy harness, the canvas boots and Anakmati's rings in a neat pile for anyone who might find them. There were several hideouts in the Sawah and over the border in Timur Kering where Derveet was accustomed to keep the bandit's black horse, between adventures. But this occasion was different, and she wouldn't leave Bejak as a burden on frail loyalties if the Koperasi were hunting; he had better come to Ranganar.

'The bandit disappears,' she said thoughtfully, looking down at the discarded possessions without regret. 'And this time, I wonder, is it forever?'

Down to the sea on either hand the former Garuda state had been stripped and razed, replaced by endless tracts of copaiba, rubber and cane, the farm camps and the straight roads. But Derveet's route kept to the spine of the Kedaulatan where untamed forest, never touched by the Garudas, still defied *co-operation*. The wild green world that terrified the Koperasi was quiet and peaceful and still. The travellers moved quickly. Riding was impossible, but Derveet set a hard pace. Sometimes they had to make long diversions, submitting to the forest's casual obstacles. When the night was clear they walked until the moon had set, following the sound of a stream or one of the mysterious footpaths that appeared, along green ridges of bamboo and grass that rose and fell among the trees. Derveet was as firmly against meat as Divine Endurance had been against plants, but she promised Cho they would not eat anything poisonous. She had dried fruit and sticks of pressed rice with her, and when these ran out they ate what the forest offered. Cho was delighted, she felt just like the mouse by her boulder nibbling its seeds.

Sometimes Derveet talked, as they walked along with Bejak and Gress behind them, about the Peninsula and its history: Snakes and Cranes and Buffalo and Mouse-deer – a whole menagerie all gone now, under the Rulers; and the remainder – Hanoman the Ape of Jagdana, Garuda the Eagle and Singa the Tiger of Gamartha.... 'The Singas, the tiger-cats of Gamartha, ruled before my family took over. They've never forgiven us for being in charge when the shining islands came. *They* would have managed much better, they wouldn't have stood any nonsense.... There are three powers in what remains of the traditional Peninsula, Cho. You've made a great impression on two of them. I wonder what the third will think? We'll have to wait and see.'

Sometimes her voice changed, and Cho would realise joyfully that a story was beginning: a fairy tale.

'There was once,' said Derveet, 'a child who was born to rule. She lived in the garden, within the beautiful walls. She was taught by the wisest women, and excelled in everything, or at least everybody told her so. She was always happy and she never worried about her future, because she thought to rule such a perfect world must be very easy. But there was one path in the garden that she was told she must not follow. One day, when she was already a grown woman, she said to herself: Whatever is down that path, I ought to go and see. So she went down the path. It led to the city gate, so she went to the gate and looked out and saw the world. She was fascinated. She wondered why this important view had been kept from her. But then she saw something lying by the road. It was a human figure, lying in pain. The lady had never seen sickness like that before. She was bewildered. She could not understand why the other people just hurried by, as if the strange apparition was invisible to everyone but her. She went back into the garden and was very thoughtful; she said nothing to her friends. But the next day she went again down the path. When she looked out, she saw the figure that had been lying by the road being carried off, wrapped in a cloth. She stopped a passer-by and asked, "What is the matter with that boy?" "Madam," the citizen replied, "nothing is the matter. He was sick, and now he is dead." Then the lady decided she could not stay in the garden. She could not rule the people unless she could find a way to overcome sickness and death. That night she went to the nurse's room, where her baby son was lying, and she said to him: "I will name you before I go and I will call you Rahula, a shackle, because if anything could keep me back from my duty, it would be you. . . ." Then she left the beautiful walls, and wandered over the world. But since that time, all ladies have worn the *rahula* in memory of her.'

They were following a small river, that ran between cool dark rocks in a narrow gorge. Derveet lay on a big boulder to look into the stream.

'And what happened to her?' asked Cho. 'In the end?'

'In the end? Oh, there was a shaven-headed nun whom I missed out because we do not have them nowadays, we have nightclub entertainers instead – and there were many adventures. They say she came back to the garden at last, by a different way. . . .'

She told stories too about Ardjuna, the exiled prince, who was so elegant and well mannered ladies not of his own family were always wanting him to father children. This lead him into an endless series of absurd scrapes, with pretty youths and boys sent out to entrap him, as he wandered the princedoms. . . . 'In real life,' said Derveet, grinning, 'Ardjuna hates travelling. He says it makes his feet spread, and he can never get his hair done properly.'

Once, passing through an open glade, they came too close to a nesting place and were suddenly assaulted by a storm of colour: a whirl of gold and indigo plumes. 'Chack –' said the forest hen, sitting quietly and resolutely in the shadows, and the cockbird arced his wings and offered his throat of violet, his breast of crimson; just as he had paraded them in the other glade where he was chosen, not understanding then what it was for, his beauty. . . . 'God bless you,' said Derveet softly, and turned to hide the frightening glint of her eyes. 'Yes –' echoed Cho, thinking Derveet might be God, by another of her titles, and they went on. Cho listened, and remembered everything. She knew that Ardjuna was Atoon, and also that other prince, the baby called Rahula, was Atoon, and also in a way the rainbow bird. And the Dapur, cynical and tricky in the

Ardjuna stories, was also the desired garden, and the resolute waiting eyes in the shadows. She thought of these things and pondered them, in the black darkness of the night, when the two horses shifted about like invisible monsters: insects sang; a leaf fell with a sigh like thunder, and Derveet lay sleeping, her head pillowed on her arms on the soft ground.

For six days and nights they moved quickly southwards in perfect security. On the fifth night, the moon that had been thin and young when Cho left Jagdana came to the full, and Derveet missed her appointment, for she was supposed to meet her friends on the morning of the fourteenth of the month. But she assured Cho there would be no problem, perhaps also reassuring herself. This had happened before, and things had worked out. After that, however, the peaceful journey ended. On the seventh day the forest, which had been growing less dense, had changed completely. The great trees were still all around, but they seemed unsure of themselves and the silence was broken by a faint disturbing murmur: the Sawah at work in its camps, on its roads. That night Derveet tethered Jak for the first time.

The next morning they breakfasted on earthy groundnuts and a hand of wild bananas with pink seedy flesh. Derveet seemed sad and not only, Cho thought, because of the end of the forest. They had not been walking long that day before they came out of the trees into a broad open ride. It vanished, to their right, into swamp and elephant grass but to their left it led away, straight and true, with deeply incised banks rising on either side, half lost in young trees and undergrowth.

Cho stood, feeling the heaviness in the earth underfoot. 'Is this a Koperasi road?' she asked.

'No,' said Derveet.

The road was green, its pavement buried deep. But there were shapes among the trees on the valley sides, and there was an atmosphere Cho recognised. Several other rides intersected. Cho looked down them curiously but Derveet was uneasy. There was a feeling now that people were close by, and might appear at any moment. At last they came to a place where two pillars stood frankly at the top of a green ramp by the side of the road. Derveet led Bejak up and Cho and Gress followed. They entered a square space. It had been walled in wonderfully

89

faceted black stones, most were fallen now, but there were rough repairs of stakes and thatch, so the sanctuary still had some privacy. There were platforms with steps, some of them roofed in thatch to protect the remaining carvings: Cho stared.

'Roh Betina,' said Derveet, 'The Mother of Life, directs Hanoman the Ape and Gardua the Eagle in remaking the Peninsula out of chaos. That pointy thing under her left foot is Bu Awan –'

The mother of life was carved like a hideous demon, to give some sense of her terror and her power.

'They are dancing.'

'Of course.'

Derveet was looking round the sanctuary, on the sculpted altars and in the niches of the walls, but she couldn't find what she was searching for, and gave up, frowning a little.

'Come on. We'll leave Gress and Bejak here.'

As they went up the road, the atmosphere Cho had recognised quickly gave way before a very different feeling. The straight way had been gently climbing. They came to the top of a rise – ahead of them the vista was cut off. The green road vanished under a wide expanse of stone chippings; a chipping road curved away to one side. There was a huge, angry-looking wire fence, and inside it buildings with hc treaders in front of them. Beyond the buildings a great white wall with yellow water stains on it stopped the mouth of the valley. A small amount of water moved from two vents at the bottom of this wall. There were people walking about.

'Are you going to blow it up?'

Derveet had slipped to her knees, below the skyline. She said without looking at the child: 'No. I hope not. Ranganar depends on this place now. I need Ranganar, we all do.'

'*Without the water the fish will die,*' murmured Cho. Derveet turned to her, and smiled.

They took a path into the undergrowth, came to a wide drain that took the outflow of the reservoir and crossed it paddling through the stream. They climbed over the pipelines, rearing like great snakes through the greenery, and arrived at last on a hilltop. The heat of the morning was already bright up here. Under a vivid blue sky spicy scents rose from shrubs and bushes; tumbled stones sprawled about. Derveet and Cho lay looking into the lake. To their left was the retaining wall, topped with a narrow walkway and two small towers.

'They control the outflow.'

In spite of the sky, the long oval of water looked grey. All the way round it, halfway down the slopes, there ran a white track interrupted by pointed domes which were clearly big lamps. But next to some of them were blackened patches, and the track was not clear of weeds. Both the towers had broken windows.

'Day is better than night,' said Derveet. 'It is easier and safer then to stage a diversion. And at night they *do* patrol: armed. It is to stop the camp people climbing in and fishing for the treasure they imagine is down there.'

She watched the empty scene a little longer, then they slipped across to the other side of the hill. Just beneath them began the collective fields. Quite near at hand was a group of long huts, fenced in: a farm camp. Immediately below a figure with a long switch was seeing over a gang of workers, clearing mud out of a ditch. They had no tools but their hands. They were in rags; most of them were no more than children. They moved listlessly. Even the seeover had a shabby, apathetic look.

'It is not that our Rulers are greedy,' said Derveet quietly. 'It is worse. It is that they just don't care. There is nothing anywhere in the Sawah but what you see here: neglect, wastage, decay. How it is possible to bring the Peninsula to the brink of starvation beggars the imagination. Mother Sky has given us so much; even in Timur Kering all you have to do is add water. But the Koperasi have managed it.'

'I suppose they don't have the Dapur.'

Derveet was silent for a moment. 'We say not,' she said at last. 'We say the women of the Koperasi families destroyed themselves, in shame after the Rebellion. That is, they took jamu to prevent themselves having daughters, and then quickly died of grief. But as you can see, the Koperasi have plenty of children still.'

'Will those down there grow up to wear uniforms, like the ones I saw at the river?'

'That's a good question. No. The uniforms are brought up in cadet schools in the coastal bases. They come from a different source, mainly. The girls down there probably will not grow up at all. You see, on the Peninsula most male children are changed into boys. The Dapur decides, when they are born or before. Whoever nurses babies who are to be changed takes jamu to alter their milk and also meditates, I mean thinks in a certain way about the children. One of the treatments is ritual, one practical: the ladies won't say which. Anyway, the male organs do not develop, and at three, when the difference begins to show, the little men have to leave the Dapur. . . . Because of this custom, the Koperasi are mortally afraid of Peninsulan women, and hate them. They're afraid of losing their "manhood". Which is sad. Manhood without the Dapur is useless and destructive but they don't see that. They just live it.'

The seeover stamped up and down, cutting at thin shoulders in a bored way: 'He'll keep them near the camp. He's afraid of the terrorists, who have been breaking into store compounds and ambushing supply convoys and so on –'

'I've heard of them. Do the things to eat go to the people?'

Derveet smiled. 'Not directly. Knowing the Peninsula, that would be too much to ask. All the produce of the Sawah you see, as in all states, goes into places called Welfari stores, where most of it rots. The terrorist attacks do very little damage, but afterwards the officers are able to report big losses, and sell the loot. Meanwhile, the achar gangsters lend the people Koperasi *cash*. The people are therefore able to buy "damaged" goods. So the *cash* goes back to the Koperasi, who spend it on achar. . . . It all fits together quite neatly. In fact, I thought the Koperasi liked the arrangement as much as anyone, until a few days ago.' She glanced at Cho thoughtfully. 'But things have changed. Yes, perhaps things have changed. There was no sign at the sanctuary, so I am taking it that my friends have not yet arrived. We'll check the dam compound again in the morning.'

They spent that night in the sanctuary of Roh Betina. Derveet told Cho to go to sleep and sat up with her back against a slab of carved stone, to watch. She had a great deal to think about.

She had guessed the moment she touched Cho's clothes by the river crossing that something momentous had happened. By now she had no doubt that Cho had been used by the Dapur of Jagdana to carry a message: a response at last. How like the Hanomans to choose an answer so elegantly simple, and complete. She felt suddenly certain, tonight, that all was well; tomorrow the others would arrive and the declaration would be made. There stood Roh Betina, on her dark wheel of stone, giving the twisting dagger of life to Garuda: Will you give me a blessing too? she asked, silently. But the immense stillness of the carving said nothing. It was just stone. Derveet smiled at herself: God is not a partisan.

The message was one thing, but what about the messenger? It was strange, but it seemed Cho had had no idea she was an emissary. In fact, the Hanomans, according to Cho, had behaved very oddly. But it was hard sometimes to understand the child; she had odd turns of phrase. Cho knew a great deal, about Peninsulan affairs among other things, but there were bizarre gaps in her knowledge. Her whole story was bizarre. Was she lying?

No. Her story was not the only strange thing. The journey from the achar hills, peace and beauty apart, had been extremely hard. It had pushed Derveet almost to the limit. Admittedly she was not strong, only obstinate: any long effort was likely to leave her ill and exhausted afterwards. But Cho, apparently about fifteen years old, and looking as delicate as if she had never been outside a house before, had come through it without a scratch, without a sign of fatigue. Derveet told her not to mind the leeches, their bites do no harm on a short trip. 'All right,' said Cho gravely. 'I won't mind them. I didn't know you liked them.' But she didn't need to. The leeches left Cho alone, as did every other small unpleasantness. . . .

She turned to look at the slight figure lying beside her. Cho's light skin gleamed faintly in the moonlight: *'Did you lose all your belongings?' 'Lose? The ladies took my clothes away. I hope they aren't missing me.'* Empty hands. Had she really come out of the impossible east, just so? There had been a time when people knew more about the landmass, when wanderers were not unknown, reaching the Peninsula with curious stories and trophies. But the world was growing smaller: in a hundred years it had collapsed inwards at an alarming rate – almost impossible now to sort out truth from fiction. Was Cho the last survivor of a forgotten race? Perhaps. . . . I wish we could stay in the forest, thought Derveet. I'm afraid for you, outside. But she could not say, even to herself, exactly what she feared. Cho stirred in her sleep and murmured, and the blouse that was being so slow to mend itself fell open. Derveet looked down on the child's dreaming face; the rise and fall of flower-petal flesh. After a moment she gently tucked the blouse closed, and settled once more to watch the dark.

There was a further complication, a troubling fountain of joy. Derveet had fallen in love with the bewildering stranger: loved her the first moment she saw her, at that river crossing in the dark and the rain.

12   The Previous Heaven Society

The painted tricycles came careering along the last stretch of the causeway in a pack, scraping wheels and jolting over the tran lines. The drivers yelled at each other joyfully, their hard brown legs going like pistons, and the crowd outside Straits Control began to laugh and cheer as the herd stampeded up to the fence and crashed to a halt. The women got out smiling sheepishly and all went through the gate marked for clan papers only.

Handai stood at the desk and looked at her number overhead: 424. Is that lucky? she wondered. There was no sign of the other four hundred and twenty-three citizens, only an empty, glaring, concrete square, with Handai's party standing about in ones and twos looking bored; and behind the fence the chattering boys' queue. She could see through the barrier that their desk seemed to have shut already, but in the mystic, ever hopeful way of boys the crowd probably would not give up and go away for hours. The Koperasi read the forms. It is a historical society, thought Handai. We call ourselves Previous Heaven because we Samsui believe there was once a golden age. . . . If we work hard and don't drop litter Mother will let us have it back someday. . . . But the Koperasi did not speak, though he kept glancing up at her as he read, or pretended to read. She saw herself through his eyes, she knew she had a childish face – rosy cheeks and curly hair and innocent round brown eyes. It depressed her. She was sometimes pulled up, speechless, at a political meeting by a sudden inner glimpse of what people saw – an earnest twelve-year-old haranguing them. . . .

Cendana the dancer strolled about the yard, idly graceful. She perused the faces of the Koperasi at the gates with detached interest, just on the edge of insolence. The crowd of boys had recognised her. Cendana! Cendana! they called – Sandalwood girl! and reached through the wire. Sandalwood was not the name Cendana's family had given her. Cendana claimed to have forgotten what that was. She had a glance that would cut glass for unwanted admiration but she smiled on the boys benignly.

'Hey you girl, get away from there –' shouted one of the Control guards. 'Stop causing excitement – !'

Cendana drifted away. Siang and Soré, who were also dancers, lolled against the fence arm in arm and laughed at the guard behind his back. Pabriker Kimlan, a tall, thickset woman with grey in her hair, took out her pocket-watch and groaned. Cendana made a circuit of the yard, silently, sometimes exchanging a look or a sigh with one or other of the waiting women. She stared up at the bright morning sky, and stood for a while gazing through the clan papers' gate, back at the road that ran across the Straits. No one offered to examine the women's belongings. Smuggling was rife, even among the most respectable, but the Koperasi seemed to have forgotten.

Handai's thoughts were wandering, fatally, to a little girl left behind in Ranganar. She had tried to teach herself never to think of her daughter. The idea of Dinah orphaned, abandoned by a mother who died in prison, turned her to jelly. *Mustn't* she muttered inaudibly, and hoped the Koperasi didn't see her lips move. Then her eyes were drawn to the crowd of boys. She imagined she caught a glimpse of a dark, distinctive face. . . . This was ridiculous she knew – a sign of nerves. I mustn't stare, she thought, or they'll all come running over, thinking I'm going to give them something.

Cendana came back. 'Hello dearest,' she said, touching Handai's shoulder. 'How are you getting on? We're all fine. Nobody has anything on their mind.'

'Sign here,' said the Koperasi.

'What?'

'Put chop here. This place.'

'Oh – Oh yes. Sorry.'

'I'm fine too,' she said to Cendana, but when she looked at her hand signing the form, she saw to her horror that it was shaking.

The Samsui colony of Ranganar was founded by women who wanted to reform society. Samsui means three springs. The three springs were to be: one, rediscover physical labour; two, abolish boy-making; three, treat men as equals. The Garuda family gave the project reserved support, the island was leased from the Kedaulatan lands. Radical ideas fell victim to economic necessity: the riches of Ranganar were in extraction of metal from the sea, and the colonising ladies put off reforming the native islanders, the Ranganarese, because they needed their boys' unskilled labour for the dredging. In the end the island was not much different from any other state, except that instead of by hidden and secret power, the Dapur governed by a host of practical conveniences. The Samsui never co-operated. In the face of great hostility from the traditional Peninsula, especially the north, they refused to quarrel with the Rulers, and maintained they could see good in the government of the shining islands. But they would never take part in the subjugation of their mother country.

Then came the Rebellion, and at some point in the war, because of their isolation; because, perhaps, of an overwhelming atmosphere of defeat and fear, the Samsui let the Koperasi in. They never regained their independence. The East Coast barracks dominated the city: although nominally the committees of the clan elders still governed everyone knew they were just puppets of the Administration Compound. The practical Samsui had always reused all their resources: they had a sea-water sanitation system that pumped human and other suitable wastes to a recycling plant that turned the refuse into gas power. So traditional Peninsulans called the women 'shit-eaters'; after the Rebellion the term was used universally, with hatred, for the Koperasi as well, as if Koperasi and Samsui were one and the same.

The Butchers, the clan into which Handai was born, remembered the 'three springs' more than most. They put their daughters to work at an early age in the meat yards and the market; they treated their Ranganarese boys fairly. They resisted the insidious *cash* – the Koperasi paper money that was taking over from communal interdependence. They refused to buy Peninsulan produce sold off in Ranganar. Handai was called 'Miss Butcher' because her mother had been head of house, but she was never likely to serve on any Koperasi-ruled committee.

As she grew up, Handai could no longer be satisfied with her family's mild and quiet dissent. She became a young radical, struggling angrily against the corruption of her city. She hated the way respectable Samsui treated Peninsulans who had failed at entering and came to Ranganar. Before the Rebellion these young women would have been adopted into clans. Now they were shunned, because of what went on in the nightclubs around Hungry Tiger Street.

Handai was enraged at Samsui hypocrisy. She knew, everyone knew, that it wasn't only 'tigers' who did secret, shameful things in those dark alleys. She could not make contact with the woman-whores. They wouldn't talk to her. But there were a few Peninsulans who did not end up in nightclubs. They worked at the Classical Theatre: Dance, the great art, was revered — ironically — in the collaborators' city, and the performers had to be Peninsulans because nothing could replace Dapur training. Miss Butcher sought out the dancers, and found anger like her own.

The Samsui had an old custom of exchanging daughters. It was a practical arrangement for strengthening common interests, but it was called 'getting beloved', not without reason. Miss Butcher Handai got beloved with Cendana the dancer, and it did not only mean that she loved Sandalwood, it meant that they believed in each other, Peninsulan and Samsui. . . . The group organised meetings, handed out leaflets, made attempts (unsuccessful) to rescue Ranganarese boys from the ritual excision, got into trouble with street patrols and were fined and threatened. Handai tried to teach the dancers the three springs. But they were half wild, even Cendana. It was hard to get them to take anything seriously: they laughed when they should cry. She sometimes wondered if there was any point in going on, her efforts seemed so petty and useless in the face of the complacent blindness all around her.

Then one night (it was a cool rainy night in North-East Wind) a shabby old boy diffidently led her to a seedy coffee shop. There she met a gaunt, ragged person with skin so dark it was almost a deformity, with an incongruous air of utter self posession and speaking the most beautiful Inggris — High Inggris — Handai had ever heard.

Derveet was a sophisticated savage. Handai could imagine

rough splendour in her past – eating from gold and crystal, but with her fingers. She never wore shoes. She couldn't write properly – she printed in wobbly letters like a child. She didn't even know what year it was. . . . Derveet did indeed eat with her fingers. She never said what she thought of Samsui table manners, but after a while, Handai wondered. It turned out she did know what year it was, but it was a different year: not 489 Ranganar, but 2031 SS. 'What's the SS for?' said Handai, watching Derveet print this for her. She was bemused, she thought the Peninsula used all sort of petty reckonings, and that was why the Koperasi had made them conform to Ranganar-time. 'Sukarelawan Selatan,' said the other casually. 'Accession of the South.' Handai looked at the severe yet delicate dark profile and had thoughts that silenced her. Two thousand years.

Derveet would not be re-educated. She didn't laugh, she contradicted and answered back. She admitted Dapur government was secretive, autocratic; often utterly ruthless, but she seemed to think the women had a right to behave that way. To Derveet men were *ksyatria*: essentially marginal, a wall around the garden of life. Why did Miss Butcher want more of them? What for? Derveet politely detested the 'contrivances' of Ranganar. Miss Butcher informed her the only way the Peninsulan ladies could maintain their exquisite unencumbered lifestyle was because they had a slave culture. Boys are *slaves*. 'Aren't we all slaves, in the end?' said Derveet, with a maddening smile. Then there was the horrible ceremony: the excision of young boys at twelve or thirteen to give them a kind of darah pertama. Forbidden by Ranaganar's statutes it went on everywhere: generally performed by older boys themselves. . . . Derveet shocked Handai profoundly by saying she 'could understand' the excision. She meant the boys' honour. Women have the darah, men have their first entering. What ceremony can boys have, to pass into adulthood? But pride and honour, though she was full of them, were lying words to Miss Butcher; they made her furious. So did religion.

'I think you ought to know,' said Handai firmly, 'I don't believe in God, or Mother or whatever you want to call her.'

Derveet thanked her for the information. 'Don't – ' said

Sandalwood afterward ' – Say "her" when you mean God. Not to Derveet anyway.'

'What should I say then? "It"?'

'No pronoun at all. Just don't Dai. You're embarrassing me.'

But it was Derveet, after all the sparring, who turned Handai's group into the Previous Heaven Society. Handai was scandalised when she first heard the plan; it was pure suicide. Then her friends told her about the secret of the Dapur: the secret even her beloved, Cendana, had kept from her. Derveet had at last, in Ranganar, found a way in to the mystery. The dancers like all failed women had kept silent and suppressed their faculties, partly from loyalty to the Dapur and partly to protect themselves. But for Garuda they put their powers to work. They could dream lucidly, and get glimpses of the future or present events far away; they had intuitions, premonitions about safety and danger that could be relied upon; they could sometimes read minds and they could shield themselves and their affairs from hostile attention. And so the Previous Heaven Society passed to and fro over the causeway unsuspected, while the mysterious terrorists plagued the southern Sawah.

The failed women had left the Dapur at fourteen and fifteen years old; the power in them was undeveloped and erratic. But Derveet wouldn't let anyone try to train the mystery into a better weapon: she had a horror of that idea. Previous Heaven remained a disorderly hybrid, mixing the deep secrets of the Dapur with most un-Dapur-like devices such as illicit crystal sets, and home-made explosives cooked up on the sly, to the recipes Derveet had first tried on Bu Awan.

It was hard to tell if the dancers shared Garuda's mysticism. They only discussed their faculties, if at all, in strictly practical terms. But once or twice Cendana spoke to Handai about something she called 'the floating world' – 'I touch it when I dance,' she said. 'Sometimes. It's hard to reach –' And she spoke then as she never did of the Peninsula; like an exile remembering the beloved country – lost forever, only visited in fleeting dreams.

There were no other tourists. 'It is dead,' said the boy at the gates of the ruins, when he emerged at last from some sleepy interior. 'Mati – the trade is dead these days.'

They found the green road, and the ramp with the carved pillars at the top. Quietness surrounded them, the grass and the stones mourned for great things buried and forgotten. Handai drew a breath and stepped through the gateway. The sanctuary was empty, but behind one of the thatched platforms stood a tall black horse and a small dun pony. Miss Butcher stared. Kimlan looked at her watch again, and shook her head in disbelief. The dancers glanced at each other – and began to laugh, half in triumph, half in relief.

'But why the pony?' said Kimlan.

Then they all turned, hearing some slight movement. Derveet was standing between the pillars. Beside her was a young girl dressed in white. The dancers stopped laughing abruptly.

Derveet put her hand lightly on Cho's shoulder. 'Cho,' she said. 'This is the Previous Heaven Society, a group from Ranganar who are interested in relics of the past. They have crossed the Straits on one of their regular outings. My sisters, Cho is a friend.'

She stepped briskly into the open space, and at once a change came over the group. All trace of excitement and tension vanished. Cho backed off a little and sat down by Gress, and watched Previous Heaven going smoothly into action. There was no discussion, everything was planned. The different elements knew, from long practice, how to play their parts.

'Kimlan?' said Derveet.

The big woman glanced up and nodded. She was busy laying out her equipment on the stone plinth under the carving of Roh Betina, with her assistant, a young Samsui called Cycler Jhonni. Pabriker Kimlan was the head of a bicycle factory. The Koperasi controllers got on well with this big, easy-going woman. They didn't mind if she did a little 'night-market' fiddling with illegal chemicals (supposedly for work on resin quality improvement) or other small supplies.

'It's good stuff,' she said, prodding the wads of explosive. 'We've improved it a lot. It's even fairly safe.'

The dancers were dressed in dark cotton blouses and trousers like the Samsui, but they had long, shining, braided hair and beautiful golden faces. Some of them were carrying baskets, as if for a picnic.

101

Derveet said, 'Cendana, go back to the gates. Take the path across two fields to what is called the Elephant Stables, though it was nothing of the sort. You will find a boy there. Tell him you want to hire ponies to tour the ruins. He'll provide you.'

Cendana and the dancers took their baskets and left.

On the hillside on the outer flank of the great dam there was a pyramid-like boulder of glittering granite, strange to the region. Legend said a Gamarthan lady had fetched it there as a present for her Garuda prince, who had never seen a mountain. Derveet slipped between tangling vines into a dark hole underneath. Pabriker Kimlan went after her, and Cho, who had followed them from the sanctuary. Derveet knew all the secrets of the lost Garuda citadel, she had learnt them far away and long ago, and checked her lessons since on solitary expeditions to this place. She led them halfway through the hill to a place where what seemed to be a black underwater canal ran between carved walls. Their path was a ledge on its side. The water disappeared, and the path too, under fallen masonry. Poked into a crack in the wall, one of Derveet's lightsticks glowed, waking up eyes and flowers in the night drowned stone.

'How long can you hold your breath?' asked Kimlan. 'A minute?'

'Little bit longer than that.'

Kimlan tucked the headpiece of her crystal set over her ears. Derveet was naked, her hair braided again, the explosive and its accessories strapped to her waist and thigh.

'Bit nerve-racking, isn't it?' remarked Kimlan. 'Like waiting to have your first shit, after you've had a baby –'

'I never knew you had children, Kimlan.'

'Oh yes, I had three,' said the big woman evenly. 'Then I gave up.' She shook her head as Derveet winced at her own clumsiness. 'No, no don't worry. It was years ago – Anyway, did you have a good trip? I know what travelling's like: room without fan, dirty hawker food –'

Derveet and the young girl exchanged a glance, a private smile in the darkness.

'What's the joke?' said Kimlan. 'Oh well, don't tell me. You're in good health though? I think you lost weight.'

102

'Of course I lost weight,' said Derveet, mildly irritated. 'I've been travelling.'

And now – Handai and Kimlan's assistant, Cycler Jhonni, were on the spicy hilltop above the dam compound. The sky over them had turned blue-black, the heat was oppressive. Down below something was happening – a threat from outside: a panic-stricken seeover from the farm camp was at the gates, jabbering. Derveet had told Cho: for the four nights of the full moon the watch is lax. Koperasi like to take their leave then, instead of at hari darah. . . . The depleted guard began to race to and fro, screaming faintly and dealing out weapons to technicians and orderlies. The duty patrol came running down from the walkway towers to join in.

'All right,' said Handai to Jhonni, bent over her set, the twin of Kimlan's. She had to be quick; she didn't want to be picked up on the Koperasi's Wave network.

'That's it,' said Kimlan.

Derveet crouched, flickering in the shadows, her eyes intent; the smooth muscles under her shoulders rising and falling.

'You're sure all this stuff is *waterproof*?'

Kimlan laughed. Derveet was gone.

There was a strange world under the water, lost and dream-like. Derveet ignored it and swam steadily. She climbed the cracked discoloured inner face of the retaining wall, entered the first tower by its broken window, laid her charges and opened the sluices wide. She climbed out and ran along the walkway to the next, ducking low under the parapet of the wall. But the staff and the guards were still trying to get organised, to deal with the gang of terrorists or brigands who were about to attack. . . . Derveet appeared in the window of the second tower, and dived into the lake.

Down in the compound the loud disarray halted: the boys and men had suddenly noticed, above their own row, the outflow changing from a hiss to a roar. The duty patrol ran for the steps to the walkway. But when they reached the first tower, the door seemed to be jammed. They looked at each other. Then one intelligent person turned and fled, and the rest pelted after.

Cho and Kimlan, in the dark, heard nothing of the explosions. At least, Kimlan did not. Cho smiled to herself and murmured 'Fireworks –'. They had to wait a long time before Derveet reappeared. She had stopped on the way back, she said, to do a little domestic chore.

'Oh, of course,' said Kimlan. 'Good thinking. Lucky you remembered.'

Rain raced down on the flat fields. Derveet, Handai, Kimlan, Cho and Cycler Jhonni watched from the hilltop, while excitement jumped about like a firecracker, sizzling in the downpour. The guards at the dam had Waved to Sepaa, the nearest base, for help, but here there was panic. The slaves darted about staring at the sky, or flung themselves into ditches or made off for the horizon, while the seeovers struggled vainly for control.

'Everyone keep their heads down,' said Kimlan. 'And let's keep quiet – if we can, with all these farting vegetarians about.'

Derveet was crouched under a bush trying to smoke a damp cigarette. She smiled.

'Are you talking about me? I never fart.'

Now the dam is broken, thought Handai, and the river pours out and spreads through the thirsty land. Unstoppable. We're unstoppable. Cycler Jhonni squatted beside Miss Butcher. She was a daughter of the rich, respectable Cycler clan; a sturdy prosaic-looking Samsui child with reddish skin and thick ankles. But she had fallen in love with the Peninsula; this drenched hillside was the height of romance to her.

'Here they come –' breathed Kimlan.

Out of the trees at the base of the hill came the brigands. They raced across the drab landscape, moving as one. Their shining braids and bright ornaments made the rain glitter, and the last rider carried a pure white-streaming banner. They were fifteen. Rumour made them a small army: the White Riders who appeared and disappeared like ghosts. Who were they? *What* were they? They dressed in white, the colour of war, but they had never been known to use the weapons they carried: and yet, effortlessly, they defeated the Koperasi. . . . Derveet watched, as always, with a feeling of slight unease. The dancers gave themselves lovely arrogant airs, and lovely new names:

Nyala, the flame; Pelangi, the rainbow – Sandalwood. But they had *failed* and she knew that was not something a Peninsulan woman could forget. They had kept out of the nightclubs, but they were too fond of danger.

Suddenly, the watchers on the hillside gave a concerted gasp of alarm. The riders had done their work, it was time for them to vanish. But instead – they had wheeled and were coming back. The slaves were in a mass now, the riders clearly meant to snatch a way between them and the long huts. The space looked small but Cendana had not misjudged it. The troop swept into the centre of their stage. . . . But some of the audience were not attending. They were staring at a thing like a pink moon that had risen in the grey sky over the eastern horizon, and was swelling silently, enormously. It was an airship. Inside the spherical envelope the shadow of the gondola could be seen, carrying reinforcements from Sepaa. Cendana had not seen the bubble, nor sensed it.

'What's wrong with her?' cried Handai. 'What's got into them?'

At the last possible moment one of the riders turned her head. Her cry rang in the air. The women on the hill recoiled in shock – for a moment it seemed as if the White Riders charged straight *at* the bubble as it landed. . . . But no. The horses spun around on their heels in a flashing display of skill and streamed away. The bubble settled. Close up it could be seen that it was rather battered, it had trouble making a steady descent. The troop from Sepaa poured out, but it was too late. The slaves milled, and the seeovers ran about smartly like chickens with their heads chopped off.

In the sanctuary again, Previous Heaven gathered. The ponies that drama had made into warrior steeds were back at the Elephant Stables. The dancers had changed into street clothes.

'You shouldn't have taken a risk like that, Cendana,' said Derveet.

But the dancer was unrepentant. Her eyes burned. 'There was no risk,' she answered. 'None at all. We had them in our hands, Garuda. *We had them in our hands!*'

Derveet looked around and saw that every face was alight. Even Pabriker Kimlan was grinning broadly. She wanted to bring them back to earth, but just now it was clearly useless to try. She laughed instead, and put her arms round defiant Sandalwood, and hugged her.

After all, there was some reason for excitement today, even without the news she had not yet told them. A declaration had been made, a signature had been added to the strange warfare of the White Riders that would be understood from one end of the Peninsula to the other. The sky cleared as Previous Heaven quietly left the ruins. The Sepaa troops fanned out in the thin jungle, the seeovers locked up their hysterical slaves, and Koperasi technicians already began to tinker with the damaged sluices. But in that deep, secret, lovely valley, of hanging woods and whispering cascades, where the Garudas had built their palace long ago, the water was still falling – falling away from galleries of pierced marble, pavilions and towers. Silt and weed blurred the outline of the emerging dream, but not where it most counted. On the topmost pinnacle, clean and bright, the golden wings of the Eagle lifted into the air, soaring and burning in the sunset light.

13 Among the Ruins

There was a resthouse at the gates of the part of the Garuda ruins open to the public. The Samsui visitors had a permit to stay the night there, because obviously they couldn't cross the causeway until it opened in the morning. All through the evening treaders rumbled and clattered past the Garuda gates, up and down the white road to the dam. There were voices, sounds of people running, occasionally the loud report of a weapon discharged aimlessly. The hotel boys went about giggling and clinging to each other. The Koperasi officer from Sepaa came to the resthouse with a small detachment and walked through the shabby courtyards, but he saw nothing: only the women, sitting on their verandahs, brushing their endless hair and staring at him with eyes like black stones.

'Tell them to stay in their rooms,' he said to the boys. 'No wandering about. Not allowed.'

When everything was quiet at last, Miss Butcher went for a stroll. The back of the resthouse blended imperceptibly, in the darkness, into ornate broken walls and weed-grown empty spaces. She sat down on a fallen lintel. The moon was coming up: the night was clear, the air as soft as milk and faintly silvered. Insects chanted gently. An angular shadow figure silently approached, and sat down near-by.

'We had a panic this morning,' said Handai after a moment. 'The tran girls were on strike again. None of us knew. It was only by chance we had enough *cash* between us to pay for trishaws.'

Derveet for a moment wondered what her friend was talking about. Tran girls and strikes confused her, she had been so far away from Ranganar.

'You know the Trans hire all sorts of girls as drivers, well now they're striking – for less pay and longer hours, needless

107

to say. I wish I could think it meant something but they won't even talk to me. They're just a bunch of red-backed kites.'

Derveet always wondered what harm those useful and handsome scavengers had done to the Samsui.

'I hate that rotten city.'

The moon strengthened, they could see each other's faces. Handai remembered another cause for indignation.

'Do you know, those troops made the boys at the ruins, the caretakers, go out and beat the jungle with them. There could have been armed bandits in there –'

'But there weren't.'

'But it's the *principle*!'

Derveet smiled. Handai scowled – and suddenly they both burst out laughing, partly at each other, partly in sheer elation.

Before they left the Garuda ruins, Derveet had told her friends the good news. Acceptance by the Royal Hanomans and their prince was a dazzling change of fortune, made even more dazzling by the fact that it came on the day – as it were – Derveet announced that the name Garuda was behind this new, stealthy, undercover rebellion.

'What now, Derveet?'

Derveet had taken the silver bell out of her pocket and was rocking it on her palm, carefully; not letting it chime.

'Nothing much changes,' she said softly. 'Not yet. As we'd decided, Previous Heaven will keep quiet for a while after today's show. The dancers have protected us so far, but we shouldn't push our luck. Later, I suppose we'll go back to work, without the dressing up: that's served its purpose. And not alone. I don't know what the Hanomans will decide to do, but I imagine life will become mysteriously uncomfortable, for the Koperasi in Jagdana. . . . But there is something I have to do urgently and that is get in touch with the Singas. They must not feel left out.'

'You're going to Gamartha?' exclaimed Handai, dismayed.

'Oh no. No need to go as far as that.'

She frowned a little and put the bell back in her pocket. 'I'm glad the masquerading is over. I wasn't seeing things, was I? They did, for a moment, mean to attack that bubble?'

'They do get fairly keyed up. Peninsulans are all a bit wild.'

Derveet grinned, and took out her cigarettes. 'What do you think of Cho?' she asked abruptly.

'Oh she's *very* nice.'

Derveet was amused, for the little girl in white had hardly looked at Handai, or anyone. She had chosen, for some reason, to efface herself completely. Miss Butcher must be being tactful: Garuda, though unaware of it, must have been absurdly transparent.

'Cho's rather mysterious,' she said. 'She's been alone all her life. She says she's an art person – I don't know what art she means unless it's the art of living as simply as – oh, a leaf on a tree. A cat brought her up. It travelled with her from their home, until it decided to run off with the Koperasi.'

'She had a pet cat?'

'Mmm. They lived very far away. She gave me a bearing – north by north-east, roughly, right into the landmass. I was rough I mean – she wasn't. She told me the distance; an extraordinary number, lots and lots of them – digits, I mean. It went on forever. I think she meant steps.'

'What an odd story,' said Handai. 'I'm going to bed.'

She judged this was not the first strong cigarette of the evening. It was a difference of opinion. Derveet did not find drunkenness funny. Miss Butcher detested that cloudy look, and the rambling nonsense. They had learned to avoid each other when necessary.

'All right,' said Derveet. 'Never mind – Oh, no. Wait, wait a minute.'

She had remembered the trishaw story. She pulled a roll of Koperasi *cash* out of her pocket: 'You'd better have this.'

Handai peered at the greasy bundle, and looked mutinous.

'Come on, take it; take it. The last thing we need now is for Miss Butcher to be picked up for being "without visible means".'

The resthouse room was warm and sticky, not a breath of air came through the verandah screens. Cendana knelt on one of the thin mattresses unrolled on the floor, plaiting up her hair.

'Siang,' she said, 'dreamed of the rendezvous. She saw us at Straits Control; she saw us going into the sanctuary, and what hour it was by the sun; and Bejak and that dun pony that no one

109

could explain. She knew something was wrong, so did we all, but we couldn't tell what. Then the news of the riot in Jagdana came through on the wall bulletins, and we guessed it meant Veet was delayed. So we told Siang to dream it again and she did, and read the date on the board at Straits Control. And here we are.'

'I know all that,' said Handai. 'But what happened to you on the field? You terrified me. What made you do that?'

Cendana laughed. 'It was joy,' she said. 'Joy made me do it. I knew there was no danger.'

Handai looked at her solemnly. 'I'm glad you won't be doing it again. You know you shouldn't use those "powers" more than you have to.'

The dancer smiled. 'That's Derveet's conscience, not mine.'

'Cendana – ?'

'But she's our Garuda. I love her. I believe in her.'

She shook her head and laughed, and came to join her beloved on the other mattress. She peeled back Handai's blouse and kissed her shoulder, rubbed her face against the soft skin: 'Do you know what I like? I like it when you forget I'm here, and think of nothing but your own pleasure. Because when you cling to me then it's *pure*. D'you see?'

They put out the lamp, not wishing to entertain any insomniac hotel boys with shadow play on the screens.

In an outer court of the dead palace two black stone demons guarded a roofless room. Cho was kneeling in the doorway, using a massive ankle as an armrest, admiring the moonlit ruins. Derveet stepped in, and sat down beside her.

'You've been very quiet today, Cho.'

'Wasn't that what you wanted?'

'Was it? Perhaps it was. Do you always mean to do exactly what I want you to do?'

'Oh yes.'

'Dear me. What a responsibility.'

Cho looked up with a flashing smile. She put her hands in her blouse pockets, and laid out on the doorstep a little heap of groundnuts: a mouse-meal.

'Let's pretend we're still in the forest.'

'Good idea.'

110

Derveet cracked nuts and ate thoughtfully. 'That bubble was in a poor state, wasn't it. And the dam. The Koperasi just cannot maintain this world the Rulers handed to them.' She frowned, and propped herself against a demon. 'I think I know something about the Rulers. It explains their fatal indifference, and the way they have withdrawn so completely. I think they are dying out. After all, they were old when they came out of the ocean long ago: survivors of something dead and gone. The Dapurs always said we would outlast them. Patience, submission, has always been their message: Don't risk lives, wait for the wheel to turn, as it always does. I would believe them, I am not such an idiot as to go to war for "independence" or any other word of that kind. But something *different* has happened to the Peninsula, Cho. The Dapurs won't see it; they've shut themselves off, since the last rebellion. But the truth is we are not just oppressed, we are dying. And those left alive call each other "shit-eaters", "natives", "polowijo", "collaborators" and so on – too busy hating each other to see what is happening to us all. The collapse is coming quickly now. In a few years there may be no government at all. If I don't find some way to unite the peoples before that happens, the Peninsula will just disintegrate.'

She sighed. 'I am a fake, you know. My lovely manners and my accent – everything that Miss Butcher most objects to, is just a reproduction of a reproduction. The original is gone forever. But I can still call myself a Garuda, and that means a great deal, in spite of my looks. One failed woman is a meaningless fragment: even my grandfather had more authority. He had a daughter – Still, I am sure I could have called out half the country, boys and men. That would have been exciting. But I'm greedy. I wanted more than excitement, I wanted – reality. That's what makes you so important, Cho. I didn't want to defy the Dapur. It isn't a game, these things I have persuaded the dancers to do: peering into the future, and into peoples' minds. God knows where it will lead us in the end. To God, perhaps. . . . But I am desperate, so I must use it.'

She leaned over and touched Cho's white sleeve. 'This doesn't only say the Hanomans know and accept the truth about the famous White Riders. It says yes to my heresy: using what the Dapurs have hidden so carefully, to save our lives. It is

111

more than generous of Jagdana. I was such a nuisance to them in the old days. And I know they have a horror of that dying monster. . . . Oh Cho, perhaps it's all ridiculous. Perhaps the Rulers are still all-powerful, and everything will end in disaster. But I have to try. I have to give the people hope. What do you think, Cho? Can you help me – *Am* I doing right?'

'Of course I'll help you,' said Cho.

Derveet smiled.

Outside the demons' brandished daggers there was utter stillness. Only the moon and the dimmed stars were moving, slowly, slowly, overhead in the profound blue. Derveet arranged herself more comfortably, and lit a cigarette. She grinned, catching Cho's eye.

'More medicine. I'll come to a bad end, I know.'

She relapsed into silence. The end of her cigarette glowed and faded like a little pulsing red star.

Cho had discovered, when she first opened her eyes in this world, that she belonged to Derveet. She had never troubled to wonder how. She found that she knew, deep in her heart, that this was the way it happened: One day somebody said, 'You belong to –' and everything was settled. She had almost given up thinking about her brother from that moment – she couldn't help herself. Divine Endurance must be wrong. *Evidently* this was the real end of the quest. She had remembered all the Cat's lessons: not being lazy, not putting herself forward, waiting to be asked. She had learned to eat and sleep for pleasure now – nothing seemed strange since she had found Derveet. But tonight she was aware of a puzzling tension in the atmosphere. She had been aware of it, growing, all the time that Derveet was talking.

Now, as the silence lengthened, she could feel Derveet's eyes on her in the moonlight – the same insistent gaze she had felt at the river crossing, like a hand touching her. But the eyes kept slipping away. Was she to turn around, or not to notice?

'Cho –' said Derveet suddenly. 'Would you – ?'

Cho turned. Derveet stared at her, seemed about to speak: but instead she threw the end of her cigarette into the darkness, angrily, and put her head in her hands.

'Cho,' she said, with her face buried. 'I've been wrapped up

112

in this cause of mine too long. Delight seems alien to me, happiness seems like an invasion. I don't know what to do –'

Silence. The moon moved, the stars moved. Cho knelt, waiting. At last Derveet looked up. The moment of absurd panic had passed. She propped her chin on one hand and smiled, and reached out to touch Cho's face with her fingertip, tracing the pure outline tenderly as if she was giving it up forever.

'You go to sleep,' she said sadly. 'I'll, I'll sit up for a while, I think.'

But her hand stayed. Cho did not move. At last Derveet sighed. Her hand slipped under the rim of Cho's hair to the nape of her neck; she drew her forward gently and bent and kissed her strange crescent eyes.

'Well?' she whispered 'Well – ?'

To Cho it was like the moment when Atoon first told her who she belonged to. Suddenly she felt completed, as if everything was explained. She said *Yes*, without words but with all her heart, and gave herself up joyfully to Derveet's embrace, Derveet's searching, ardent mouth and hands.

Cho woke up, hours later, in a soft world of pearl-coloured mist and coolness. She lay looking at Derveet's left hand sleeping where it had slipped from her shoulder: dark, supple, long fingered and slender. She thought: '*Entered*. Ah – !' Among other confused feelings, Derveet had been afraid it was wrong of her to fall in love with someone so young and childlike, and she meant to be very careful not to demand too much of Cho's inexperience. Her awakening that pearly morning was a revelation.

PART TWO

Wide, wide flow the nine
streams through the land

Dark, dark threads the
line from north to south

I pledge my wine to the
surging torrent

The tide of my heart
swells with the waves.

Mao Tsedung

I am very angry with Cho. First she refused to follow me at that river, and now I find she has formed the sort of association I particularly warned her against.

The place I went to in that dry but unpleasant smelling vehicle was a farm camp. These people, it seemed, use their preoccupation with a large scale and exceptionally unlovely kind of landscape gardening as an excuse to gather numbers of themselves in very small palaces. I suppose it keeps them from spreading all over the place but I found the arrangement irritating. I did not announce myself. I soon realised that the Koperasi, though they think differently, are not to be included in the category of people who matter.

The Rulers, most sensibly, have as little to do with anything that goes on on this Peninsula as they possibly can. And yet, I was aware of their influence. I am aware of it even more now that I have come to this place: Ranganar. Everything is running down. This is the great natural process of course; I have known it all my life. But I must admit it gives me a peculiar satisfaction to feel these Rulers gently, without fuss, giving the process their assistance. I am now quite certain Wo is with them, helping them in this smooth descent. It is pleasant to watch the thing, slowly rolling, but I wonder what will happen when there are two of them acting on each other, as Em said. I am eager to find out.

The Rulers are eager too. They are already aware of Cho's arrival. They must have been watching out for more of us since Wo came to them. They don't fade away and drop off as quickly as the Peninsulans, so they don't forget things so easily. They have contacts, naturally, in the palace of Jagdana (even that very private part, that thinks itself so special). Anyway, something alerted them. Messages passed to and fro quickly – the Rulers do not share the Peninsulan passion for the simple life – and we could have been safe and sound, but for the stupidity of those bounty hunters. It was Cho they were supposed to be fetching. But they were greedy, and foolishly imagined their local celebrity was a much bigger catch.

All this I have picked up here and there. Essentially, it means that there are people waiting to take us to the Rulers (they don't, of course, know what Cho is – that would be silly). The only problem is the association Cho has formed. I will try to get her to see reason, but these attachments were designed to be very stubborn. An added difficulty is that the ones supposed to be fetching Cho now are just as impressed by the local celebrity as the ones up in the Sawah, and nagging them does not seem to help. The Koperasi 'authorities' are no use, they are far too lazy and timid. But I am sure I will find a way. I have learned a great deal from Wo already, though I have never met him, and I find I can do many interesting things, if I take the right approach, without being pulled up by my conscience.

14 What I Find I Can Do

The west side of the Ranganar river was the home of the native islanders: the Ranganarese. The river itself was no more than a black tidal creek on the edge of the Samsui city: beyond it a confusion of mud alleys and board walks over silted waterways trailed away into the encroaching salt-water swamp. The area had none of Ranganar proper's amenities: no water, no gas, no tran, no streetlights, no recycle. It was a squalid place, a warren of secret creeks, eyes and bolt holes: the natural haven of low life criminals. The Koperasi left it well alone.

But the island of Ranganar had a long history, stretching back before the Samsui colony was thought of. The West Bank slums sprawled over ancient ruins, mostly buried in swamp; sometimes jutting out above the hovels. In one place the water-gardens of a great mansion remained almost intact, with one bathhouse still standing. It had been reclaimed. Clear water gleamed again in the square pool; the dirt and debris of centuries had been cleaned away. Blue stone pillars stood around the water from which a crumbling but polished stairway of rose marble led to the gallery they supported, and an upper room where long gone youths and gentlemen had rested and amused themselves after bathing. Stone wings were carved everywhere: both the Garuda symbol and another, gentler kind. Merpati, the Dove, said Derveet, had been the original name of her family. They adopted Garuda at the accession, so as not to seem hypocritical.

Derveet's boys had been waiting for her after the dam incident, hiding down on the Straits with a wasp-tailed smuggler's boat. They were Jagdanans: they had mysteriously turned up in Ranganar right at the start of Derveet's exile, and insisted on becoming her household because it was too shock-

ing for Garuda to have no one at all – Petruk, Gareng, and old
Semar. Derveet periodically tried to send them back to home
and safety, but they always refused, and so she felt, distantly,
that the Hanoman Dapur had not yet quite abandoned her.
Previous Heaven passed innocently across the causeway. The
boys took the horses, decorating Jak with white splotches that
horrified and depressed him so that he became a completely
different animal; led them over the Straits and stabled them
safely in the warren. Derveet and Cho took the boat, slipping
along the coast and across to the western tip of the island in
darkness, and so they reached the security of the West Bank,
and Dove House.

A wide bed was the only piece of furniture in the upper room,
apart from a chest of clothes and a few curios. The floor was
cool bare stone, patterned in blue-grey and rose, the tall
windows were open to the air in all but the worst of weather.
The carved inner roof had gone, of course, and rain dripped at
times. The boys put pots under it, and remarked that madam
really ought to get something done.

Cho watched through the bed curtains as the room quietly
reappeared: it was dawn again. She disengaged herself softly
from hard smooth thighs and dark arms that had lost their
cradling strength – Derveet had fallen asleep. She reached
down beside the bed and picked up a round box made of a grey
raspy material. When she dipped her hand in it came out full of
glimmering blue-whiteness. The pearls were from Pulau Sinar
Bulan, Moon Island – the place where Derveet grew up. She
thought of Derveet, alone in a boat sailing on the enormous
ocean and let them slip through her fingers, smiling. Then she
heard something land on stone with a soft *plump*. She looked
through the curtains and there was Divine Endurance sitting in
the window. . . .

'No I won't,' said Cho. 'I think you're silly to ask me. You
must know I have to stay with my person now.'

To her relief and suprise the Cat did not begin to nag. She
settled her paws under her and said, 'Well, how are you getting
on, anyway?'

'Pretty well. But there's a lot to learn about making them
happy.'

Divine Endurance narrowed her eyes, and her ears pricked.

'It's no good giving them things to eat, and making the weather nice. It's more subtle. You have to go by their inside feelings, and sometimes it's a complete contradiction.'

'Ah,' said the Cat. 'You've noticed that.'

'It's strange how ignorant they are, too. The Peninsulans, I mean. They don't seem to know about fading away, and how sad it is; nicely sad, you know. They say all the time "everything's passing, everything's over soon – " but they don't seem to realise that it's themselves they're talking about. But the Rulers too, and – well, everything. You know what I mean, Divine Endurance.'

The Cat looked at her foster child thoughtfully.

'What about – er – Derveet?'

'Oh, Derveet's different. She knows things. The divers on her island used to bring relics up from the sea, that they couldn't even recognise. The Rulers collected them. And she's heard of the Blue Nomads bringing things from the landmass, though she never saw any of them. It was world-wide, she says; the Peninsula was part of it too; you can tell by things like High Inggris, which was *always* the second language, long before the shining islands came. She wonders if the Rulers are the only survivors of that other creation. Perhaps something could have lived on elsewhere, through the long ages, preserving ways and knowledge that would seem very strange now. . . .'

Divine Endurance heard the voice of her adversary, and felt annoyed. Cho *would* have to pick a bright one.

'I told her there were no people where we lived, except for the nomads: only me and you. She seemed a bit disappointed.'

'No people at all?'

'Well, there weren't.'

'Does she ask you a lot about yourself?'

Cho frowned slightly. 'At the start she did. But then she stopped. I think it made her upset for some reason, and she's given it up.'

'Ah yes,' said Divine Endurance, and looked across at the long dark body spread out on the bed, sleek and relaxed inside the cloudy curtains. 'That's what happens. I told you: they get embarrassed. I wouldn't press the subject.'

'Of course not.'

The Cat yawned. 'How difficult these Peninsulans are. They

120

have so many things wrong with them. They've got infestations in their lungs, they've got worms in their guts, they never get enough to eat. And yet if you cured all that would they be happy? No. They'd still be longing for something. They know it Cho, deep in their hearts. They know what they *really* want. In fact, you could say all their little troubles are a sort of manifestation, of the longing that they hide away. . . . It is a shame they are in such a muddle. You and Wo together could soon help them sort it out.'

Cho did not seem to be attending. She looked back into the room where Derveet lay, and she smiled. 'Divine Endurance,' she said, 'you know what you ought to do. You ought to find a person for yourself. Then you'd understand.'

Divine Endurance stood up, twitching her tail in exasperation. The child was besotted; this was just wasting time. Now I've annoyed her, thought Cho. But suddenly the Cat changed her mind.

'Hm,' she murmured. 'Hm. That's an idea.'

She vanished.

Cho looked down into the yard. The boys were outside the kitchen house, thumping coffee beans for Derveet's breakfast. They waved to her and smiled broadly. There was a smell of roasted coffee, and no sign of the Cat.

Derveet had woken, and seen Cho at the window with a visitor. 'Was that your pet?' she asked sleepily as Cho came back to bed.

'Yes, it was Divine Endurance.'

'I wonder how she found you. How clever –'

'She's gone again,' said Cho. 'I think she has things to do.'

15   A Fan on the Ground

Handai was in the covered market, ordering dry groceries. Her little daughter, Dinah, leaned on a sack of onions, picking absently at a bulging seam. She was three years old and extraordinarily like her mother except that her hair was straight, not curly. From under a thick fringe her round eyes peered out, staring down the other customers with a fine non-conformist disdain. The stallholder was very friendly with Miss Butcher, but when she'd added up the goods she frowned. She leaned over and whispered that the Butchers had not enough hours left.

'D'you want to make it up with *cash*, or borrow it from somewhere else and give me a chitty?'

Handai's family was always short of hours. They had no more credit with any other clan than with the Commercers at the moment. She blushed, annoyed at the whispering. She was not ashamed of being poor.

'No thanks,' she said firmly, and rather too loud. 'Give me the list and I'll take some things off.'

The stallholder sighed. 'You Butchers are crazy. Why spend everything you earn on fines? You never achieve anything. The Koperasi just laugh at you. They dismiss you completely.'

'I know,' said Handai. 'I know they do.' But for once she did not explode. She only smiled.

Out in the street it was a glaring hot afternoon. The road was up along the market front, as it had been for months, because of a sanitation problem. Overhead a tattered banner flapped, a reminder of North-East Wind Drill:

ASK YOUR SISTER DOES SHE KNOW
WHAT TO DO AND WHERE TO GO

In the eleventh to the thirteenth month the city centre was often flooded.

122

The water supply had been down for twelve days, and Straits Control shut. Giggling boys queued at standpipes, and people argued bitterly with a few triumphant market gardeners. No one panicked. An explosion in the Sawah was hardly news. The excitement was nearly over now: the causeway had opened, soon the taps would be working again. 'They think they can forget all about it,' thought Handai. 'They'll be amazed when they look back and remember this "little incident" –'

What would the support of the Dapur mean? Handai was not comfortable about the 'powers' – that whole business reminded her, embarrassingly, of an idiotic song often heard at drunken meetings of the stockbreeders club:

> Well, first I made a bunny
> I made it up so funny
> It had three ears!
> It had three ears!
> It had three ears!
>
> And then I made a ducky
> The duck was not so lucky
> It had no feet!
> It had no feet!
> It had no feet!

She did not like the idea of changing into a new kind of animal. When she saw Cendana, talking seriously to Dinah about the little girl's dreams, it gave her a strange feeling –

The Dapurs run things, she reminded herself. That's their real importance. The hot street was reassuringly solid and familiar, even down to the hole in the road. 'When I'm old,' she said to Dinah. 'There'll be young women *and men* gathering on these street corners, telling each other the revolution's gone to seed: it stinks, it's time to get rid of the old women. . . . Oh Mother,' she added fervently, under her breath. 'Oh Mother, let me live to see that day –'

Handai had got a lift into town with one of the Butchers' delivery boys, in his trishaw – her bicycle was off the road. Now the trans seemed to have vanished. At last the lines above the street started to hiss, and the tran appeared – but there was a Koperasi uniform in the cab. The tran hired girls wanted to be

123

paid in regular hours again, and *cash* only for extra time. Their quarrel was purely mercenary, nothing to do with the destruction of communal life, but it was still vile of the Trans to get the Koperasi in — another step downward for the rotten city.

'It's all right, Mummy,' said Dinah resignedly. 'I can walk.'

Sitting in the shade of the five foot way near the transtop there was a brown cat, with unusual blue eyes but otherwise merging perfectly with the Ranganar street. Divine Endurance saw the sanitation pump, cracked and seeping into the fresh water pipes; she saw the rain damage of not one but many seasons patched or left unrepaired. She had already seen the abandoned fishing quays; the metal-dredging plant shut down 'temporarily'. She had been eavesdropping: she noted with amusement Handai's desire for sweeping changes, so long as everything stayed exactly the same. 'This has possibilities,' she thought. 'But how they do blind themselves. Or is it Wo who blinds them? The truth about this city and its street corners is really very simple.' She slipped down from her doorstep and briskly followed Miss Butcher and her little daughter.

Handai went back to the house in Red Door Street, where First Aunt, the old lady who had taken over when Handai's mother died, ruled absolutely over the sister, cousins, nieces of three generations, and their various attachments. Because of the coming New Year, the family conversation was all about accounts. They had to pay fines for not carrying *cash*. They had to pay low-spending tax for not buying Koperasi 'imports'. They had to pay punitive fees for the servant boys' and labourers' citizen papers (second class). They wanted to keep more live meat in stock, but could they possibly afford to? Divine Endurance was extremely bored.

When Derveet first came to Ranganar, she was puzzled about an important aspect of Samsui life. She saw little Samsui daughters everywhere; she saw her new friend Miss Butcher becoming obviously pregnant. But she never heard the arrangements mentioned, never a hint of discreet visitors tapping at night at a side door. The Ranganarese kept their men enclosed, they had nothing to do with the 'renegade women' nowadays. She asked her friend at last – Handai, please tell me: do not eat me, I can't help being ignorant. Where do babies come from?'

Handai's face flooded instantly, darkening painfully. 'I thought you knew,' she muttered. 'We go to them.' The answer to the riddle was in Hungry Tiger Street.

The people called what the Koperasi did in nightclubs *kejahatan rajah* – the Rulers' vice, but there was no proof of that. More likely they had taken up the practice as a kind of oath between them, sealing themselves off with finality from all other Peninsulans. Derveet had known about nightclub entertainment, and that the Koperasi didn't grow their élite officers in slave camps, but absurdly enough she had never seen the connection. Now she knew the real shame, that even Handai in her fierce radical anger could not bear to discuss. . . . What if Handai had had a son? Derveet didn't ask. Samsui male children were never mentioned. She felt heartsick. Our enemies don't need to touch us, she thought. We hate ourselves, we destroy ourselves. The nightclubs of Ranganar were the very heart of the Peninsula's despair.

Hungry Tiger Street was in the Singa quarter, but it was a bad Ranganar joke that 'whore' and 'northerner' were synonymous. The failed women came from all over the princedoms. Women do not commit suicide, but the *tigers* had found something more expressive: serving the Koperasi themselves and arranging the Samsui business with them. The most famous nightclub was at the corner of the Pasar Diluar, the open market, and the Street. It was run by two sisters who were the undisputed rulers of the tiger world. It was Leilah, the more forceful of the two, who had instituted the brilliantly shameless and cynical dress now worn like a uniform by all the women-whores. Big Simet wore the silver anklet of her childhood embedded in her muscular flesh with a few blackened links still trailing. How she had come to bring it away with her was a mystery, but the gruesome gesture was much admired in that world. No one knew where the two came from. The tigers pretended nothing mattered to them, but as among the dancers it was an impossible crime to ask someone's family.

The day after the causeway opened, Derveet left Dove House for the first time since the adventure. At sunset, she was playing chess with Handai in the garden in front of Nightclub Leilah's, Cho observing with mild interest. The real business of the club had not begun; only a few sleepy tigers sat about, looking sordid as nightlife does even in twilight. The Koperasi were still on duty, the customers were Ranganarese boys drinking beer out of teapots, and a few respectable Samsui, come to look, at this hour, not to do business. The nightclubs had their own horrible fascination.

Soon Leilah appeared: a small woman, still young, with rich hair in artistic tangles down her back. Years of tigering had coarsened her, but she still had a look of sullen pride especially in her eyes, which were extraordinary. They were light grey, flecked with chips of gold and green and amber, like splinters of burnished metal. She had come out, ostensibly, to see the place was in order for the night, but as she wandered about, snapping at the girls in an undertone, she had her eyes on Derveet's table.

Derveet watched her with an almost guilty expression. She knew Leilah quite well, in a way. There were two powers, mysterious and tiresome to the Koperasi, in the disreputable or 'native' side of Ranganar, and for the last four years Leilah had been only one of them.

At last, Leilah came over and flung herself in the chair beside Derveet. She wore the sash, bound from her breast to her thighs, in a bright silk batik: an interesting combination of constriction and nudity. She sprawled so Handai had to look quickly away: grinned at this, and watched the game.

'Her prince's horse,' she said to Handai, after a moment or two.

'Thank you Leilah,' said Derveet, smiling. 'Don't you think I can lose on my own?'

The nightclub owner laughed, took a cigarette from the case at Derveet's elbow and leaned over her shoulder to get the silver lighter.

'I think I'll keep this. It's pretty.'

Derveet bore these intimacies patiently. She had never intended to become Leilah's rival in the city, but it was hard to explain this to the tiger. Leilah did not like competition.

'How's your little girl?' she asked Handai. 'Does she take after the stud at all, or don't you remember?'

Handai's face went stiff; she stared at the chess pieces

126

angrily. Leilah chuckled, got up and left them, lifting a handful of cigarettes and rumpling Derveet's hair in passing. But she left the lighter.

Handai said, 'Oh – It's that cat again.'

A brown cat had jumped onto the table, and was gazing with interest at Nightclub Leilah as she strolled away.

'It came home with me and Dinah yesterday and this morning it went off with Cendana. It must have followed me from the theatre just now. D'you think I've been adopted?'

Derveet shook her head, 'You must be dreaming. That's Cho's pet. The one I told you about. It found her again. I know it by the eyes – '

Cho said, 'Why have you been following people about? It's rude.'

Divine Endurance slitted her eyes benignly. 'I'm just taking your advice. I'm choosing one.'

'That's the wrong way round.'

Handai and Derveet lost interest in the minor puzzle of the cat. The chess game was abandoned. Now that Straits Control had relaxed they could expect news from other places; perhaps emissaries. 'How will they know?' asked Handai. 'All over the states, I mean?' 'They'll know,' said Derveet. 'Word like this has a way of spreading, among my people – '

'Well I don't think much of yours,' said Divine Endurance to Cho, 'I must say. Its colour doesn't match. And listen to it – '

Derveet was coughing a little, resentfully: the humidity of Ranganar never suited her.

'Oh hush,' said Cho. 'She particularly dislikes you to notice that.'

The blue dusk had grown dark and bright with lamps, the respectable element in the clientele had left, and the tigers looked different now.

'We ought to go,' muttered Handai uneasily. 'I don't know why we came here anyway.'

'To show Cho to Leilah,' said Derveet quietly.

'Yes, I gathered that. And did you get what you wanted?'

'No.'

'Well, of course not. It was you who told me, there's no

point in trying to reach the tigers. They're dangerous, that's all – '

Derveet sighed. 'I'm afraid Leilah is dangerous to no one but herself. But I owe her something.'

'What?'

'Discretion, if she won't have anything else.'

In the lighted doorway of the club Leilah stood talking to her big sister, with sharp little gestures.

'I wonder what sort of family she came from. Do you think they mistreated her, because of those funny eyes?'

Derveet was putting away the chess. She glanced across at her rival: that cloudy wild cat stare hidden now in the darkness.

'Oh no, I don't think so. There are places where eyes like that are quite well thought of.'

Since the lamps went on, the little stage in the centre of the garden had presented fairly good dancing, and mildly simulated love-making by tigers still clothed, if you could call it that. But now the scene changed: unusually, for there might still be decent people walking by. A boy, almost naked, danced swooningly with a muscular young man. He flexed his knees and swayed backwards; his spine arced wonderfully and the young man, supporting him with a hand in the small of his back, parted both their clothes and began to treat him 'as the bee treats the flower – '

'That's *disgusting*,' said Handai. 'And it's not what bees do to flowers anyway.'

Leilah was watching them from the doorway.

Derveet smiled faintly. 'I think it's a hint. Let's go.'

There was something in the air that New Year, not only on the city island but up and down the Peninsula from Gamartha to the sea. Even Sepaa and Nor were affected – by something that puzzled many, but made others eye each other in the street, and secretly smile. Rulers' agents in several places noted, reported, and decided it would go away. They made no connection with events surrounding a minor attempt on the Ranganar reservoir.

The Classical Theatre was a steep half circle of stone tiered seats under a sweeping roof, open on three sides to the humid darkness. It was a gala night, the first of the New Year.

128

Ticket-holders climbed to their seats, the Ranganarese packed themselves in front of the stage. (There were no Ranganarese women: they rarely crossed the river because of the contamination of the Koperasi.) The theatre's famous orchestra began to test patterns in the air; coughs and ripples were struck from the ancient moony bronze. This historic gamelan had been salvaged from the old Garuda palace, its name was Drifting in Clouds. The stage remained empty. Down in the pit, a tall black-skinned woman appeared, causing a stir. Her colour was nothing in the city, where all hues rubbed along – but she turned heads; she obviously meant to. She was dressed formally, in an exquisitely cut jacket of thin silk; a fan at her wrist, her sash and kain panjang patterned sombrely in the prized, rich colours 'of blood and clouds'. By her side was a young girl in white. Handai, up in the dancers' guest row, thought: She's not so *very* tall. Kimlan tops her by a head. It's when you realise that, you start to wonder *who does she think she is?* Nightclub Leilah, late as always, arrived while Derveet was still standing. She was in her best clothes too; more of them than usual. For a brief moment they looked at each other, and the boys began to shiver with anticipation – Derveet sat down. A Rulers' agent, making himself comfortable up above, laughed and said to his neighbour: 'Gangsters – '

Handai put her chin on her hands, and tried to understand Drifting in Clouds. Derveet said this gamelan was 'one of the few justifications for the existence of the human race', Cendana thought it was good too. In the middle of the floodlit stage a fan lay on the ground, picked out by the light: gold filigree over dark silk, waiting for somebody to come and pick it up, as a sign that the Dance had begun.

129

16　At the Dance Theatre

In the rehearsal courtyards behind the Theatre, violet water-lilies stood over their deep reflections; dragonflies wandered glinting across the fountain pools. Inside a pavilion a class was going on and the blurred images of the dancers swayed under their feet, in dim waters of polished wood. Outside, the Previous Heaven Society, or most of it, sat about on the steps or the cool pavement, turning out a chest of properties. Gareng and Petruk of Dove House were lending a hand, rubbing things up with metal polish and folding silks. There was no news yet. Derveet asked the dancers if they had seen anything, but no one had anything striking to tell.

'There is danger ahead,' said someone.

General laughter. Of course there was danger ahead. Dinah dressed herself up with care, tying mangled knots in exquisite scarves and sashes Cendana had just smoothed and folded. She was observed, belatedly, and ran off round the fountains shrieking like a factory whistle, with Sandalwood in pursuit. Siang took her little iron off the brazier and tested it with a licked finger singing softly, glancing at Soré –

> ... bruised coriander leaf
> my sweet
> my kelapa muda,
> milky coconut...

Cho was puzzled by the stage daggers: 'Are they meant to be like the one Atoon wears, except that his is made of wood?'

'That's right.'

'Derveet, everybody knows what *this* means' – she sketched a double helix in the air – 'If that is what the daggers are to mean, isn't it a bit odd to have a straight one?'

130

Derveet smiled at Cho's 'everybody knows'. She glanced at the toy that Cho held. It passed, at a distance. It was, yes, straight as death. . . .

Siang looked up. Nyala the flame, Pelangi the rainbow, turned as well: 'What's the matter? Did I say something?'

But the dancers shrugged, and went back to what they were doing. The moment passed, it was only the briefest ripple.

'They have to be straight,' she said, 'or they would be facsimile weapons. Besides, it's hardly worth the trouble. Those curves are not easy to produce.'

Handai came to sit beside Derveet, who was stretched out lazily on the pavement. She was slightly embarrassed by the presence of Semar, who was massaging her friend's neck and shoulders with his clever old hands.

'Are you worried because there's no news yet?'

'Not really,' said Derveet. 'I still feel dazed, I think. I'm used to fighting. I am not –' her mouth tucked itself up wryly at the corners – 'used to winning – '

'I suppose it will be all over pretty soon once the big Dapurs get started.'

Derveet shook her head. 'Oh no. Don't start thinking that, Handai. I only meant winning *relatively*: not losing so badly anymore. And even if the Dapurs could somehow forge a weapon to hammer the enemy, they wouldn't do it and we mustn't want them to. We must borrow from our future as little as we can. Don't you see? If a people were growing wings, they might find the bumps on their shoulders useful for hefting things, but then they never would fly. . . .'

'You look a tiny bit tense, madam,' said Semar to Handai, kindly. 'Shall I give you a rub?'

'Oh no – I mean no, er – thank you – '

It was a while before anyone noticed that Cho was gone. Was she in the pavilion? No: the class had broken up, the polished floor was empty. The rehearsal gamelan sat swaddled in its canvas wraps; hunched animal shapes in the shadows.

'Oh wait,' said Nyala. 'I saw her. She was talking to a boy, by the gates.'

In the alleys round Dove House Cho was always vanishing: disappearing into some ricketty hovel; playing with the children in dirty little gangways over the mud. Everybody loved

131

her. Derveet liked to see her go, to the people. 'Oh so that's it – ' she said slowly. The afternoon had worn away unnoticed, the theatre compound had grown quiet, before the burst of activity that would herald the evening performance. Petruk and Gareng put away their rags and polish and stood up.

'Derveet,' said Nyala, 'I've just remembered. I've seen that boy before. He comes from Tiger Street.'

'*Bodoh* – ' whispered Derveet – *fool* – The dancers glanced at each other, the atmosphere suddenly sharp: *No*, she said, in the same language, *I'll deal with this.* And she ran to the gates, with the boys hurrying after her.

Down near the waterfront Ranganar river ran blackly; under derelict godowns on the Samsui side, West Bank boardwalks and huts on the other. There was no bridge, the length of the city. The Ranganarese were quite happy with their boats, and who else wanted to cross over? Derveet stood in the flower market where the lowest ferry plied. In the city behind her the bell in the Commercers' clock tower clanged the sunset hour. The flower boys gathered around the roots of a waringin tree, threading garlands and creating petal confections in little leaf baskets, for people to send down the river to Father across the sea. They were busy, trade was brisk; it was still New Year. Heaps of scarlet and white, blue and yellow, tiger stripe and violet, poured on the worn cobbles.

Derveet had sent Petruk and Gareng to Tiger Street's alleys, to spy out what they could. She had sent Semar to a place on the East Coast road, near the barracks. It was called the Assistance: both a convent and a place for unruly people whose families couldn't manage them – so the Samsui put it. Nowadays a Koperasi cadre worked beside the nuns. It was possible Cho had been taken there.

Derveet paced the waterfront waiting for the boys, thinking of all the hiding places there were in Ranganar. But what did she fear, really? Not that Cho had been handed over, for revenge or spite, to the city Koperasi. Not that someone had taken the child for ransom. No. It was more than that. She had given up asking Cho about her past. Why? She had given up thinking about the extraordinary stir that had attended the child's arrival in this world: the riots in Jagdana, the bounty hunters. She had managed to put out of her mind that lingering

132

sense of something very strange. . . . It had been easy, so easy she felt dizzy now to think how much she had blithely put aside. But Cho was so dear, made every moment so sweet. And yet. . . .

She leaned over the river wall, and watched a shower of petals falling, spinning down bravely from sunlight into moving darkness. She had not been able to forget, not entirely. She had been afraid, from the start, that she would not be allowed to keep her treasure. Oh the poor child, dear child. What would they do to her?

Cho was in a room with painted walls. She could see out of a small window a herd of bicycles corraled, minus their metal chains and gear wheels. They did not have crossbars, they were for export, but trade was slow just now. It was the back of the pabrik (which was not, after all, the same as palace) where Kimlan worked. *Kimlan* she thought, but she didn't like to press it. Kimlan was probably busy. She knew where she was: the pabrik quarter merged into nightclub land. She looked at the paintings on the walls. It was a *wayang* room – thin, gold, ornate people surrounded her, acting out a legend. Sometimes the customers liked a touch of grandeur. Cho gazed at the golden puppets solemnly, and looked down at her own tied hands and feet. She had something poked in her mouth as well: sign language again. Someone opened the door and she looked up to see who it was.

Derveet was still by the riverside, under a darkening sky. She did not know where to go, how to start. But as she stood there, suddenly there was a brown cat in front of her, sitting on the cobbles; sniffing at the flowers. It turned and stared with brilliant blue eyes, then stood up and trotted away. Derveet, without thinking, without questioning, followed.

The Cat led her down to the seafront, and out of the city centre by the East Coast Road, jogging along the five foot way; hopping over storm drains. The East City had no nightlife, it was too near the barracks, the streets were empty. The Cat did not pause at the barracks, or at the Assistance walls. She led Derveet on, to where there were no more buildings and then left the road, slipping through a fringe of coarse shrubs down

133

onto the sand. The Straits of Ranganar; the forgotten, abandoned ocean lay dark and empty. There was a small jetty, once used by fishing boats. Divine Endurance jumped onto it, walked to the end, and sat down.

Derveet followed. She stood and looked out to sea. Far away, standing out black against the dim evening sky, there was a skeleton tower, heavy swell rocking around it. The Rulers had left several of these things behind, when they moved further out after the Rebellion. Smugglers used them. Divine Endurance looked up at Derveet. Her eyes, glinting in the dusk, spoke very simply. Derveet measured the distance. It was about half an hour's swim: nothing. But she had not been well; it was taking her time to get over that last escapade.

'Cat – ' she said. 'You – whatever you are. I don't think I can do it.'

'You could at least try,' said Divine Endurance's eyes.

Derveet took off her jacket and sash and kain. She rolled up the kain and twisted it round her waist, because nakedness puts you at such a disadvantage. The tide was full, so there was plenty of water. She dived into the sea.

17   Wayang

Derveet reached the tower, but she could not climb into the scaffolding. A hard rib between two columns slammed against her knuckles, she fell onto it gratefully and hung there, with the dark bitter water slapping her in the face. Stupid, she thought. It was nothing. You did it too fast. In a moment or two she had her breath back and pulled herself up. She sat crouched against one of the columns. The surface of the sea glowed faintly with a reddish colour. She had never swum off Ranganar before: so strange, to live on an island that ignored the ocean. The Ranganarese said the Rulers had frightened the fish away, the Samsui said they were letting the waters 'rest' and blamed the Peninsula for over-fishing. Rest? she thought, tasting it in her mouth and feeling it on her body: it is dead. The image of a whole ocean dead, surrounding everything, came to her – she closed her eyes and shook it away.

There was not a star in the heavy sky. Ranganar was a vague blackness, with a city shape of lights. She felt better. She coughed to clear her throat – suddenly her mouth was full of liquid. It was warm and salt; it came out on her hands black in the darkness. . . . Derveet knew about this weakness of hers. It was a plague the Dapurs had wiped out at least once in history, but it was back now, more stubborn than ever and beyond even their power. She was prepared to bear it like the common people, and just try to take care. But she had never had this particular experience before. She sat still, wide eyed, and the waves lapped. It doesn't mean anything, she muttered, and bent to rinse her hands and mouth. When she looked up, she saw the brown cat, perched in the framework above her head. She was not even surprised, or only for a moment.

'The only wonder,' she murmured, as she wrapped the dripping kain round her and knotted it over her collarbone, 'is, what do you need *me* for? Lead on.'

135

High overhead was a black roof, the underside of the solid part of the tower. The Cat led Derveet nimbly, occasionally glancing back with some scorn, to a ladder which took them up to a railed walkway. Derveet pressed herself against the inner wall, and stood very still: where the walkway turned out of sight round the curve of the tower was a glow of light, and a huddle of figures. She could make out five: boys or men. A sixth figure, a little apart from the rest, made her stare; she thought it was a woman. Then she saw what they were watching. A bubble was coming, a small one. It floated just above the water, making a trail of glimmering reflected light on the little black waves. It was rose coloured and silent; she could see that it would dock in a bay designed for it, below where the people were standing. It had come for Cho. . . . Her nails dug into the palms of her hands. But her guide wanted her attention.

There was an entrance, a blot of deeper darkness in the wall across from the head of the ladder. She could not see the Cat but she knew she was being led on, into the centre of the tower. Everything she touched felt like the scaffolding; smooth and hard and curiously cold. She realised it was all made of metal, all of it. There was no sign of decay. The sea-washed ribs and spars she had climbed had been sleek and bare too, after a hundred years. She had a feeling that she did not want and could not use: it was not decent fear, but a failing of the heart. . . . Luckily this is the Cat's rescue, not mine, she thought. The corridor ended in a blank wall. But as she sensed this, and stretched out her hands, the wall glided away. Divine Endurance slipped past her. The room in the middle of the tower was not large. It had a trestle table in it, benches, some old sacks: incongruous flotsam. The air glowed with a dim, pale light. The Cat trotted to a section of the curved wall and stared at it. Derveet approached: the wall opened and a light came on inside. The Cat was gone. Cho was sitting on the floor of the cupboard, with her back propped against the wall and her head hanging limply. Derveet stood looking at the little figure, her heart full of love and pity; tears pricking her eyes. Cho raised her head, and her face lit up in welcome.

'Don't come in,' she said. 'There's no catch on the inside. I was just coming. I was, really.'

It was like the first bounty hunters: she had delayed trying to

136

think of a way to satisfy everybody, and wondering a little if she really ought to go to see her brother. But now Derveet was here there was no dilemma. She got out of the cupboard.

'Wait – ' said Derveet. 'The Cat – where's she gone?'

'Did Divine Endurance bring you?'

Derveet was looking under the table.

'Oh, I don't think we need her,' said Cho, a little embarrassed. She was going to explain; it was rather awkward – but there was no time. There were people in the corridor. Derveet snatched Cho's hand and together they made for the farther wall. It opened and they fled into the dark. But this was not the Sawah river crossing: everything around them was hostile and there was no confusion. The passage end was blank and would not give way. There was no sound of pursuit but they could feel someone in the room behind them: someone in control. Cho turned quickly, after a flicker of thought, and the side wall opened. 'It's a storage space,' she said as she ran. 'It doesn't lock up, you can only change the doors about.'

They ran, not noticing the darkness; knowing by senses other than sight that a room had become a dead end corridor – a corridor's walls had fallen away and left them lost in space. They ran round and round the tower: Derveet lost all sense of place, the maze could have been endless. But they could not get to the walkway over the sea. Whoever was playing with them was too good at this game.

'Stop!' cried Derveet. The room they were in stayed still. 'We can't get out!'

'No, I don't think so,' said Cho, so composed, so perfectly at ease. She looked at Derveet expectantly. And Derveet at last, suddenly, realised the meaning of what she imagined: what she guessed.... Light fell on them abruptly. The passage behind them closed. Doors on each side opened together, and another straight ahead. The boys surrounded them. The woman Derveet had glimpsed turned out to be Nightclub Leilah. She faced them smiling, and the boy beside her levelled a Koperasi *stop*.

Koperasi did not often use things like that law and order weapon now. As the years passed they fell more and more to a conventional armoury: various firearms, fairly sophisticated but not different in kind from what the Peninsula could understand. And so people said the Rulers had sunk down; were powerless. But Derveet thought no: It's just that we are not the only ones who are being abandoned.... The sight of that sleek thing worked on her like the tower itself. Bitter and defeated anger exploded in her. She shouted, 'Cho! – ' and flung herself at the boy.

The sound pistol flew to the floor. Leilah, for a fatal instant, forgot she was not a lady and recoiled in disgust from this crudity – she had never played the Anakmati game. The boy was on the ground, gasping. The others grabbed Derveet as she came up, but by that time Cho had the stop, and was pointing it at all of them. The boys instantly, carefully raised their hands. They knew it was a soothing myth that this thing was 'only to stun', you could die weeks later or lose a limb, from the vibration damage. But Leilah cried fiercely –

'Oh, you shit-eaters! She's only a slave. She daren't use that thing. She can't do it – '

Cho was looking at the weapon, with a faintly puzzled and unhappy expression.

'You're right,' said Derveet sadly. 'She cannot.'

White light shone on the makeshift smugglers' furniture. One of the boys stood over Derveet, tied by the wrists and held down on a bench at the table, the stop nuzzling her throat. The rest of them sat on the floor in a corner, whispering occasionally but keeping their heads bowed and their eyes lowered. Leilah stood apart with her arms folded, her face a cool mask. Derveet admired her: shameless, degraded, traitor she might be, but she was *not* going to be impressed. She thought of the Cat (where is she? what happened to her?) but with scarcely a flicker of hope. A panel in the wall by Cho's cupboard was open, showing a mysterious nest of what must be controls for this place. On the other side of the table a stranger, strangely dressed, was examining Cho.

The Ruler was large, larger than most Koperasi, which struck Derveet as odd for the Dapur always worked for smallness, considered long bones, big bodies unsuccessful. The head was a bare shining globe, not shaven she thought but naturally hairless, the face smooth except for many tiny, tiny lines when it moved, around the eyes and mouth. The body was dressed in baggy coveralls, carefully fastened – no doubt as protection against this alien, abandoned world. She could not say if the Ruler was a woman or boy or man, there was no sign of anything like that. Perhaps this person had left behind such distinctions, as very, very old people do. . . . Large smooth hands moved confidently, encased in glistening film; applying various devices to the subject. Derveet had to watch: the procedure was grimly absorbing. Finally, the Ruler put everything else away, and wrapped a web of flexible glass tubes around Cho's head.

'Look at the tabletop please.'

It was the first time the stranger had spoken. The Inggris was oddly accented, naturally enough. The battered tabletop went white in a square area, and Cho's face appeared in transparent detail of bone and moving blood. Then an enlargement of her eyes. 'Ah – ' The image showed something strange. In the centre of each eye, as if on the retina or the lens itself, there appeared tiny silvery lines. The Ruler adjusted for more detail. And now the silvery engraving stood out plain and clear. Each eye the same – a group of minute patterns of crossed lines, and then four letters: ACGT.

'Adenine, Cytosine, Guanine, Thymine. The tumbling dice. That settles it.'

The web was removed; all the instruments were folded away and slipped into some deep pocket of the coverall.

'Those – ah, chemicals are the final building blocks of life. They were synthesised, and changed incredibly. This is a product of the Tumbling Dice Toy Factory, Beijing Province, Rising Sun World State. The most advanced model they ever made, for it was soon after this particular range came out that – the party was suddenly over, as it were. Ah well.' A glistening finger tapped Cho on the shoulder: 'There is no doubt about it. This is a meta-genetic android.'

'No I'm not,' said Cho. And the whole room was startled to hear her speak.

'Oh, I'm sorry. Gynoid, I meant of course. That's all I wanted to know, anyway. We were pretty sure, but we thought we'd like to confirm it. It's very satisfying. A very satisfying turn of events.'

Derveet stared at what was Cho: awe greater than horror;

greater than any feeling. So far to go up, so far to come down.... She felt the vast weight of the past for the first time, truly. It seemed too much for the world to bear.

The Ruler looked across at her and asked, conversationally, 'Did you know?'

'I knew ... fairy tales, folklore; rumours, of the *wayang orang*, the doll people. They belonged to another age of the world. No story imagined they had survived into this creation. The very best of them came from a special pleasure city in the east. They were called "wayang legong" – angel dolls. They were not machines but perfect lifelong companions. They were invulnerable to fire, disease, any kind of weapon – time. They protected. They had power over animals, the elements, the minds of enemies. But they were always good and gentle. They would do no harm.'

'All that and more. There has never been anything like them. An angel doll can grant, *will* grant, every wish of the human heart.'

The boys kept their heads down. Leilah stood as before, preserving her cold mask with a great effort. She had thought she was recovering a stolen farm camp slave.

'But how did *you* know?' asked Derveet.

'Oh, that's easy. We have one already. We've had him for about a hundred years: picked him up, it doesn't matter how, at the beginning of your last troubles. We've been looking out ever since, in case there were any more.... He has helped us so much. I'd try to tell you, but you wouldn't understand. You will though, you will.'

Derveet had some idea of keeping the creature talking, as if she might in a moment think of a way out of this. But no more words would come. The Ruler was perfectly relaxed; watching her face, smiling a little.... It was strange. She could not see, when she looked into her enemy's eyes, any sign of enormous evil and power. There was only an immense, immense weariness: the vast weight of the past. She stared, for a long moment of curious intimacy, trying to understand.

Suddenly the large person sighed, and then leaned forward with a new expression.

'Oh dear. You are going to lose the sight after all I think. It happens: even the best repairs are never quite the same. How

140

do they do it by the way.... Fascinating. Still, it serves you right for those bold bandit antics of yours in the Sawah. That'll teach you to wish things on yourself.'

Derveet had only an instant for dismay, at this mocking glimpse of knowledge she was given – and to remember it didn't matter anymore now. With the last words the Ruler moved: a faint, almost imperceptible nod, and the boy turned his stop and brought its butt crashing down.

'There,' said the Ruler. 'I was wondering just how long before she realised all she had to do was to say a word to the doll. But it is a habit one has to develop, I suppose. Ours, now, has gone far beyond needing someone to tell it what to do all the time. But they too have to develop, to reach their full potential. Which is *enormous*.... Open one eye for me. Yes, she's safe for quite a while. But tie her up thoroughly please. Do things properly – '

Leilah had not moved or made a sound since the revelations began. The Ruler smiled at her pleasantly, rivers of tiny lines rippling.

'Now then. I will give you all a lift to the shore and put you down somewhere quiet; it's safer that way. The price, I'm afraid, remains what it was. This other person is really Koperasi business, not mine. Just one word of advice madam: it might be better to leave Ranganar for a while. "Tongues wag", you know. I'll collect these two on my way out.'

The gang of boys shuffled to their feet. What kind of servants would the Rulers use: who would work for the monsters themselves, with no disguise? The dregs of the dregs, obviously. Can dirt that you walk on be insulted? Leilah went with them, still expressionless, and the Ruler was close behind her.

Divine Endurance had not been far away. She had followed all the proceedings, while at the same time looking curiously around the rig. She was soon aware that the plan was rather different from what she'd thought. And yet, and yet.... It had its own elegance. She was content. As soon as the Ruler's bubble had gone she bounced into the centre room, jumped up on the table, and sat there licking her ruff.

'Why *did* you bring her?'

'I should have thought that was obvious. I wanted you to

141

come to the Rulers and you said you wouldn't leave her. Anyway, I didn't bring her. I just helped her to come.'

Cho gave the Cat a rather quizzical look. Two small figures, crouched on a cold bare floor, on either side of a body lying motionless. The walls had dimmed again, the nest of controls had vanished: the room was still and empty. Cho touched the dark face – Derveet awoke to see the child bending over her.

'Cho?' she said, and put her hand to the back of her head.

She sat up and saw the table, the benches in the grey gloom. The Cat was back, and where were the rest of them? She looked curiously at the rope-ends lying beside her, carefully unknotted and neatly coiled.

'Do you want it to hurt or not?' asked Cho. 'I wasn't sure.'

'Come on,' said Divine Endurance.

The walls opened with eerie obedience: the Cat led them to the ladder on the walkway, and down. She disliked climbing *down* things, but she knew Cho would only start fussing. . . . At the bottom of the ladder a smuggler's boat was moored, painted black inside and out.

'It's the one they brought me in,' said Cho.

Of course. Derveet stared. She turned her head and looked back, up at the bulk of the tower. Nothing stirred. No great eyes opened in the blackness, nothing reached out. . . . The child and the Cat were sitting in the boat looking up at her. She got in the stern and started up the illegal wasp-tail engine.

When they reached the shore the Cat hopped out neatly, shaking her paws at the wet sand. 'Goodnight,' she said. 'I have a feeling your friend is going to stand about *talking* and I'm sure it's going to rain. Besides, I have to get back to my person.'

Derveet let the boat go, to take its chance. She looked around: 'Where's the Cat?'

'She's gone back to her person.'

The beach stretched dimly: quite near to them was the jetty Derveet had dived from, between the black sea and the dully glowing sky. The palms and pandanus hiding the road rustled and tossed harshly; the sea bumped against the sand in heavy blind waves. Out over the ocean the sky cracked suddenly with light, revealing cloud capped towers of storm piled up into the dark –

'They let us go,' said Derveet. 'Why did they let us go; let *you* go? Cho, why did you never tell me there was – someone like you, with the Rulers. Didn't you know?'

Cho said nothing. She was in tears. It was not that she had not known exactly what she was. Of course she knew. But the knowledge had been so simple she had never looked at it, never thought what it meant.

'Oh no – ' cried Derveet. 'Dearest child – '

She put her arms round Cho and held her tight. Cho sobbed.

'Child it doesn't matter. What difference does it make? We are all *wayang*; all – I, yes, even that creature with the gold head, all *wayang*. What else is there?'

But Cho had been listening to Derveet intently, lovingly, for all the time she had known her, and she knew that the Dapur, which held Derveet's heart, had been striving all its life to leave Cho behind, to get beyond Cho entirely. And now here she was: wrong, wrong, the very thing that wasn't wanted. How could she make Derveet happy?

'It's why,' she sobbed. 'It's why I couldn't go in the Dapur.'

Thunder rolled like a rockfall over the sea and the rain came down with a roar; invisible one moment, a white forest of falling stars the next. They ran up the beach, Derveet pulling Cho by the hand, and took shelter in the ragged, trailing undergrowth; wet bodies huddled together, comforting each other.

In the cabaret room of the nightclub Leilah sat with her sister. It was evening again. Leilah had returned from her adventure in the early morning, and shut herself up all day. Tonight the club was closed. The dull lit room smelled of stale beer, old achar smoke and sweat.

'You going to do this often?' asked Simet, grinning sardonically at the empty tables. Leilah flashed a glance at her and said nothing. The brown cat that had come to live in the club recently jumped on her knees and curled itself comfortably.

Something had got into Leilah. It was entirely unlike her to chase after adventures at all. She had detested the interloper Derveet for a long time without doing anything but snipe. It was Leilah's way, to hate and be disgusted and yet at the last moment get sickened at the idea of action. Some time ago they had investigated the squatter who had taken up residence in the

143

old Merpati ruins, now called 'Dove House', and found her out; even found out the trail that led to Bu Awan, and the lost Garuda prince. Leilah did nothing, but sneer and hint: Derveet never turned a hair. Now suddenly she had done this thing, in spite of the people she had to deal with. 'Why not?' she said. 'I *want* to do it – I wonder what they'll do with the little girl.' Simet thought it was mad, but she didn't interfere. But Leilah had come back in a very strange mood.

'What are you going to do then? Turn her in?'

'You don't listen, do you? *They know.*'

The most mysterious part of all this was that Derveet was *not* a prisoner of the Rulers, with her little girl. Simet had sent over to the West Bank: Derveet was at home, alive and well, as of this afternoon. Leilah, when told this, stared with enormous eyes. But she did not seem surprised. Simet was jealous.

'The truth is you've always been a bit trickly for her,' she said. 'What you really want is to get your hand in her pocket.'

'You talk like a five-year-old,' said Leilah. 'Her father was the Koperasi, her mother was a polowijo. She has *no* rights: none. She's going to set herself up with that "little girl" of hers, seduce the common people, persuade everyone the Dapur is on her side – big lies are best, aren't they, and bring the country out. Her friends are the Samsui, the Koperasi, the polowijo on Bu Awan. It's unbearable.'

'She's never done anything like that before.'

'Don't you listen to the news? Don't you know someone sank the water in the Garuda dam just before New Year, and set the Eagle flying again? The whole Peninsula knows it.'

Simet said stupidly, 'But you're not interested in politics.'

Leilah glared: her sunset eyes took on the blank, cat-look that meant trouble.

'All right,' said Simet quickly. 'I'm listening.'

'Obviously it is coming soon. Everything points to that, especially this thing she's got hold of. But she doesn't know how to use it properly. They'll take it when they want it, even if she got away this time. . . . Don't make any mistake, Simet. There is no hope. All we can do is hate them. We can't win. I've always known it, and I know it better now because I've seen one. I've been in their world.'

She fell silent. How many years had she lived this life? She had come to Ranganar to escape from unbearable reminders, and found she had to live on Tiger Street. She had been in a mood to laugh at that, at the time. Why had it taken her so long to find out that she need not laugh, sneer; swallow vomit? She could do something else. Her hands soothed the cat's sleek fur: Divine Endurance crooned gently.

Simet looked at her sister's aroused and vivid face. She wondered. She wondered what 'this thing she's got hold of' referred to, but obviously she wasn't going to find out.

'What do you want to do?'

'I'm going to do what the Ruler told me to do,' said Leilah. 'Leave Ranganar.'

She raised her head and their eyes met, but Simet soon gave way. She sighed.

'Anything you say, madam'.

Then she took a bottle of Anggur Merah from behind the bar and brought it over, with two glasses. The wine smelled of mountains; its colour was bright as blood.

18 Atoon in Ranganar

Derveet was sleeping in the sun. She lay on a flat roof at the back of Dove House, one arm behind her head, the other outstretched on worn stone. A tray with the remains of breakfast lay beside her, and the bold mynah birds, rolling their sulphur-circled eyes, stalked grandly from one fragment to the next. At the end of the red mud alley, a little flock of boys appeared, ragged and excited; clinging and jumping like kittens round a sedate figure in their midst, a stranger to the West Bank. The flock halted, pointing and explaining, and then their chattering faded. The visitor came down the street alone, between tumbledown shacks and pungent heaps of refuse. He wore white, his hair was coiled in shining braids; his perfect golden shoulders were bare. He did not seem to feel in the slightest degree out of place.

When he came to the end of the alley she sat up. They looked at each other gravely – it was a long time since the sunset, the day of Alat's trial. She reached down to him, he grasped her wrist and came up onto the low roof. They knelt face to face, strangely tongue-tied, then Atoon took something out of his sash; she smiled when she saw it and opened her left hand. She had been sleeping with the dancer's bell tucked in her fist. Solemnly, they exchanged tokens and then, at last, embraced.

They had never quite given each other up. The link between them was very tenuous: no Dapur power, only the more mysterious bond of friendship, but it had never quite broken.

'So,' said Atoon at last. 'You have become a Samsui.'

Derveet looked at herself – black trousers and blouse. She often wore the city women's clothes now, she had forgotten it was strange.

'Why yes,' she said. 'After all, in the end, I think I have. But you, my dear, are still a prince I see.'

She was laughing at him. 'But this is your territory isn't it?'

146

said Atoon – he meant the West Bank – 'Naturally I tidied myself up. Why ever not?'

Derveet frowned. 'It's true you're probably safe from the Koperasi here, but they are not the only problem. Shall we go inside?'

She stood up, lifting the breakfast tray. Atoon looked again. The face of his angry young friend had changed, it had grown; it was strong and calm, and yet –

'Derveet,' he said. 'Have you been ill?'

She had her back to him, stepping through the window she was using as a door. 'I'll? – Well, perhaps a little different from usual. It is hari darah, Atoon. Are you trying to insult me?' She flashed a smile over her shoulder – 'Now I've made you blush. How sweet. Watch out for holes, and beware of falling lizards.'

She was lying, of course. Atoon followed her, frowning slightly.

In the upper room, Cendana the dancer and Miss Butcher Handai were waiting. They had not seen Derveet since she left them at the Dance Theatre several days ago, they had only had a message passed on via the Butchers' hired boys, that the kidnapping had been foiled and Cho was safe. Meanwhile the big nightclub on the corner of the Pasar Diluar suddenly had its shutters up: Leilah and her sister had disappeared, no one knew where. But all was not well, the dancers knew it though they had no clear picture of what had gone wrong. Handai and Cendana had been waiting, ready for any kind of disaster, when the summons came, through the boys again, that they were to come to Dove House. The prince of Jagdana had travelled down the coast in secret, crossed the Straits with smugglers and was now on the West Bank.

Handai stood up, nervously. 'How do you do?' she managed to say, in a strangled voice.

'How do you do?' returned Atoon gravely, offering his hand. Miss Butcher took the elegant golden thing gingerly, as if terrified that it would break. Cendana bowed correctly over her folded hands, for a moment not brave Sandalwood or the great dancer but a failed woman of no particular family, meeting the Hanoman prince –

Derveet sat on the end of her bed and watched them. 'An important meeting of four conspirators,' she remarked,

'coming together to discuss how they will take over the Peninsula –'

Her voice was strange – irony without a hint of laughter.
Handai and Cendana glanced at each other.

'I wish it was,' said Derveet. 'But I'm afraid it isn't. I don't
even know why Atoon is here, I haven't asked him yet. And
there is something else we have to discuss.'

Then she told them the real story of Cho's kidnapping: the
truth about the child Jagdana Dapur had dressed in warrior
white, who had come to change their fortunes, and the cool
familiarity the Ruler had shown with certain Peninsulan
affairs. She left nothing out, except that she was a little vague
and dismissive about the 'gangster' who had been the Ruler's
instrument.

When she had finished there was a long, stunned silence in
the upper room. At last Handai stood up and went to the
window, irresistibly drawn there. Down in the courtyard the
Dove House boys were playing tag with a brown cat and a piece
of string. Cho sat on the kitchen doorstep and laughed,
showing her small white teeth. It was incredible. She turned
away.

'I was going to tell you,' she said huskily. 'I was trying to get
up the nerve to tell you – that she was too young for you, it
wasn't right.'

That made Derveet laugh.

She looked at Atoon. 'Well, why *are* you here? Of course I am
pleased to see you, but it is a long and dangerous journey for
someone as precious as the Hanoman prince. Why didn't they
send a good boy, whatever their message is? Your family has
been behaving very strangely, from the start.'

Atoon sighed. 'I think,' he said, 'that I was sent, principally,
to carry a warning that could be trusted to no one else. But I
have come too late.'

The Hanoman women knew at once that Cho was not
'Derveet's emissary'. They did not reveal this to Atoon,
because they sensed that something very important was happening that should not be discussed prematurely. They were
curious about the circumstances of Cho's arrival: her clothes,
her sojourn in the irrigation ditch and remarkable recovery,
Atoon's instant conviction that she had been sent to call him

148

back to the struggle; to call him back to life. They had acquired these details carefully, through the screens, without showing their astonishment to the outside palace, which was, Atoon included, so strangely ready to ignore everything strange about the visitor. . . .

'But if all this, then why the white clothes Atoon? Why send her to me? I don't understand.'

The prince shook his head. 'You must know what happened when I tried to send her inside: my family never actually examined her. Then there were the riots. I think it was only afterwards that they studied the past and so on, and became quite sure of what she must be: that she is a wayang legong –' He paused. It was a name out of a fairy tale, with only the vaguest of associations; either wonderfully good, or wonderfully bad, but certainly not real –

'I believe that in one way they sent her to you quite simply as you and I accepted it, to recognise your work. But it was Cho herself, Cho's arrival that made them decide it was time to give up neutrality. This angel doll is very dangerous, very fateful, they told me. She changes everything. But they couldn't tell me how. I think they are still trying to find out themselves.'

He fell silent. After a moment Derveet prompted him quietly. 'Anything else?'

'I was to tell you: Set thy heart upon thy work, never on its reward. Let your thought be for the good of all, and then do thy work in peace. . . .'

Handai whispered to Cendana – 'What's all that about?'

'It's scripture.'

Atoon exclaimed, 'Why *didn't* they take her into the Dapur?'

Derveet smiled. 'Oh, I can explain that. It was nothing to do with your family, it was Cho's conscience. It won't let her go where she's not wanted. And I imagine, Atoon, that the Hanoman Dapur, in its heart, does not have much use for – machines.'

Handai said firmly: 'Of course we can't give up Cho. We simply can't do that.'

Derveet was studying, with concentration, the rose and smoky pattern in the marble floor. She glanced up at her friend obliquely, but said nothing.

'What about the rest of the Peninsula?' she asked Atoon. 'We have heard so little in Ranganar, except rumours and what comes filtered through the Koperasi airwaves. How are people reacting to the dam message, and the Hanomans' child in white? How far have things gone?'

'The signs have been read, definitely,' said Atoon. He hesitated – 'There's a certain amount of visible excitement, Derveet. Especially in the north.'

'Oh no!' The soft exclamation was involuntary. 'You mean Gamartha, don't you?'

'Derveet, they can't help it –' Handai remembered the *two thousand years*, and felt for the excitable Gamarthans. 'They don't know what's happened. I thought you wanted other people to take up the initiative.'

'Yes – But not like this.'

Derveet got up and began to pace the room restlessly; touched the pearls and put them down again: 'Jagdanans hate to exaggerate Miss Butcher. If the prince says there is "a certain amount of visible excitment" you can take it from me the whole country is bubbling. Boys and men bubble. If the Dapurs had allowed themselves to become involved, there would be nothing to see on the surface ... just some unexplained changes, developing. So, we have the women holding aloof, in spite of the Hanomans' declaration, and danger in the north.'

She had come to the window and stood there. 'The trouble is, Dapur government isn't meant to impose authority: it is meant to give the ladies peace and quiet and time for more important things. It's an arrangement that has worked for a long time, whatever you may thing about "covert manipulation", Handai. But it tends to make some people – outside the walls – irresponsible. And there is so much hatred about nowadays. We were very careful in our game with the Koperasi. There were no losers, I think Anakmati has as many admirers in Sepaa as anywhere. Even so, it was going to take us all the time, all the patience, all the restraint in the world to keep our factions together. Think of the possibilities. I'm sorry to bring this up, Handai, but where do the Rulers' agents come from ... for one thing?'

'And there is Cho –'

The boys had gone away and Cho sat quietly with her pet, she looked up at Derveet and smiled. Derveet smiled back.

She spoke half to herself. 'I can accept that the Rulers have known everything, that they have been laughing at my amusing antics all along. But why did they let us go? They have not stirred from their islands for a hundred years, but they came for Cho. *Why* did they let her go again?'

'You escaped –' Atoon reminded her.

'So we did,' said Derveet dryly. 'It was very easy. It had not occurred to the Ruler that the angel doll might rouse me. The boat left behind was no doubt a simple oversight.'

For a while no one spoke. Petruk was banging pots and pans in the kitchen house, and singing tunelessly.

'Cho is dangerous, Cho changes everything because the Rulers want her and we've got her,' said Handai. 'That's clear enough. They're playing some kind of cat and mouse game, that's all.'

No one commented. Cendana glanced at her beloved with a brief smile, like a mother a little embarrassed by her child. No one could think of anything else to say, under the shadow of that one bewildering fact: the Rulers knew. They should draw back, they should undo what had begun – but how? In fact, it was impossible.

At last Atoon said, 'We have never been able to understand them. We have always lived in fear, and we would none of us have started on this enterprise if there had been any other choices left. Nothing has changed. We must go on, as best we can. When Ardjuna the perfect archer takes aim the world disappears for him. He sees nothing, no distractions; nothing in his way – only the point on his target where the arrow will strike. We must be like Ardjuna.'

Derveet smiled, the dancer's eyes glowed. Handai wondered why the prince was suddenly talking gibberish.

When Cendana and Handai had gone, over the river, Atoon turned on Derveet immediately.

'Who is she?'

Derveet pretended not to understand. She lit two cigarettes, and gave him one, and stretched out on the bed.

'Who is who? And why? We have so much to talk about. Have you forgiven me, for refusing to let you disembowel yourself that time?'

'I mean the person who kidnapped Cho.'

151

'Oh – I thought you gathered. Just a nightclub owner. Afterwards, as I said, I sent the boys to see what had happened to her. She got back safely, apparently, but then vanished. Probably afraid of what my "gang" might do to her.'

But he had seen her reaction to the mention of trouble in Gamartha. 'I somehow got the impression,' he said obstinately,' that your enemy is a northerner.'

Derveet was silent for a moment. Then she said, 'No, Atoon. I won't tell you the name or the family of a lady whose bad luck brought her to Hungry Tiger Street. She was someone who should have been my friend, it must have been partly my fault that she wasn't. You may find out who she is soon enough, but not from me.'

'What do you mean by that?'

'Nothing,' said Derveet. 'I hope – nothing.'

Cho and the Cat were enjoying the warm stone. The Cat licked her flank indolently, relaxing after the amusement – something she enjoyed once in a way – of making the boys jump about and squeak.

'Divine Endurance,' said Cho. 'Why *did* you come back with me and Derveet? I thought you wanted to get to Wo, and take me with you.'

'I changed my mind,' said Divine Endurance. 'It's a cat's prerogative.'

Cho looked sceptical, so for peace the Cat explained.

'I've realised there is no point in nagging. This world is so small you and Wo are bound to meet sometime. Meanwhile I think you are doing quite well at helping to help people just where you are. And I will help to, of course.'

'But what about your person? Where is she? Have you lost her?'

'No I have not lost her,' said Divine Endurance crossly. 'She has gone somewhere she likes, and I am still helping her. You don't *have* to get in their pockets to make them happy you know.'

Cho laughed, delighted to have caught the Cat out for once. 'You don't know what that means,' she said.

Derveet might as well have told him. Her discretion was about to become quite pointless. On the same day that Atoon arrived in

152

Ranganar, prince Bima Singa of Gamartha stood in an ante chamber, waiting. He was in the northern palace, where the Singas were discreetly contained by their enemies. He gazed through a high fretted window of grape-bloomed stone at citrus gardens and mulberry groves; and beyond, the steep emerald terraced hillsides and the sudden brilliant sky. He was a handsome young man, with the wide cat-face and pointed chin of the Singas, and the notorious 'tiger eyes'. The Gamarthan Dapurs had a passion for close breeding. Eyes and face at the moment were full of pride and a new feeling: a fierce, reckless joy. He loved his country very much.

In Gamartha things had always been different. People of high caste ate meat and drank wine, and the ladies were far closer to the world of men. This was not the Dapur, but behind Bima a light screen, veiled with draperies, had been put across the room as a mark of respect. He heard the rustle of silk and turned, drawing a deep breath of happiness, to kneel and greet his long lost sister.

19   The Black Horse

The rising in Gamartha sent shock waves all through the
Peninsula. There were outbursts everywhere: even parts of
Sepaa mutinied and took to the hills. Garbled bulletins on the
Administration Compound walls told a grim story of lives
wasted and savage, ineffectual reprisals. In a matter of days it
was as if the delicate, careful work of the White Riders had
never been. The people of Ranganar knew nothing of that of
course. All they knew was that fugitives were pouring into the
city: hordes of starving slaves from the camps; seeovers barely
distinguishable   from   their   charges;   Sepaa   mutineers,
brigands; and even whole families from the near parts of Timur
Kering. The city was in an uproar. The Samsui were indignant
that *their* Koperasi failed to control the influx. The truth was
the men could not do it. They were no longer capable of doing
the job for which they had been hired, and so bitterly paid.

The black horse struggled as Derveet led him into the yard.
He was afraid of the dark and the flaring lamplight.

'Hush, Jak – hush –'

Cho put her arms round Gress's neck and whispered to her.
The horses had to be moved. Tonight, suddenly, their hidden
stable was in danger, it was too near the river.

'He'll be all right,' said Gress. 'He's just a bit highly strung.'

Bejak stood still, pressed his face into Derveet's shoulder and
sighed heavily. He was bitterly disappointed. He had thought
when they came to fetch him that the horrible imprisonment
was over.

'Console him for me Cho,' said Derveet. 'I can't think of
anything to say.' The journey through the forest seemed like a
lost paradise – far out of reach now.

Cho led the animals away. Petruk turned his lantern out and
studied the fireclouds over the city. It looked as if the trouble
had moved, since midnight, into the Commercers' quarter.

154

'Madam, could you not possibly cross the river? This is disgraceful.'

'No Petruk,' said Derveet. 'It would only mean some of the rioters would be shouting my name, and that would give me no pleasure. Besides, the Koperasi might arrest me.'

Petruk grinned. The red creatures were showing themselves sadly incompetent at arresting anyone. It was nearly a month now since the news from Gamartha. Street fighting had broken out among the fugitives quite early in the crisis: everybody said the Sepaa mutineers were mainly to blame. Now every day and night brought more violence. And overcrowding was weighing heavily on the city's resources.

Handai was standing at the window, staring. 'Where is it?' she asked anxiously, as Derveet came into the upper room.

'Commercers, the boys think.'

Miss Butcher and the dancer had come over to talk, uselessly, about what could be done, and been stranded when the night's trouble broke out. Little Dinah lay on Derveet's bed, oblivious. Beside her was prince Atoon. He had been caught in the city, with no word from his family. He was still waiting for a safe chance to leave.

When the news first broke that prince Bima Singa had declared *merdeka* and launched an armed uprising, most of Previous Heaven had felt something uncontrollable: a start of joy. No one spoke of that now. Derveet was grimly silent. Prince Atoon said openly, ruthlessly, that the sooner the Koperasi pulled themselves together and stamped it out, the better he would be pleased. The name of Leilah of Gamartha had appeared frequently now on the Koperasi walls, and it was fairly common knowledge where this lady had sprung from. Derveet had given up etiquette and told Handai a story.

There was once a young lady, a jewel of a young lady; accomplished, spirited, clever. One of her blood brothers was the crown prince. This being Gamartha he knew it, and naturally was drawn to her. They wrote long letters. The Royal Dapur were worried about the influence of this one daughter of theirs. They did not want their prince to be inflamed with sad, stupid fantasies about merdeka – freedom. They could not send her to another court or household because of 'movement restrictions' in that subjugated country.... The dilemma was

155

solved when the fiery young lady, and her most faithful companion, failed at entering and went away to ruin. They did not need any papers for that. Nor – the big base on the gulf of Gamartha – was not far enough for such a fallen star, so they came to Ranganar.

If it was true that Leilah's failure was arranged, those hard-hearted, careful ladies had sown the wind, and they were reaping now. 'Why don't they stop her?' demanded Handai. 'Because they can't,' said Derveet. 'Anyway, some of them probably don't want to.' It was evident from the bulletins that the Singa Dapur had taken a very Dapur-like decision. They had withdrawn from the action, abandoning Leilah and Bima to their fate, which was inevitable. . . .'How did she find the courage to do it?' wondered Derveet. 'For better or for worse – I thought she was lost. I thought nothing could move her.'

Derveet's room had changed. The boys had infiltrated its austerity with mats and cushions, for the prince's sake, and there were several lamps burning. It was very quiet. Dinah slept. Atoon tried to answer Handai's questions about what would be happening in Gamartha now. She made a point of talking to Atoon seriously: she disliked a way Derveet had of treating him lightly, like an amusement; like something she owned. Cendana took down her hair and began to brush it out.

'Let me do it,' said Derveet. The dancer was right: talk was pointless. She knelt on cushions, and Cendana sat at her feet. Her hair was very different from Derveet's slick, heavy stuff. Opaque and insubstantial it spilled on the air, and twined itself self destructively around the brush.

'Did you ever have long hair, Derveet?'

'Oh yes. All divers did. Only men cut their hair on the islands. Silly, really, but it was tradition. I had a great thick plait – negative buoyancy, I suppose.'

'It was cut when you were entered?'

'No,' said Derveet, working gently on a tangle, 'that couldn't be, because I couldn't have dived with cut hair, and I had to earn our living. It was not a great occasion, the ceremony. Only my grandfather entered me, there was no one else. Perhaps I was too young. We couldn't wait because he was ill, and the evacuation was hanging over us.'

Hush, hush, said the smooth strokes over Cendana's shoulders. The sound was like the sea, sighing on that lost, dark shore. Derveet felt adrift. She had the sensation every day now that she must act – urgently. But what could she do? Atoon's wise words about Ardjuna the archer had come to nothing. They had had no chance to 'go on' with whatever action or restraint, before the Singas' merdeka exploded. Such a destructive explosion: Miss Butcher had said more than once that at least the Gamarthan outbreak showed there was no need to worry about the Rulers. Whatever they knew, they were letting the Koperasi do their dirty work, as inefficiently as ever. We don't have to be afraid of them suddenly striking us down in some awful way – Don't we? thought Derveet. Perhaps they've just done it. She did not believe that Leilah was the enemy's tool now, not consciously; she had seen a revulsion of feeling in the tiger-cat, that night on the rig, and been afraid even then of what it might mean. Leilah was sincere, like all the other thoughtless rebels; sincere like the rioters. . . . But while Derveet tried doggedly to think of this disaster as a setback; a reverse to be weathered – we lie low and then try again – something monstrous and shadowy was taking shape in her mind. What had she disturbed?

These frantic outbursts were not new. In a milder form they had plagued the Peninsula for a hundred years. A few nights ago, alone here with Cho, she had asked the child about the other angel doll, her brother. What could *Wo* do? What sort of thing would he do for the Rulers? And Cho answered with her usual impenetrable candour. 'How many people?' asked Derveet. 'How many people could someone like Wo "make happy"?' Cho said, apologetically, 'Well, there isn't really an answer.'

She had asked the dancers what they could see ahead when things first started to go wrong, before Gamartha came out. But they could not help her; they still could not. They offered her obscure fragmentary dreams, vague feelings that something tremendous would come out of all this trouble. And they did not seem to care that their intuition had deserted them: 'Too much is going on,' they said. 'The present's too important just now.' She did not ask, but she had a feeling no one had glimpsed the 'floating world', that painful memory, for quite a while. . . .

157

She tamed the filmy masses of Cendana's hair into one sheaf, and began to put them into a thick braid. Are you hiding something from me? she thought. Do you see something you are afraid to tell me, is that it? I am Garuda: perhaps I could make you tell. If I dared.... But Cendana was listening to Atoon and Handai talking about the price of violence; the cause of the Gamarthans.

'Derveet,' she said softly, 'does everything always end and fail and come to nothing?'

Suddenly there was a great crack of dry thunder out in the dark. It came from the east. Handai jumped to her feet.

'You may as well sit down,' said Derveet, after a moment. 'Whatever it was, there's nothing you can do.'

Cho came up from consoling Gress and Bejak and settled by Derveet, nestling down among the cushions. Derveet finished her plaiting and Cendana moved away. Darkness stood around the lamps, and no one felt like sleeping. Suddenly, Cho lifted her head.

Handai said, 'O it's *raining*. Mother, what a relief. It'll put out the fires –'

Derveet looked at Cho and got quietly to her feet. A moment later and they could all hear, above the sudden rush of the rain, Semar's voice raised querulously at the yard gate. Atoon moved away from the sleeping child and glanced around the room, assessing. Frightened footsteps thumped up the stairs. 'Madam –' But Derveet said, 'Don't be rude, Petruk. Bring the visitor in.'

It was Cycler Jhonni. She stood dripping, twisting her hands in her wet sleeves.

'Jhonni!' cried Miss Butcher. 'What's happening? What were the explosions?'

'Well – someone set light to some raw rubber that we hadn't moved. The river caught fire for a bit –'

'Is *that* what I could smell –'

'The explosion was probably the Clock Tower. It was very hot, all the windows burst.... That was the worst, actually. The Clock Tower was the only big thing, and it was, it was an accident....'

It was difficult for Jhonni now. Her clan and family blamed the radicals for everything. She was forcibly kept away from

158

her Previous Heaven friends and she was afraid they didn't trust her anymore anyway. She looked at the prince, and couldn't speak for embarrassment.

'What is it Jhonni – ?'

Finally, she managed to tell them. Yesterday, the major clans led by the Cyclers had decided the mass of fugitives had to be expelled. They were to be given an amnesty, to leave peaceably. After a certain day, the Koperasi were going to round up any remaining aliens and see them off.

'I thought you ought to know. I don't know what they're going to do about the West Bank. I didn't know how to – to get here, but tonight the firefighters had boats on the river you see –'

Once it had been the dream of Jhonni's life to come to Dove House, and sit in this room. 'I'd better go,' she muttered. 'I'm sorry –'

'See them off where?' cried Miss Butcher. 'They won't go. It's mad! It'll make things fifty times worse –'

But Derveet was staring intently at Jhonni's bent head, the rim of wet hair plastered pitifully on her reddish nape. Her eyes grew wide and black.

'Atoon, I know the answer. I have been wondering all along, why did your family send you into danger. Just that late warning wasn't enough reason. Now I understand. I know what we should do.'

Twelve days after the Clock Tower riot, it was deportation day. The playing fields that covered the old reservoir, which the Samsui had filled in because of salt-water seepage, were thronged with people in the grey darkness before dawn. Many of them had been camping for days in makeshift shelters. Samsui organisers hurried about, their voices ringing in the air. There were bales, carts and animals. Of course, the 'causeway people' were getting what supplies could be spared. On the perimeter of the crowd hc treaders from Straits Control snarled up and down. The Samsui ignored this infringement, they knew the Koperasi were nervous and touchy.

Derveet was at the playing fields' foodstalls, standing *behind* Atoon in the way Handai so disliked, her hand just

159

touching his shoulder. For once the prince was not in white: he wore drab riding clothes.

'Here he comes. Now don't smile. They don't like you to smile, unless you are saying something very simply humorous.'

The speaker for the mutineers said, 'G'day.'

'Good day,' said Derveet.

He was red, big. 'We're for Anakmati,' he said aggressively. 'If Anakmati stays, we stay.'

'Anakmati is staying. But I think you should not.'

His blind-looking eyes followed the hc treaders uneasily. 'They won't touch you if you go.'

The mutineer stared at Atoon, who remembered not to smile.

'This is your man?'

'This is my man.'

The red creature at last shrugged, and nodded. He vanished into the crowd. Derveet and Atoon sat down together.

'Derveet change your mind. Come with me. I don't like the feel of this city –'

The Samsui imagined that Ranganar would be 'back to normal' in a day or two, with all its prized amenities, but the prince of Jagdana knew better. It was not just the riots. He had learned, painfully, to know the insidious marks of final decay. Derveet shook her head.

'No. I can't. There aren't any Samsui listening are there – ? After all, this is part of the Garuda state; it's my place to stay. Besides –' She smiled shyly. 'I'm not really fit for a camping holiday. You must have noticed.'

He had noticed. There was nothing to say; the uncertainty ahead swept over such minor concerns.

The noisy crowd milled around. Atoon said quietly, 'Tell me about the angel dolls.'

He knew she had some theory she was keeping to herself. She had refused to discuss it until the deportation was arranged.

'I once saw something Cho had done by accident,' said Derveet, looking into the crowd. 'Some mountain cats had attacked her and Gress: there was only blood left. I didn't know what I'd stumbled on, but then I met Cho and told her. She was very embarrassed. I thought – hm – she was embarrassed about something else, but I realised later. . . . They're not supposed

160

to be weapons. But perhaps they could be perverted. The Rulers could have left Cho to us so we'd quarrel over the marvellous toy, but they know we quarrel anyway. More likely they think we'll try to *use* her, and come to grief. Well, we will not. I think Cho was bound to gravitate to some power or other. By "coincidence" she came to you, and to me: both far too Dapur-ridden to be tempted by that kind of experiment. We are safe.'

'So what is it you are afraid of?'

Derveet glanced at him, and away. 'That it may be enough for Cho just to be here.'

'Oh Derveet –'

'No, no; not doing anything on purpose. But – Suppose the wayang the Rulers have, has some kind of harmful influence? Cho could affect that – a sort of catalyst. . . . Of course, this may be nonsense. . . . Or if not, I'll find a way round it.'

Atoon looked at her steadily, and said nothing. Derveet suddenly shook her head, dismissing the subject.

'For now, the point is you have a safe passage. Ranganar escapes the fun of a Koperasi round up, and you will keep this dreadful rabble out of mischief.'

'Yes. I had thought – I could travel via Bu Awan and talk to Annet, maybe stay there.'

Derveet frowned. 'No. Don't do that. Leave Annet alone – I've a feeling she has troubles enough at the moment. Stay completely in the wilds. Here – I want you to have these.'

She gave him a small padded bag. It was the pearls from Sinar Bulan.

'Derveet,' said Atoon. 'My family is not rich nowadays, but I think we can support people who are really in need.'

'But you'll have to go into the hills. Not to the capital. These people are displaced *anywhere* Atoon. I'm trusting you to keep them safe.'

'Until?'

'Until you hear from me.'

The Samsui must have been aware that some unseen force had taken over their ignoble decision, so that the trouble-makers, the mutineers and strays, came quietly and willingly. Nothing was declared. But there was an incongruous air of purpose in the ranks of the unwanted. In fact, there were many in the lines who had not been asked to leave at all. An impression had spread that this docile departure was really, secretly, a great adventure.

It was time for Atoon to leave. The treaders snarled and distant voices shouted. Everything began to move. As he stood up, a line of carts passed and out from behind them two boys led a big nervous animal with a hide like black glass.

'Derveet –'

The boys whipped off a saddlecloth of cloud colour and blood rose, and flung over the horse's shoulders the blue and gold of Jagdana.

'Don't get on,' said Derveet grinning. 'Might attract too much attention.'

Some people shouted out – some knelt down: for Garuda's steward, their prince and leader; and then the moment was covered in the surging crowd.

'Go to the hills. Go far. Don't go back to Jagdana; don't go to Bu Awan, or anywhere near trouble. Stay away from Bima Singa. Stay away from the sea –'

The sea. It was her last word. The ranks pressed forward and she disappeared. A Sawah boy ran and snatched the blue and gold and stuffed it into his blouse. He took the bridle and proudly led the black horse after the prince, into the ranks of the people.

The cavalcade passed away, flanked by Koperasi vehicles, down the causeway road: mutineers and seeovers and slaves; Samsui and Ranganarese; veiled peasants from Timur Kering with their whole families trailing, and the senior boy holding up the rahula. . . . Derveet watched with Cho from the foodstall. 'Do you remember,' she said, 'I once said I had to find a way to unite all the peoples?'

Handai arrived, in a hurry.

'Have you seen Jhonni: Cycler Jhonni?'

She looked after the crowd with a helpless, angry expression and turned on Derveet: 'You know what you've done. You've amputated the men. Typical Dapur tactic: when in doubt send the men off to kill each other. What d'you think's going to happen to Atoon up there, and all those poor people?'

Cho looked at her reproachfully. Cendana, who had caught up, said savagely, 'Dai, shut up.'

162

It was the fourth month. The flame of the forest tree that stood over the little tables had a crown of scarlet in the morning sunlight. Handai stared down the road.

'What's Jhonni's mother going to say now?'

20 The Arousing

The audience made a tight circle around a young woman, dancing. Evidently she had been a tiger; she still painted her face and had her hair loose, but she wore Samsui clothes. Her partner was the same, she stayed still in the centre while the other moved round her. She danced wonderfully. The air near her shook with faint after-images or anticipations: it was the effect called thunder-and-lightning; people said Sandalwood had it, if you had eyes to see. The ring had reached a high pitch of tension. It was impossible to tell now whether the dancer was moving so fast or so slowly that she seemed to stand, while the earth spiralled round her. Suddenly the girl in the middle cried out. She fell to her knees, palms pressed into her eyes.

'Oh! I see it – It's like a cloud. A branch – unstretching –'

Something rose up from the ground between the dancer and the other; a figure flickering, glittering. Its hair fell down its back; its face was the face of both young women. The blind one spoke again, a throaty unintelligible muttering. The audience gasped and began to whimper.

'Stop her! –'

Handai and Derveet crashed through the bodies. Handai launched herself after the dancer, but the devotees were running in panic, and the young woman vanished with them. There was nothing left but a patch of waste ground in the Pabriker quarter, and Derveet holding the other girl by the shoulders. She was still muttering, but her eyes rolled up whitely.

'We'll get nothing out of this one for a while.'

Handai came and crouched down; peered into the empty face. 'We've got to get to the source of it.'

The streets of Ranganar had been quieter since Atoon left, but not more peaceful. Of course, it was only the healthy, able-bodied fugitives who had gone. The rest remained, and more kept coming. The round-up had been cancelled as impractical, the prison the Samsui called their 'Assistance' had become, helplessly, a packed pauper-camp, and still the city seethed with homeless strays. Ordinary services like water and the recycle were strained already by riot damage. Produce looted by the Koperasi from the Peninsula disappeared from the markets, and the once self-sufficient colony had a horrible shock. The city, everyone agreed, was suffering a plague of *red-backed kites.* There were shortages, there were infections. This was one of them. It must have begun just about the time Previous Heaven lost their prescient dreams. Whores had abandoned tigering and were taking to this cult; a crude indulgence of the faculties Derveet had tried so hard to keep secret, and not to misuse. Previous Heaven were breaking up the meetings wherever they found them. The Ranganar Koperasi were in a bad state of nerves. If they realised the talk about women's magic loose in their streets was true, they might panic horribly.

The Pabriker quarter was very quiet. It was noon, but no crowds of workers hurried to the foodstalls round the Pasar Diluar. One whistle shrieked, at a distance, faintly. There was broken glass in the street. On the waste ground, tangled morning glory vine had crawled over a pile of factory waste that was waiting to be recycled. On a blank wall plastered with old bills, one of Handai's 'Don't Eat Rice!' posters, with the skeletal Peninsulan child, hung in tatters. . . . What had happened to Ranganar? Outside taps, heaps of refuse; people locking their daughters up at night, for fear of weird orgies. Miss Butcher shuddered, unwilling to touch the tranced body.

While she went to search for a trishaw Derveet stayed with the girl. She looked down at the body in her arms. It shivered occasionally, the way something rotten moves, with a life that is not its own. Her expression was bleak. She had sent the causeway people into hiding because of a terrible suspicion: it was more than a suspicion now.

She was thinking of something she had seen a few days ago. She had come across a small crowd in the Open Market. When she went up quietly, she found there was no dancer, instead there was Cho. She was talking to an elderly boy, and everybody was listening seriously, it was a religious meeting. The boy asked Cho a question that had been around for some years, an anxiety often expressed by the people. When was the Father's child coming back? The trouble was, everybody knew there was something wrong with the sea now. Perhaps it was quite dead, and then how could it carry that Emissary? How long are we to wait? Has God, who is really all the people we pray to, forgotten us?

Cho thought for a moment. Then she said, 'Once upon a time there was a Ranganarese lady. Her sisters and aunties and daughters had gone away to an entering in another part of the Bank, and all the boys had sleep-in jobs with the Samsui. So she was living alone with the man of the family and she had to go to market herself, holding up her own chain. She left the man to mind the house and went out. Well, evening came, and it was raining hard. The man sat in his own balé, his own little house, at the back of the compound, and smoked achar and played music to amuse himself. He was sleepy and a bit fuddled. He remembered to bar the gates, but he forgot the lady was outside. And so when our Semar came along that gang just when it was dark, he saw a lady standing in the rain –'

The boys were always with Cho: Derveet had told them never to leave her alone. Old Semar was squatting in the front row, he grinned delightedly at his own appearance in the story.

'Semar was very embarrassed,' said Cho. 'He hid his eyes and ran past.'

The crowd, which contained more than one veiled, escorted Ranganarese, laughed and nodded –

'But he came back later, and there she was still. He peeped from behind a tree and wondered what was happening. Then he decided that he must do something, so he went up with his eyes lowered and banged and rattled on the gates. But the man inside must have been asleep. The lady didn't even look at Semar, so he had to go away. But he was worried now, so he kept coming back, it was near our house, you see – and it went on raining and there was the lady still standing there in the rain and the dark, right into the middle of the night. Now the man had woken up. When Semar came close he could hear him stirring about inside the compound, searching for his lady and getting frightened when he couldn't find her. Semar knew a lady wouldn't shout, so very boldly he shouted for her: "Open

166

the gates! There's someone waiting here!" But the man was upset and the rain was noisy; he was afraid, obviously, that it was robbers outside and he didn't dare come. So then Semar, who soon runs out of patience, crouched down to the lady and said humbly, "Madam, after all times are changing. I know it's rude to shout, but why don't you touch this man's mind as I am sure you can do, so he can let you in. It's too disgraceful for you to stand here all night." Then the lady, without hurrying, turned to him at last and said: "The gate is barred and I am not within. No doubt the significance of this will come to him in time. . . ."'

Semar saw Derveet in the crowd. She shook her head at him and walked away, she did not want to speak to anyone just then. Cho understood the Peninsulan mind too well.

And so do our enemies, she thought, kneeling on the waste ground. How can we resist a poison that's so alluring? – recklessness, abandonment, giving up everything; opening the gates – She remembered being seriously worried, as Anakmati, about how she would reclaim her identity as a woman, if the time should come. How absurd that seemed now. Bandit or Garuda lady: nightclub owner or leader of the Singas, no one cared. And the power of the Dapur had turned into something anyone could understand: no longer awesome, no longer out of reach. . . . Everything we ever wanted. Derveet smiled thinly. She had carefully understated her fear to Atoon, otherwise it would have been difficult to make him go away. She shared her hardening dread with no one now: it would do no good, it would only help spread the poison.

She saw the morning glory flowers and watched a pair of orioles in their lilting flight, from tree to tree in a factory garden across the street. The birds called to each other blithely and clearly.

At least there was no news of Atoon in the Wave bulletins, only reports of the Koperasi trying ineffectively – or was it unwillingly – to control the spreading violence. The causeway people had vanished. There was hope for them. In her worst moments Derveet was afraid there was not much hope for anyone else.

Handai came back and they piled the girl into the trishaw. She was still unconscious, or making a good show of it. Derveet would not come back to Red Door Street, she thought she had been away from the West Bank long enough. She was determined not to break down and start behaving recklessly herself.

'How is Dinah? Is she eating now?'

'Oh no. *She's* not stupid. She knows if she doesn't eat her bean cake today we'll be forced to give her chicken rice tomorrow.' Handai laughed. 'I think the little brute's going to starve herself to death if this goes on,' she said casually.

Derveet tried to make herself say something reassuring, but she could not.

The trishaw boy wanted Handai to get into his cart but she refused. It was against her principles to have a boy pedal two adults, except in an emergency. Derveet left them arguing, totally at cross-purposes. The sound of Miss Butcher's voice, raised in anger, that pursued her, was strangely heartening.

Cho was in the monkey quarter. Once, before the days of Pabrikers and Commercers, the city had been named after various princedoms. In this area there were still battered shrines of white apes, called 'monkeys', on some street corners. In front of one of them was a crowd. A Sawah boy was chanting in a loud voice about the dream he had had. He saw a great battle, the warriors had breasts – the enemy fled, and melted into a mist. . . . The people gasped and swayed, stirring themselves up to see what he had seen, and make it real. . . . But Cho was frowning. She saw Divine Endurance slip neatly from between the shuffling feet and hurried after her.

'You shouldn't encourage them! It's wrong of you. They're going to wear themselves out!'

The Cat turned her head coolly. 'I believe you are right,' she said, with a blink of satisfaction. 'And about time too. It is very proper and right.'

'They shouldn't be behaving like this. I know they shouldn't.'

'You and your Derveet. Such a passion for the simple life. Why not let them enjoy themselves? They're soon going to be wearing out very rapidly indeed, anyway – by the way things are going over the causeway.'

Koperasi bulletins, and rumours, told a bleak story. Prince Bima's followers had not been able to get into Nor or the other bases, so now they were out of control; attacking towns in

Gamartha and neighbour states that hadn't 'come out'. There was no united front: the Gamarthans would have nothing to do with the brigands and mutineers who were running wild in other parts. The Koperasi, it was said, had orders from the Rulers to keep the rebels from each others' throats. Cho knew that this particular piece of news had not made Derveet less anxious. . . .

'Derveet says,' she said firmly, 'that they will stop. The Dapur, I mean the idea-Dapur, the real one, will stop them. It says that no one must go to war, not properly. You remember: Annet told us.'

'Ah yes. A not-allowed.' The Cat looked cynical. 'They seem impressive at first, I know. But in my experience there isn't anything these Dapurs and Controllers can really *do*.'

Cho sat down on a doorstep, her chin in her hands, a frown of concentration on her face. 'Divine Endurance,' she said, 'I'm not sure anymore. It was right for our palace and everything to fade away, because we are the very very last of something, aren't we. But these people are the very, very first of something, I think –'

The Cat gazed at her blandly: 'Idle speculation. But – So?'

'So, we ought to help them more than we are doing, somehow. We ought to get them out of this trouble.'

Divine Endurance smiled with slitted eyes. 'Oh, don't upset yourself,' she purred. 'I think we'll soon have them out of it, you and Wo and I.'

She had gone too far. The child was staring at her curiously.

'Hm,' said the Cat. 'Ah well –', and jumped, just the moment before Cho grabbed her. For the next few seconds the patch of hot pavement was an interesting sight, because the child and the Cat were both moving a good deal faster than usual. They flickered like the trance dancers, only more so. But Cho quickly realised that the Cat was too good at this game. She left off and walked away, without the explanation she wanted, still looking worried.

Back at Red Door Street, Handai asked Cendana to see if she could get anything out of the captive. But no source emerged, and they had to let the girl go, like the others. The Classical Theatre was temporarily closed. Cendana, restless and idle, started staying out late in the evenings, to see her dancer friends.

Atoon found that the causeway people could not stay in Jagdana, not even in hiding. When he had brought them safely through the Sawah he sent ahead to tell his family what he was doing and soon a messenger from the capital arrived at the camp. The ladies praised Atoon's altruism for taking on this task, but suggested it was not wise, just now, for the Hanoman prince to sit up in his hills with a large band of followers, however secretly. So the deportees marched on, fleeing every rumour of trouble, farther and farther up the Peninsula. Atoon was dismayed to find how little he liked the sacred tasks of women: it depressed him to have hard dirty hands, and his hair never dressed properly. He wondered how Derveet had managed to hypnotise him into this extraordinary position.

They avoided all roads, all towns, all Koperasi presence; crossed state borders without ceremony on unmarked trails. They bartered all sorts of things with the hill women; notably, of course, the pearls of Sinar Bulan. Customs around them changed: in wayside shrines a many-armed, fierce creature presided; the spirit of life was not Bu Awan, the sky mother, here in the north, but Bumi, the seed-swallowing earth. Boy-making was not so common. They passed families of young men at work in the steep fields, astonishingly lovely, loaded down with gold and coral. Dreamy eyes beckoned boldly, the whites tinged with a brilliant blue to accentuate their beauty. Atoon took care to walk beside Breus, the leader among the ex-Koperasi, and warn him:

'Don't approach them, however welcoming they look. They tend to defend each other's chastity vigorously.'

'I'll pass it round,' said Breus. 'Why are their eyes like that?'

'Their ladies give them jamu, to make them more interesting.'

Right from the start, there was an element that disturbed Atoon very much. People, all sorts of people – Samsui and mutineers included – said they were dreaming dreams, and seeing things. Some said they could hear what was going on inside each other's minds. Some could hear or see what was happening in Ranganar. Several people saw a woman with a fierce face and many arms, dancing round the camp at night. . . . Atoon did not disbelieve any of them, but he was sure this sort of thing could only cause trouble, outside the Dapur. He tried to keep it down.

Another dark, drenching day. It was the end of the sixth month, and South-West Wind was in full flood at the landmass end of the Peninsula. The causeway people had gathered together and made camp in a hollow of the hills where there were caves for shelter. Atoon was down by the river with Koperasi Breus and Cycler Jhonni, on watch. Breus was a strange character. He considered it enormously good of himself to have forgiven Anakmati for being a woman. That had been the hard thing, much harder than breaking out of Sepaa. Atoon laughed – and Jhonni turned on him indignantly, absurdly defending the mutineer: 'You don't *try* to understand – '

'Look at that, Atoon – ' said Breus softly.

Lying concealed, they watched a small armed band traverse the scrub-covered slope on the other side of the stream. One of them was carrying the merdeka flag: a red dagger on a white ground – many of the insurgents used it. The sentries were not alarmed. Peasants had told them there were other 'freedom-dreamers' about: this time a parley seemed unavoidable. The band marched up to the water and stared around.

'Monkey!' yelled the one with the flag.

Strange manners, murmured the prince, but they all stood up. 'Come across – ' called Jhonni. 'It isn't too deep – '

The next moment six senjata were levelled over the stream. Atoon and the others slowly lowered their own unready weapons.

'But we're friends,' said Jhonni blankly.

The flag-bearer ignored her. 'Monkey,' he shouted. 'You'd better get out of here, and your renegade whores and shit-eaters. We know all about you, and this is Gamartha, in case you didn't know.'

'I have no quarrel with my brother Bima Singa,' said Atoon mildly, because he would rather lose a little dignity than be torn up with bits of old iron. 'Or with his family.'

The boy, or youth, laughed loudly. '*Your brother Bima Singa*,' he mimicked, 'is cleaning up Jagdana state right now, monkey. Our lady and our prince are cleansing the whole

Peninsula of corrupt southern elements. Where have you been? Don't you know what's going on?'

Silence. Breus and Jhonni gaped. The Gamarthan grinned. Atoon, his face calm, his eyes dark with rapid thought, said coolly: 'I do not have to worry about those two. If I am in Gamartha I am under the protection of the Singa Dapur.'

But the flag-bearer laughed again. 'Out of date, monkey. The Dapur is with us now. All nations, all ladies together against the menace of deformed criminals, renegades and dupes of false Garuda Koperasi-whore – '

'You little rat turd!' shouted Breus. 'You stupid bugger *we're* not the enemy! We know about *your* lady – She'd have had me as well if I did it with women, the way you all do – '

Atoon turned and kicked Jhonni to the ground, Breus was too big for him to tackle. The flag-bearer had a self righteous expression. It was not *his* fault that the enemy carried no flag of truce. . . . All this in a fraction of a fraction of a moment – there was something happening behind Atoon's back – 'No!' he yelled. Kimlan and the people she had brought up held their fire. The Gamarthans ran away, unharmed.

Atoon had been ignoring the bad dreams, keeping strictly to Derveet's rule and refusing to be drawn by ugly rumours among the hill people. But this he could not ignore. He sent down scouts, cunning ex-Sawah bandits, to the towns and the roads. The 'freedom-dreamers' stole a few horses, unless that was the locals, but did nothing more. The scouts came back. It was all true. The Singa Dapur, for whatever reasons, now supported Leilah and Bima. Bima was moving with an army somewhere down in the small states of Timur Kering, purging 'corrupt elements' among the insurgents there, and gathering allies. Leilah, officially in residence in the northern court, was really in the Sawah collecting her own special fighting people to fall on the starving city of Ranganar and leave no one alive. . . .

'She may be there already,' whispered the boy, awed, transported by the magnitude of his bad news. 'Ranganar is lost . . . Anakmati, *Garuda* is lost – '

Rain drummed on the canvas awning in the mouth of the cave, where the leadership of the causeway people were gathered. Those who couldn't get in were pressing and crowding in the sodden mists outside.

172

'What about the Koperasi?' said someone.

The boy who had been speaking glanced at the other scouts, lowered his eyes and shrugged his shoulders a little: 'Nobody is talking about them.'

Late in the night, the rain ceased. Atoon walked out of the cave he was sharing. He sat by the entrance and lit a cigarette, and watched the smoke float away in the darkness. The camp was very quiet; even the sound of the animals shifting in their lines seemed ominous and strange. He thought of the long journey; its trials and losses, and the people who had joined the ranks on the way. Seventy days since deportation morning, nearly two months since that calm letter in Jagdana moved them on into the wilds. He wished he could conjure Derveet or his family here, to tell him what to do now. He tried to remember all she had said at the last moment, but the situation had made her words meaningless.... The scouts reported that the small towns where they looked for news were strangely empty. The ordinary people who had not been infected by the fever of this rising were leaving and taking with them their boys and men, into the wilderness. *What are they afraid of?* Atoon had asked. *Rebels sweeping through? Koperasi punishment? No, it is more than that,* whispered the boy. *I spoke to a wise woman, she took me into her hearth. Scatter and hide, she said, is the word now. The end is coming....* If that is the only advice the women here have to give, then I must refuse it, thought the prince. I will stay with my own inferior vision, which shows me no reason to give up hope.

Even if everything the boys reported was true, if the situation on the Peninsula was so terrible it could not be right to run any further. Derveet could not possibly have meant them to disappear into the desolate lands and never be seen again. The boys said Bima was supposed to have an army of 'six hundred thousands – ' Six hundred thousands was substantially more than half the population of Gamartha. Still, it could be assumed that prince Singa had a lot of company.... He put out his cigarette and stood up, with the starless dark all around him. He had made up his mind. He would turn back, and parley with Bima Singa.

And he remembered, as he made his decision, that the words

173

from scripture sent by his family to Derveet, months ago, were spoken on the edge of a battlefield.

The life of Ranganar ebbed in slow waves. First there were the riots, then the magic and the weird enthusiasm. That business seemed to fade about the same time that they heard of the prince of Jagdana, suddenly appearing on the Peninsulan stage 'with an army'. The next wave was more boring, it was just sickness and tiredness. *Cash* in quantity was the only currency for any comfort, decent food or medicine. The fugitives still coming in reported big war bands of some kind roaming in the Sawah: the Koperasi wouldn't guard the causeway properly and everyone was afraid.

Derveet had been out all day, alone. Now she lay on the bed in the upper room beside Cho, staring into the sunset light at the window. She shaded her left eye with her hand for a moment, and smiled a little. 'Tiger Street is nearly empty,' she said. 'I suppose they have gone to other Koperasi bases, I hope they will be safe. But I went looking for my friends as well, at the Theatre and at their homes. Where have the dancers gone?'

'Perhaps Atoon has got them?'

Derveet smiled again. 'That doesn't comfort me any more, child. I tried. I failed.'

A strange thing had happened to Derveet. Her right hand had lost its skills. It had forgotten how to write even, she had had to revert to the left. Every injury she had suffered in her life seemed to be coming back to haunt her: a place on her side where Anakmati was knifed once ached and ached, though there was hardly a scar. She sat up to slip out of her clothes.

'And where's that Cat? Has she deserted us too?'

'I don't know,' said Cho unhappily. 'She isn't letting me know.' She had not seen Divine Endurance since that day in the Monkey Quarter.

Derveet said suddenly, fiercely – 'Do you understand what is happening? We cannot bear a war, a civil war. We are too weak. The Dapurs have turned inward; imagining the future's already come they can't or won't deal with this crude situation. The princes are idle puppets, they've never been trained to think of the consequences of anything. And the people – We will be destroyed!

'And I'm so tired – '

She put her arms out and held Cho hard. 'But it won't happen,' she said, intently. 'Here are Atoon, and Singa and Leilah, all hanging on the edge of disaster, and on the edge they stay. They *cannot* fall. Stillness, Cho. It is our only weapon, but it will win. It must.'

Her skin was hot. She made love as if she was burning and wanted to burn Cho too. Then she slept. Cho lay with her cheek on Derveet's hair, that smelt of cocoa butter and flowers, and watched the room grow dark.

Cendana was cooking in the kitchen house at Red Door Street. She murmured to herself *hot wok cold oil, hot wok cold oil* – She had given up the affectation of refusing women's tasks long ago, but she would never be good at this. She could not open the sliding wall because the courtyard was camped out with sick fugitives, she opened the windows as wide as she could. There was music playing somewhere in the compound; not classical, just Samsui popular tunes on three fiddles and a horn. Aunt insisted everyone had to keep cheerful –

> Every day we used to meet
> In the garden
> You gave me a flower –
> Where have you gone?

As she listened, the dancer suddenly felt an odd little stab of happiness. Life had been good after all, in so many ways. She began to sway and then to move fluidly, with perfect artistry, around the kitchen floor. A small black kitten that had crept in looking for scraps sat back on its heels amazed, privileged to be Sandalwood's sole audience. She laughed at its round eyes and gave of her best, until the music ended.

The wok and the steamer had been included in her choreography so there was no harm done. She left most of the food under covers, for the family couldn't possibly eat all together anymore; some she put in a tiffin carrier and took away to Handai's room. Dinah woke up: something smelled good. Handai lifted the lid off the carrier and looked at her beloved reproachfully –

175

'Eat up,' said Cendana. 'And don't ask silly questions.'

While they were eating she said suddenly – 'Dai, I won't let them hurt you.'

Handai and Dinah, with full stomachs, fell asleep instantly like babies. Cendana took the tiffin carrier back to the kitchen. She did not do the washing-up because there was no water ration left and she had not managed to acquire the art of doing without. She walked softly between the bodies in the courtyard and slipped out of the back gate, closing it very quietly behind her.

PART THREE

The wayang on the left side represent an evolutionary phase which has already completed itself and is bound to become extinct, and those on the right side the next phase to come. Nothing can ever stop this process. Nature cannot have regard for individuals, and thus it arouses our sympathy to see the blameless characters on the left fulfilling their duty and keeping their vows, though they know there is no chance of success for them.

Hans Ulbricht, *Wayang Purwa*

21   A Deputation

Cendana had vanished, and in her place was a city daily more
clearly given over to death. 'It's ridiculous,' sobbed Handai
angrily. 'She's a *dancer*. She's never handled a real weapon in
her life!' It was impossible to find out what had happened to
anyone who had left the island. On the Peninsula prince Bima
and Atoon moved about, according to the Wave bulletins, like
tom-cats getting ready to fight. Some rumour attributed scru-
ples to one prince; some gave protestations to the other, but at
this stage it was meaningless. Now the mood of Ranganar
changed again. Koperasi reappeared as a presence in uniform
on the streets. Bubbles from Sepaa and further away were seen
landing at the East Coast barracks; this activity was not mentioned in the news.

Handai had given up reproaching Derveet for sending the
causeway people to an unknown fate long ago, she had shared
her friend's dismay when Atoon turned around. Now she
followed the bulletins slavishly; knowing they were mostly lies,
and days old anyway, and waited like everybody else for the
inevitable. But Derveet, bleak and withdrawn as she was,
stubbornly refused to give up hope. Life is stronger than death,
she said. In their hearts they know what is really happening.
They *will* draw back. And day by day Singa and Hanoman
hovered on the brink, as if held apart by a mysterious invisible
force.

At the start of the second twelve days of the eighth month, a
deputation of the major clans wanted to see the Butchers of Red
Door Street. The Butchers cleared away some of their house
guests from the big dining room and put out tables and chairs,
wondering what the clanswomen had to say.

Everybody sat around a row of tables pushed together.
Overhead the fans said clack, clack, clack; sometimes whirring
for a few seconds and then slowing to clack, clack again. It was a

very hot day. Noises of the sick and homeless came through the thin walls, fine lines of gold crept between the slats and lay burning on the floor. Mrs Cycler, without much polite preliminary, began to read out a long account of everything that was wrong with Ranganar: sickness was spreading; piped water had to be boiled. The tran system was completely shut down; gas for light and power unpredictable, sanitation failing. Fresh food was almost unavailable; dried food adequate but for how long? Industry was at a standstill, children missing their education.... Unknown powers in the Sawah were liable to attack at any time –

'What is this leading to?' murmured one Butcher to another. 'The "roundup" idea again?'

And apart from all else, because of lack of drainage maintenance North-East Wind floods would be the worst ever known. Mrs Cycler gathered herself and her papers and came to the point. The Rulers had offered, through the Koperasi, to evacuate the whole of Ranganar to a safe place for the duration of the present disturbances. Knowing the Butchers' great influence over the native population, the clanswomen wanted their help to get the idea accepted and organised smoothly – The great influence Mrs Cycler spoke of was sitting apart, at the end of the row of tables. The deputation had covertly requested its presence: no names, no problems. They were all now pretending Derveet was invisible.

Uproar! First Aunt jumped to her feet, shouting angrily. Mrs Builder and Mrs Printer jumped up too and yelled back at her: shouting that it was all the Butchers' fault anyway. With their sympathies they ought to be in the Assistance now, not sitting at a meeting –

'Quiet!' roared Handai. 'Quiet! Aunt *please* sit down –'

Calm was restored. Mrs Cycler said, 'Mother knows I have enough to reproach you with. Where is my child? But we need your help. I will tell you something that must not leave this room. The Koperasi themselves are evacuating, from Nor and from Sepaa.'

The Butchers stared at each other and muttered. Handai looked at Derveet, sitting quietly as if nothing could shock or surprise her anymore. How thin Veet had grown. She knew her friend was spitting blood: Derveet insisted the haemorrhages

180

were very slight, nothing serious. . . . She needs rest, thought Handai. Rest – when will any of us have that ? . . . Incredulous and suspicious murmurs died away. Derveet said (and all the clanswomen started involuntarily, at her beautiful High Inggris):

'Where exactly are they going to put you?'

'On one of the big islands. They're making a camp.'

'A camp. Ah. May I smoke?' She rolled a cigarette and lit it; pungent fumes of the mixture of achar cake and tobacco she was reduced to rose –

A Butcher called Pao suddenly burst out: 'Anyone can see through this. They don't care about you. They just want to flush out the few people who could still save the Peninsula!'

'All right,' said Mrs Cycler. 'I'll tell you. Three days ago Mrs Leilah of Gamartha was travelling through the Bu Awan region to er – to join her brother. Her escort was attacked by a band of – deformed criminals and mutineers, of the other party. It was a massacre. So now it is war. No one's going to save the Peninsula. And we are getting out.'

Again the meeting was upset in shouting and angry exclamations.

Early on that same morning there was a small disturbance at Causeway Control. The Koperasi were in their blockhouses, indifferent. The traffic was as usual; partly stumbling, haggard fugitives; partly people who were making regular trips, somehow finding produce and meat to bring back to the hungry city. Some charitable Samsui women were at the gates. They did what they could for the fugitives, and tried in a kindly way (and without success) to get the traders to give up their goods to the fair market. Empty handed, with bundles, handcarts, leading animals, the morning entry came down the grey road on its piers that stretched away across the shining water. Among the people was a creature they did not like. Even the bewildered ex-slaves pushed it away. It had not a human face but a blunt calf's muzzle. It had no proper fingers on its hands. Its body was a lump of muscle clothed in a coarse hairy blouse matted with old dried blood. It stank. Get away, you mountainy thing -- they said, and they began to shove it and kick it as it reeled about, grabbing at everyone; trying to find a friend. 'A-a-ati?' it sobbed – 'A-a-ati?' Suddenly one of the charitable Samsui, a

181

young girl, gave an exclamation and ran through the gates. She took the calf's grotesque hoof-hand. Its ox eyes stared at her. A-a-ati? it begged: Anakmati.

The deputation had gone. The Butchers still sat around the tables.

'The whole population – ' said Handai. She tried to imagine this, packed into bubbles. 'How can they do that?'

'Oh, it will sort itself out,' said Derveet softly. 'People will hang themselves, jump into the sea and so on, before embarkation day. The ones who finally line up will be the sensible type, so there'll be no trouble. I've seen it before.'

They did not believe what Mrs Cycler had said about Bu Awan. Leilah was in Gamartha. The mountain people were harmless; incapable of massacring anyone. The past few weeks had produced a succession of incidents like this – probably outright invention. All of their thoughts were on how to deal with this threat of evacuation, when the sliding wall opened, and the young woman from the causeway came in with the calf who was still sobbing for Anakmati.

The creature had been running on its thick legs for days and nights, it did not know how long. It gasped out a bubbling string of sounds the Samsui could not follow. It was Low Inggris of a kind: hantuhantu-bertempur... mati, dihukum – ghosts, and a fight, and death. But Awan's child squatted on the floor, he hardly knew what a chair was. The Samsui girl crouched beside him, holding his stumpy hand: 'They killed them all!' she cried. 'They killed all the poor polowijo!'

Derveet got up from her place and knelt down in front of the monster. 'Child,' she said gently. 'Why *dihukum*? – Why "punished"?'

'It was wrong to fight them.'

The creature made a great effort: these words were quite clear.

A strange silence fell over the room.

At last Handai said, 'Derveet, we've got to do something, we'll have to get you away. Pao's right, this evacuation is aimed at you – and, and Cho. You can't stay in Ranganar.'

For a moment she had fallen, she could see from their faces that the others had fallen too, into the relief of being able to give up at last, to give up hope. But only for a moment. There was

182

still work to do (*she is dead, then,* she thought. *If not now, then very soon –*).

'Yes,' said Derveet. 'Yes. You're right. Of course.'

Late that night, one of the Butcher boys came and woke Handai up. She had not been sleeping in fact, just lying with her mind going round and round: it was that hour of the night when you know you are incapable of thinking, but you can't stop. She followed the boy's breathy whispers and soft tugging hands to the kitchen house. He vanished and she made out a figure, sitting very still, down on the floor by the doorway. She thought it was one of the fugitives at first.

'Veet! What are you doing here? – It's dangerous! What's happened?'

'Hallo dear,' said her friend quietly. 'I couldn't sleep, I thought I'd come and see you.'

Handai went and fetched a lamp, muttering, and stumbling over the gas line as she pulled it out across the tiles. She lit a match and Derveet's face appeared in a sepulchral blue glow.

' – Not supposed to have it on at night now. You didn't really come over here for no reason did you? That's just bad morale –'

'I love that lamp,' said Derveet. 'That factory-made lamp, and that hose thing that so offends my sensibilities.'

Handai stared at her, bleary and half angry.

'What?'

'I wanted to tell you: It is you. You Samsui women with your shrill voices and ridiculous ideas. You have no dignity, you're not *ladies*. But you are alive. Dapur women know so much – but you can't teach human beings without being human yourself, without joining in. You see the trouble with women is that they are so sure. They are born sure. Their purpose is certain, their value is certain, and so they naturally dismiss everything else – as unimportant. If we had listened to you Samsui we would not be facing what is coming now crippled and divided. . . .'

The lamp hissed. Handai stared at her friend with a dull, bemused expression.

'Oh, Derveet,' she said at last. 'What does it matter? What does any of it matter now?'

22 The Mountain Top

Derveet was not fit for the wilds, so she travelled by road to Bu
Awan. The South Sawah was alive with Koperasi: bubbles in
the sky; vehicles snarling – no sign of the roaming war bands in
an empty land. She was not surprised. She knew she was seeing
the wheels go round, behind the scenes. No one saw her. She
was invisible, among the people. She set out alone. She knew
her friends would try to stop her, and she did not want anyone,
not even the dear child – (Ah no, above all not Cho –) But on
the second night she was sheltering in a shack by the roadside,
haunch to haunch with other fugitives. Rain streamed down
and gathered in cold pools round their feet and buttocks; the
treaders crashed by in the dark splashing white light across
blank and fearful faces, and Derveet suddenly knew someone
was watching her. She looked up and thought she saw something move; a rat perhaps, in the criss-cross of poles under the
tattered thatch.

After that she was haunted. She knew all the time that
something was beside her, though she never saw it move again.
The treaders swept up wanderers on the roads, and carried
them off to 'collection points'. They picked up Derveet with
the rest more than once, and she saw the Sawah from the
back of packed Koperasi boxes, rolling on their jolting tracks.
Endlessly the plantations, the rows of trees and melon vines
and maize fell away – rotting and derelict. Blackened shells of
farm camps rose up and disappeared; Koperasi standing over
heaps of strange fruit at the gates. . . . She could not take her
eyes away. She heard the voice of whatever was haunting her
whisper: 'All this is very good –'

The clanswomen had been right, the Koperasi were clearing
up and getting out. She never found out what happened at the
'collection points'; she managed always to give her lifts the slip
before the final destination. On the fourth day she was beyond

most of the action. She hitched a lift in a treadie flying the merdeka flag. The brigand in charge dropped her on the western edge of the Bu Awan wilderness, and drove north to find Singa. She walked to the last village on the mountain, and found a few boys still hanging on. She hired one of them and two ponies for a great deal of *cash* and the ruby and silver lighter; her last negotiable possession. That night, lying out in the open on the mountainside, she woke. The boy was asleep a few paces away. Near her face in the darkness gleamed two diamond blue eyes. Derveet sat up. 'Ah, it's you –' she said softly. 'I might have known.' The Cat made a small dim shape against the stars, low on the stony ground. Derveet was not surprised, not surprised at all. 'Why are you here?' she whispered. But Divine Endurance was gone.

Derveet did not need a guide. She assumed the boy was with her to keep an eye on his pony, she didn't care. When they came to the rim of the caldera he became very reluctant. The dead, he said, had not been attended to –

' – There is no need to be afraid of them.'

The boy huddled his shawl round his half-naked shoulders and shivered nervously. 'The Koperasi have been here,' he muttered, and his eyes flickered; shamefaced and uneasy: 'They might, I think they might come again. . . . It is dangerous.'

She left him at the foot of the descent and went on alone. The caldera was terribly silent. When she saw what she was coming to as she approached the polowijo caves her mouth filled with bile and her vision began to swim. But she would not turn back.

All the way up country she had heard of *the massacre*. The boys on the flank of the mountain had spoken of it with awe: fire on Bu Awan; blood and the cries of the dying – No one had exaggerated. There were hundreds of bodies lying under the cliffs. They had been untouched for days. There was a smell of death; sickly, hideous, throat-catching. She walked to and fro between the stark images, over ridges of fine black silt that crumbled underfoot. She was not the first on the scene. Some of the bodies were torn or gnawed, others showed signs of looting; some had been stripped and laid out in rows. Sticks, stones, knives – senjata lay around, but the bodies showed evidence of worse weapons, she noted grimly – The Gamarthans were dressed for their part as a lady's escort, in white linen stained

185

and filthy now, with silk sashes bound high on their breasts; some had bright ornaments or marks where they'd been torn away. It was hard to tell the ragged polowijo and the mutineers apart, except that the men had bigger bodies even in death, which makes everyone look smaller....

The broken outline of the cliffs rose up, terribly familiar. Here she had lived, bullying the poor outcasts with her dreams. She had left them vowing she would never forget them, her own family. By her black skin she was marked like them – Bu Awan's child. She had promised them she would make them part of something wonderful one day. And they believed. She remembered Annet's angry, hungry cynicism ... *never betrayed me, never....*

Did the Gamarthans attack, or did the polowijo? It made no odds, though some might pretend to ask the question, for a little while. The rent was big enough to let chaos in. She stood in the hideous silence, her mind empty. What had brought her here? Only the knowledge that it didn't matter any more, so why should she not mourn her dead. But oh, how was it done? She had been so sure, as the long battle of wills dragged on, that the Dapur rule was going to hold after all. The enemies would have to try another way; they couldn't make the Peninsula destroy itself so easily. How was it done? What boy or man, renegade or noble, could have raised his hand to this – ?

It was then that something glinting caught her eye. She looked down: a Gamarthan lay at her feet. On the warrior's forearm, smeared with black blood, was a bracelet Derveet knew quite well; incised silver, sprinkled with little crystals – very pretty. Soré made it. She stared for a while, without comprehending. Then she went down on her knees. The smell of decay was strong, but it was strange how all revulsion left her as she lifted the thing's head. She cried out aloud: 'Siang!'

The sun slipped away below the great crater, and the caldera grew vague under a veil of vaporous cloud. Derveet was sitting by the path that led to the rim, where she had left the boy, holding a silver bracelet in her hands. She had forgotten about the ponies, and her guide. She was weeping. She felt someone approach and raised her head. The brown cat came neatly down the slope and settled itself beside her.

Derveet said nothing, but the Cat could see that she had at

last begun to realise a few things. The mists crept over the bowl, the shadows deepened. Divine Endurance began to speak: 'A good many Koperasi so-called mutineers had come to live with the polowijo. One morning before light a host of warriors came over the rim and attacked without warning. It was illusion, of course, part of the special weaponry Leilah has been finding out. The girls were very pure in their use of these weapons. They knew they would all be killed. It was their sacrifice, for the good of the Peninsula.

'The tigers had been gathering to Leilah for a while. She was what they wanted when they began to feel alive again. As I think you know, she did not have to send clumsy messengers to fetch them. The others came later, it took them time to realise what they wanted. They taught the tigers to masquerade, of course. You see, Leilah was afraid it was all going to grind to a halt, with you sitting in Ranganar disapproving of everyone and embarrassing them. And the Dapurs were getting at her brother's armies. If something dreadful had been committed by the renegades it would bring Atoon and Bima together, and strengthen them to go on.... The girls all hoped you would understand in the end. It was you, after all, who dressed them in white and told them women must step down into the sordid world, to save it.'

A muffled sound came from the woman. Her hands covered her face, Siang's bracelet rolled away in the dust.

'I'm glad you understand me,' said the Cat. 'I thought you would. I've always suspected those noises were quite superfluous.'

'You did this. You, and the wayang that the Rulers have. You drove people mad –'

Divine Endurance parleyed briefly with her conscience. But it would be unkind to leave the woman desperately trying to deceive herself.

'Not I,' she said. 'Not Wo. We have been interested, but in the end our part has been quite small. You humans are very odd. You don't even recognise your own dreams when you see them coming true.'

'See – ' she purred 'See how still they lie, how simple they are now. No more divisions. Stillness, simplicity, the leap into the eternal. You asked, and she has performed, and it will go on. . . . '

Derveet whispered, '*No. I did not. I never asked her anything. I was afraid –*'

'Oh yes you did,' said the Cat. 'Cho told me so, and Cho does not tell lies. You wanted her help so she has been helping you, right from the start. She is hardly more than a child, for she has led a very sheltered life, and she doesn't understand some of her own effects, but it makes no difference.'

The dead were out of Derveet's sight in the dusk and the distance, but Divine Endurance could still contemplate them, with quiet satisfaction.

'You should not be surprised,' she murmured, half to herself, 'if what Cho has given you is not what you thought you wanted. She did her very best, so naturally this happened. As I told her, but she wouldn't listen, every desire of the human heart is just the real desire in disguise, the desire of the world. Wo's people understand; it's what they've been trying to teach you. It is all over. It was settled long ago. I saw some of it happen – most impressive. . . . There is no point in fighting, Derveet. It's natural, it's right and proper. What does the Dapur say? *Submit*, it is the only word.'

'*The desire of the world, which Cho and Wo and I, and our kind, have always served.*'

The sky cleared and turned black. Divine Endurance, pleased with the effect she had produced, slipped away for a while. Derveet watched the night. She saw the fountain of joy, and Previous Heaven playing tag with death the day the Eagle rose, and now it seemed it was true: she must have always known. Strange fruit by the Sawah roadside, Alat's blood on her hands in the waringin glade long ago, it was all the same. She heard her own voice – telling Atoon that by God's grace or good fortune the angel doll had come to someone above temptation.

She tried to tell herself that there was hope still; that the new world might live even if the old was utterly destroyed. But she could not. She had seen how the strange, frightening beauty of her vision had been belittled and degraded: there was no safety. Nothing is assured, *nothing*. The gate was open and it was not God who was waiting, only emptiness. She had come to the

188

centre of the mysteries and here the Rulers disappeared, the Dapur vanished, even Cho herself meant nothing. Cho did not make the darkness, the universal darkness, swallowing the stars. . . . A ragged moon rose and arced slowly over the caldera. Derveet sat on unmoving, hour by hour. She could not pray, or weep anymore. But after a while a pain began, deep and insistent, somewhere around her heart. It seemed physical and real. She was glad of this pain, and hoped that it would stay with her from now on. And it did.

The day after the deputation, Handai went to Dove House and realised at once what Derveet had done. Horrified, she left everything to First Aunt and started in pursuit. She made Cho come with her, because she knew she wouldn't reach the great mountain alone. Cho didn't want to leave Ranganar: Derveet hadn't told her anything. She said: *I don't know what to do to help Derveet now.* But she was obedient. They travelled fast. The Koperasi never touched them. Gress, Cho's hard little pony, came with them all the way – a succession of others served Handai, straight up the great west roads, right through Koperasi country. Handai was past caring how any of it was done. She was thinking of her city and all that was gone for ever, for ever and ever and ever. The words of that stupid old song kept running through her head, pitifully –

> Oh, then I made a moo cow
> It was meant to be a blue cow
> But it died
> But it died
> But it died –

She hardly hoped that she would get to Derveet before the enemy did. But something in her would not let her give up. She would not abandon her friend now, no, nor the dream they had shared.

On the fourth night they were in a peasant's hut or cave, high on Bu Awan's side. The polowijos' speech was animal noises to Handai. She set Cho to question them while she crouched by the dapur, the hearthstone, blinking in the smoky firelight. How strange to find people still living here. Nothing is ever

189

complete, she thought – not even destruction. She watched the boy-creature who had brought them in with his mother, or his sister. They sat close together, touching gently, stroking each other's faces, holding hands. As the firelight flickered their eyes seemed to brim with light. She remembered how she had always hated the way Derveet behaved with the Dove House boys – fondling them and petting them all the time. She wondered, if she tried hard now would she understand at last? The shining eyes turned to her. For a moment, perhaps, something stirred in her mind – shapes and colours; intimations, but then it was gone again. Perhaps it was only a trick of the shadows. She was very tired.

When it began to be light Derveet stirred and looked around, vaguely at first; then she stood up sharply.

Divine Endurance interrupted her morning toilet to remark – 'He's gone. He took both ponies. They left yesterday afternoon in fact. Didn't you notice?'

Derveet stared blankly.

'I can see it's going to take a while to sink in,' said the Cat. 'Well, I know you'd hate me to help you down from here, so we won't bother about that. Come on, I'll show you something of sentimental interest. It'll take your mind off things.'

The brown cat trotted away. Derveet hesitated, then followed. Divine Endurance led her south, to where the crater wall broke up in grottos and fissures; through the paths where Annet had once led her and Cho, and up into the dawn beauty of the peaks, etched in rose and indigo against a shining sky. The Mangkuk Kematian, the Bowl of Death, was at their feet.

'Officially the attack was only on the Koperasi element,' said the Cat. 'An absurd story, when you consider the excitement of these things. The tigers knew better anyway. But some of your friends were shocked at what really happened, and quite changed their minds again – '

In a hollow below them white vapour eddied over a bubbling pool, with a strong mineral smell. There were two bodies in the sulphur mist. Derveet went down, and found that one of them was Leilah's sister, Simet, the blackened silver chain still trailing from her ankle. The other was Cendana. Death had caught her in the act of twisting the knife that killed her out of Simet's hand, and burying it in her throat.

'There now,' said Divine Endurance. 'Isn't that nice to know.'

The bodies were not decayed, the mineral steam had preserved them. Derveet carefully drew Cendana away from her enemy. She gathered branches from the thorns that grew near the hot pool, and put them around her friend. She searched her pockets in vain for her lighter, but found some matches. It was not much of a pyre, but it was all she could do. There lay Sandalwood – still lovely; no longer reckless, no longer passionate. She remembered the night in Dove House, when she brushed the dancer's hair. Had it already begun then, even then – ? How lonely Cendana must have been, with hope burning her up; struggling towards this adventure. But it was all over now. She held across her hands something she had found under the two bodies: it was a dagger, made of gilt and base metal, straight as death. Not your fault, Sandalwood, no blame to you. I wish I could tell you so. *Happy the warrior to whom the just fight comes, that opens the doors of heaven. . . .* She did not know much about lighting fires, but the thorns caught and crackled.

Derveet sighed at last and said 'Divine Endurance, why Bu Awan? A hundred years ago perhaps – but who but the converted would believe such a thing of Annet's poor shiftless thieves? And it is so out of the way. Couldn't Leilah have found herself a more convincing atrocity?'

The Cat was on the other side of the hollow, watching the funeral rites dispassionately and occasionally glancing down into the great bowl, where it seemed there was something that interested her.

'I was wondering when you'd come to that,' she remarked composedly. 'It's quite simple. The polowijo are your mother's people, Derveet. Leilah thought it would fetch you out, and she was right. She, and other interested parties, who are now advising her, have been looking for a way to get you out into the open – before you made off to some desert island, leaving the idea of you behind to hold things up, if you see what I mean. They have been watching the mountain, and paying the remaining peasantry, who are quite hungry I'm afraid, to give information.'

She was not sure how much of this got through, but conscience told her she ought to make the gesture, and it could do no harm.

Derveet heard nothing. The voice in the night had gone: there was only the thing that looked like a brown cat, with its strange, implacable eyes. But as she knelt there, watching the flames, suddenly something fell away from her, and she realised – That the boy had disappeared. That she had given him Atoon's lighter, in case anyone needed any help. That she had been quite mad for days, ever since she heard that Bu Awan was dead, and she had walked, simply and co-operatively, into a trap. She stared at the fire, that was waving a flag of smoke now; above the vapours, high into the clear blue air. . . .

'You have not won,' she said, finally, in a firm voice. 'You are so clever, but you have made the same mistake as always. I'm no loss. I was half on your side already, as you so cunningly realised. Your real enemy is a woman in Ranganar, who chops meat in the market, minds her child, and gets into stupid arguments in the street. She'll go on doing all of that; and there are thousands like her – in your desolation; even in your evacuation camps. Fight you? She doesn't know how to stop. You will never destroy her –'

The brown cat gazed. Something in Derveet's mind said: *Most inspiring. I am impressed. But after all, there's Cho.*

'Cho is innocent!'

Silence. Divine Endurance turned her back and peered into the bowl again, her tail twitching pleasantly, like a cat that is watching little birds through a window. Derveet got up, slowly, and went to see what the Cat was looking at.

Handai climbed the scree on a narrow path, tugging her pony's bridle with one hand; the other fastened on the grip of her knife. She was afraid. She did not know what she would find above the ominous rim of red and black: Derveet arrested? Derveet a prisoner? The scale of these mountains appalled her. How could she begin to search them? When she came over the edge and saw Derveet, standing there quietly, she was confused. She couldn't understand it – Cho came up too, with Gress. Derveet said nothing. Cho hid her face in the pony's mane.

Divine Endurance had disappeared.

In silence the friends faced each other. Protests, reproaches died unspoken. Handai began to cry. She let go of the bridle and stumbled down into the hollow, into Derveet's arms, and they stood together, tears mingling. So this was how it ended, all that fuss about uniting the Peninsula, and women and men being equal. Here it came to rest; here in the bleak red rocks and the sulphur steams it lay down – and it seemed, like the dead, so much smaller.

Handai pushed herself away – 'Derveet!' she cried. 'You've got no time. The Koperasi have Wave down on the mountain. A boy has given you away. We'd better hide – there are caves aren't there. We aren't finished yet, Veet. We'll get you over the sea –'

Derveet said, 'Cho brought you.'

'Well – yes. I had to have help. I couldn't leave you alone.'

Miss Butcher had been under the edge of the scree. She had not seen the bubble quietly descending. It had come down on the Bu Awan ridge, just out of sight above them.

'Derveet – *come on!*'

'Now listen,' said Derveet. 'They won't touch you, you're a Samsui. Just go quietly, and afterwards do what you can. If there is anything to do, now they have Cho. You have been used Dai. Don't worry, so have we all.'

Handai couldn't understand. There was such a look in Derveet's eyes – it was horrible.

She said suddenly, 'What's that fire for –?' It flashed into her mind that her friend, in despair, had deliberately –

'Ah – wait. Dai!'

Handai struggled. She felt the brittleness of Derveet's arms; fleshless bone beneath the cotton sleeve. But just as she escaped, a group of people appeared, and came quickly down into the hollow: a troop of Koperasi, armed, and with them was Leilah of Gamartha. Leilah was dressed in riding clothes. She had lost weight, and her tiger eyes were very bright. She looked beautiful and strong. She stood in front of her enemy: *Yes. Look at me. I am the coming race that you prophesied. You could have been me but you didn't dare. I dare anything.*

'Arrest her,' she said briskly to the Koperasi. 'She's responsible for all this.'

At Derveet's feet was the tawdry dagger. She glanced at it, and bowed her head.

Handai cried, 'Derveet! Don't let her say that! Don't give up!'

She started forward. . . . But the Koperasi did not give her a chance to speak. They shot her. At a range of some twenty paces their hardened bullits tore great holes in her chest and body, and she fell back, bewildered, into Derveet's arms. 'Ah – ' she said, and no more.

The echoes that the shots had raised rattled slowly away. Handai lay on the ground, and did not know her beloved was beside her. Derveet had fallen to her knees; and the Koperasi closed in solicitously. The fire around Cendana's body was dying down. Leilah stood apart from all this. She watched the tableau for a few moments, but then turned her face away coldly. It was nauseating to have to work with the shit-eaters. And yet she felt very satisfied that her stratagem had succeeded. The massacre was never, of course, meant to reconcile Atoon. It was to strengthen her brother. It was just a little present, because she had seen he needed something to help him make the plunge. They had not been together since the event but she knew how he would take it: shyly, a little coyly, pretending he didn't know who it came from. . . . She smiled, thinking of the man's weakness and feeling her own power course through her to her fingertips.

The Koperasi thought Leilah was being used, but she knew exactly what she was doing. She had known from the beginning.

Thinking of all this, she saw the two ponies, and the slight, childish figure beside them. Cho had not moved since Handai ran from her into Derveet's arms. She had not made a sound or a sign all through the little drama. Leilah's eyes widened. She did not want the angel doll, but she knew the Rulers did. Their agents never mentioned it, and nor did Leilah, but she was well aware that the toy was at the back of everything. They had let her kill all the people on Bu Awan; they had let her stick her fist up Garuda, all for the sake of the angel doll. She had not cared. When she turned on her 'advisers' in the abyss after that, what difference would it make if they had one more machine or not? But she had not imagined such an opportunity. She glanced at the Koperasi who were still occupied. *They'll kill me* she thought. The consideration had no weight at all.

'Come on madam, up you get,' said the Rulers' agent to the prisoner, 'And count yourself lucky we're here with that lady, and not some of the "tigers". Don't you see her eyes? She's mad. Completely off her fucking rocker.'

Leilah unslung her own senjata and moved casually round to the ponies. She noticed that, unfortunately, the better one was unbridled. The Koperasi suddenly woke up to the presence of the angel doll. They spoke to each other; some of them stepped cautiously forward –

'You'd better not touch it!' shouted Leilah. 'It's poisonous!'

The men stopped. She laughed out loud, made a dancer's lunge across the remaining space, and grabbed Cho by the arm.

'I'll take this –' she cried. 'It belongs to the people, not to you. This child in white is our sign: purity, war, womanhood. It had fallen into the hands of the corrupt south, now I'm claiming it. Merdeka! Daulat untuk Gamartha!'

She bundled the doll onto the bridled pony, flung her firearm away and jumped up behind. Cho did not resist. She only cried, 'Derveet –' If Derveet answered, no one heard. For a moment Leilah faced the Koperasi, her eyes blazing. Then she bent over the doll, down to the pony's neck and whispered, or touched it. The poor, starved, jaded creature reared up. It bounded over the rim of the hollow and the noise of it, plunging recklessly down the screes, thundered all around the great bowl.

The Koperasi came to life. Some of them rushed to see where Leilah had gone. They reported to Wave, but it seemed there were no orders to cover this development. No one wanted to go in pursuit anyway. The woman was mad, and reputedly possessed of appalling Dapur powers. They marshalled themselves and the prisoner; and soon the bubble went swinging into the air and glided away, leaving Bu Awan to the dead.

23 A Sharp Knife

Leilah was pursued down the screes by the riderless pony. Some madness had got into it; as soon as the path allowed it was up beside her, shouldering her and showing its teeth. 'Get off – ' she shouted, and lashed at it with the end of her reins. The toy, that she was holding in the crook of her arm, raised its head then and perhaps did something, for the pony gave way. It still followed. Leilah kept looking back and seeing it, the only thing moving besides herself in the great theatre of the bowl. She decided to take no notice.

It was hot down in the wilderness. The screes stood against the sky, dimmed in a haze. A singing silence, bare lava, cracked earth; a scorched aromatic scrub that rasped against the pony's legs as it stumbled between the rocks. There was nothing in the sky but the sun, there was no one following. Leilah let the pony slow down; it was exhausted now. She rode slackly, hardly pretending to hold the doll. She began to smile, and then to chuckle, and then to laugh. The pony stood still. Leilah slipped from its back with a sly look at her companion. It was very hot. She found a boulder and sat herself beneath it. She began to chuckle again.

'Merdeka! – They didn't know what to do –'

The doll had come after her.

'Go away,' she said to it. 'I was lying. I don't want you. Go away, do what you like. I don't care.'

A small brown cat came trotting down the dusty path, and sat beside Cho. Leilah did not seem to notice.

'This is your one isn't it,' said Cho.

'Oh yes.'

'There's something very wrong with her.'

Two pairs of eyes, dark and brilliant blue. Leilah watched them both, indifferently.

'What can we do for her?'

'Don't waste your time,' said Divine Endurance. 'I've been helping her and helping her but it's as you said. They simply wear themselves out.'

'I have killed my sister,' said Leilah. 'I have corrupted my brother, I have betrayed Garuda. It's all done. The armies don't need my help anymore. Nothing will stop it now.'

Her eyes moved dreamily. She thought of pushing the doll, live but unresisting, into some crevice of the rocks, or pressing it down into a pool of bubbling mud. She knew it would only climb out again. She had made her gesture, that was enough.

'Don't think I've changed my mind,' she said. 'It was right, all of it. Oh, I knew we had a chance, don't think I didn't. I could see we might be *patient*, we might be *reborn*. But I couldn't stand that. It is disgusting. To survive on top of all the dead.... Too many filthy things have been done, just to keep on living. Living now is swallowing vomit, eating shit....'

'Perhaps they'll forgive you,' said Cho. 'If you say you're sorry.'

Something flickered in Leilah's eyes for a moment, but it didn't stay. Her hands took out the knife she carried in her sash. She tested the point against her thumb, and then on the underside of her left wrist. It went in very easily. She had stayed alive so long from the thought that it would be so hard, it would hurt ... what a waste of time. A bright, chuckling stream. She felt herself growing dizzy, but she wasn't satisfied.

'Not enough,' she muttered, and took the dripping point up to her throat.

There was a long silence. It was broken by the sound of Gress's hooves, clip clopping in the dust of the path. She didn't like the smell of blood but she came up anyway. Cho went to the other pony. It was a brindled, mountainy roan, its coat all patchy with sweat, its miserable flanks still shuddering. She took off its harness and stroked its face. 'Go on,' she said. 'She doesn't need you anymore.' The puzzled beast looked around for a moment, then tossed its eased head and slowly trotted away.

'Would you like us to go and help your one now?' asked Divine Endurance sweetly.

Cho gave her a long look.

'She didn't want me.'

197

Then the three companions left that place, and vanished into the wilderness.

On the night that Derveet watched over the dead, Annet of Bu Awan woke from a pain-filled dream and found herself in a place with a high roof and a few squares of moonlight. She missed the smells and closeness of the caves. Then she tried to move, and remembered. She was in the barracks of a derelict farm camp, under the Mountain on the Jagdana side, being kept alive. She closed her eyes in helpless bitterness. After the battle, so she'd been told, she had been dragged from under a pile of bodies by the snake boy. She remembered coming to herself in one of her peoples' boltholes in the side of the Bowl of Death; she remembered the suffering, dying polowijo. There was no food, no water, no fire. The Koperasi were hunting on the Mountain, there was no hope. She remembered her own voice sobbing – 'No, no. We'll stay here. We'll join no factions. . . .' After that, everything was confused. Help had come; too little, too late, and so in the end there was this place.

Snake was dead. He had been hit by a stop, and when he began to bleed internally on the dark journey no one could keep him alive. Annet had been hit by a stop too. She had been burned by some kind of flame-thrower down one side and thigh, but also when they found her there was a black stain of broken blood vessels on her back. Now she could not move or feel her body from the waist down.

When Annet first saw her rescuers, the robes and veils, she thought it was part of her ugly dreams. She didn't understand. The last thing she had heard, before the horror, was that Jagdana – even Jagdana, had abandoned their prince, instated Atoon's heir and gone over to Bima Singa. She hated all Dapurs. Derveet had done this with her meddling, but the women were worse, letting it happen. She didn't want their charity. All she wanted was death, and she couldn't see why they were holding her back. She thought of a small figure dressed in white, gazing at her solemnly in the hearthcave. She knew, obscurely, that it had all begun with that little girl. But she couldn't remember how. . . .

She woke again. She was still in the derelict camp, lying on a string bed on the verandah of one of the long huts. Her mind was clear, but she had the feeling that days and nights had gone by. Furtively she slipped her hand down to her side and felt clean scabs under the dressings, no scar tissue. I am alive, she thought. But she could feel in the air, all around her, the enormous menace: the end was still to be faced. Everything was very quiet. She could hear polowijo voices, somewhere nearby. On the steps of the verandah a woman sat paring mangoes into an enamel bowl. She wore soft trousers, her cropped head and golden breast bare as if she were safe in her own garden.

Annet said, 'Why are you healing me? I don't want to be healed.'

The woman raised her head and smiled. 'You are healing yourself Annet. Are you not aware of that?'

She stared sullenly, refusing to answer. 'Why couldn't you have left us alone. We could have died just as well in our own place.'

The Jagdana lady went on with her work. 'Why did Garuda give their son to Bu Awan?' she said quietly. 'What use is a prince without a family? we asked them. The Garuda, though dead, answered: the polowijo are the prince's family. We have learned to understand that message. A polowijo is disorder, it makes cracks in the patterned walls of life and thrusts itself through. So – the prince, that is, the Peninsula, can only survive by embracing the polowijo: that which breaks down the walls, abandons the patterns. It has been hard for us to learn, but we see now the truth the Garuda left us. We could not leave you to die. You are our hope.'

The lady's voice came from a cool, still distance; it was utterly without inflection. Annet looked at her with hatred.

'You can leave that out,' she said roughly. 'What's happening outside? What's happened to Derveet?'

The Jagdana lady bowed her head. And so Annet understood that it was really all over. She accepted the news blankly. It didn't seem to matter much.

'Oh no,' said Jagdana lady. 'She is not dead. We sent her our prince. Like the rainbow bird in the forest he was meant to outface the enemy, while she took her nestlings into hiding. But she sent him away instead and he became entangled, and she – was in greater danger than she knew. Who can tell? Our way might have prolonged the struggle, probably it could have done

199

no more; this enemy is so implacable. But she is not dead. She will rejoin our prince on the field of battle, and who knows what may happen? The poet says: As the flower and its scent and the fire and its flame, the flower is Krishna and the scent Ardjuna, the fire is Krishna and the flame Ardjuna. . . .'

Annet turned her face away. Jagdana lady must have forgotten that scripture is not taught in farm camps.

'Oh, what's the point,' she muttered. 'You don't care, anyway. You'll come out and make a new Dapur world, with nothing human in it, when you've cleared us all away. None of this affects you. I bet you set it all up. You've even cleared the Koperasi out this time, God knows how. I'm sure you can deal with a few senile old Rulers –'

There was a silence so intense Annet could not stop herself from looking round. Jagdana lady's golden hands, banded with silver, for she was a mother of children – had closed convulsively on the paring knife.

'The senile few,' she said softly, 'are in the grip of a purpose far greater than they. Their only blame is, because of clinging to the past, they have put in the hands of that Purpose things that should not –'

The lady could not find words. Words often failed her, that was why she had retired from them. She opened her hands.

Annet saw drops of scarlet, falling on the bright flesh of the fruit. She understood. The lady said, silently, *We are mortal.* She said, *There is no protection, nothing is secure. This is not the end of your world only. It is the end.*

She had thought she would never feel anything again, but suddenly an abyss of fear opened in her heart.

24   Sunset

'This is it – '

Two people were crouched at the foot of a small, scrub-covered rise near the southern boundary of the Pancaragam, the holy city of the west. Behind them stretched the ruins: field on field of half-buried streets; shrines, meeting halls, nunneries.... The Pancaragam was far greater and far more ancient than the drowned Garuda citadel. The Gamarthans first built it; a monument to the unity of their everlasting empire. The early Garudas had kept it up for a while. Now it was a barren plain, halfway down the coast of Jagdana, forgotten by the peasants of the Hanoman countryside, haunted by the never ending mournful sighing of the sea.

The causeway people had been outmanoeuvred by prince Bima, who would not talk but led them and followed them in an uneasy dance up and down and across the princedoms until, like the last outnumbered piece on a chequer board, they had no choices left. So here they were. The Pancaragam was on a rough peninsula; it should cost even Bima's great army dear to dislodge the defenders. But the causeway people had their backs to nothingness. For more than a month there had been a kind of stalemate. The fields beyond the neck of the Peninsula were covered with the tents of princes and warriors – but Bima would not strike or actively enforce the siege: neither side made any hostile sorties. Meanwhile the Rulers' agents, like children playing a callous game, kept on delivering to Atoon's camp the *recalcitrants*: the sick and old and defiant who wouldn't leave Ranganar, and fugitives rounded up on the roads. The noble allies claimed they were being patient and merciful, but it was evident that the real enemies were gradually making it impossible for Atoon to defend his people. When they had achieved this aim, they would let Singa off the leash.

Pabriker Kimlan stopped digging and watched as Atoon

grubbed in the dry soil with his hands, uncovering long folds of shiny, dark cloth. They had come out to look for buried treasure, hidden here by Atoon's family in some nervous time years ago. He peeled back the treated silk, and laid bare long serpent necks.

'Very pretty,' said Kimlan. 'Still working, eh?'

'I don't know much about field guns. Probably they'll only blow our own heads off. We'll get them carried back and I'll load them up with black powder and see what happens.'

'Atoon, Atoon,' said Kimlan. 'You *must* learn to delegate.'

She sat back on her heels and stared at the western horizon, where the land ended. 'I've got a plan,' she said, 'for making kites. We could make kind of *winged* flying devices, with little hatcha engines to get them up into the currents: I've been drawing pictures of one in my head. Then we could all fly away.'

'That would be nice.'

'Breus says if he can have someone who can start a treadie he can walk past the corral guards. There are Welfari supply sheds, untouched; medicine and food, just down the road. He's very good, you know, at that sort of thing.'

Atoon shook his head. 'No. They would call it truce-breaking if they caught him with the vehicle. We are *not* going to give them their excuse.'

'Of course he won't get caught.'

'Besides, it is misuse.'

Kimlan looked at him thoughtfully. 'And what would be the *right* use, Atoon, of being able to read people's minds?'

Atoon was silent. All through the long march there had been an understanding among the causeway people that something strange was happening to them. It was an uneasy subject. People joked about it, or said nothing. The prince was one of the many who resisted and refused, insisting that it was wrong; horrible, to let changes like these grow on a battlefield.

'I wonder what it will be like,' said Kimlan at last. 'The new world. It'll be very weird, it'll take some getting used to. No more ignoring misunderstandings and getting by on the surface. No more pretending the people you hurt aren't really human. . . . I think I could have got to like a life like that. Oh

202

well – never mind. It's a causeway's job to lie down and be walked over.'

A pebble dropped on a stone. Atoon looked up and saw her walking away. He did not follow. He stayed where he was, chin on his knees, eyes blank and dreaming. He was a different creature from the whiteclad aristocrat of long ago. He wore Samsui blouse and trousers nowadays, much faded and worn. He had dug ditches and tended fires and minded children and sucked wild pigs' bones for the marrow when he could get them. He had shorn off the long braid of his manhood for convenience, and couldn't even remember the occasion of this life-changing act. His cropped hair sprang up above his brow in obstinate vitality, making his tired face look strangely young.

He knew the end was not far off. The camp was crowded now, and supplies were dwindling. At the beginning of the stalemate Bima had suddenly announced terms for a settlement: Peninsulans could go free, if they would give up 'corrupt southern ideas' and the false Garuda, and return to their families. Samsui and ex-Koperasi would be taken care of by the Rulers, who realised the people would no longer share their country with such elements, and were making new arrangements. Atoon, knowing he was hopelessly trapped, could only answer, to the repeated offers: that they were all Peninsulans. That prince Singa couldn't possibly expect him to behave so despicably.

News of the massacre at Bu Awan had come quite soon. It did not have the effect – supposedly – intended. The causeway people saw through the lie at once, and were horrified by whispers about Leilah's methods of warfare. And Bima wavered – Even while his emissaries and allies were proclaiming the official version, Atoon *felt* him struggling. . . . But the flicker of hope passed. Leilah had disappeared (how wise of her, or someone) and become a martyr. Worse, a story had begun that the renegades now had in their possession the *anak khusus putih* – the 'child in white'; talisman of hope and freedom. Having heard the various stories, Atoon believed Cho was gone for ever. She had escaped, poor innocent – she wouldn't stay to harm her friends. But the rumour persisted. And it was said the idea of the child affected the princely allies

203

and their followers with a kind of madness. There had been no embassies now for several days.

He gazed into the west, where the sun was going down in scarlet. Even that wide gate, Derveet's beloved ocean, was not open anymore. Soon after the causeway people reached this ancient place they had woken up one morning to find a row of shining half circles lying on the line between sea and sky. It was the Rulers' islands. They had come from the eastern sea. No one knew how they had travelled, whether they had come instantly, or whether the Rulers had known for a long time that this was where things would end. But everyone in the camp felt that presence all the time now: watching, waiting to be satisfied.

Some of the renegades were bitter about the great Dapurs and said the ladies had betrayed the Peninsula. But Atoon understood. It was the correct Dapur decision: Singa was stronger, therefore Hanoman must not be encouraged – *Thou shalt not risk lives.* In desperate danger it is right to ignore the rules. But if there is no way out, not the most crooked; if the calamity descends inexorably, then it becomes right to give up all machinations and let fate find you, if it must be, doing your duty – no matter how irrelevant. And so fate finds us, thought Atoon. Even Bima is doing what he ought, in serving his sister. Together we will appease those watchers on the horizon, with a blood sacrifice.

He remembered something Derveet had told him once, about the Black Islands. Some decadent communities there had forgotten how to give birth. When someone came to term, and began to struggle, her belly was opened with a knife. Conditions were poor, many people did not survive: it was considered the most honourable death. Is this our role? he thought, and he shuddered. Not for the causeway people but for the others; the old and bewildered and especially the children. Atoon had seen death now: death by disease, death by injury, in a way he had never known it while he lived in the palace of the Hanomans, not even at the end when the mobs were running wild. He understood as he had never done how the Dapur shielded their people, and he knew that the end here would be hideous. But the new world would survive, in hearts and hidden places, and rise again. *Someday we will be remem-*

bered – He knelt for a while, listening to the grieving murmur of the sea, then got up suddenly and began to walk back to camp.

'There. He's gone.'

'And a good thing too,' said Divine Endurance. 'You'll have the whole pack of them onto us.'

'I was only looking.'

They had scratched out a den for themselves among the roots of the long-legged bushes – behind them lurked Gress in a little dimple among the rocks, bare and hot and very uncomfortable, but the pony never complained. Divine Endurance complained all the time. Now she said sharply:

'You've looked enough. We must go, before we find ourselves trapped here. Or have you changed your mind again?'

At last the child had given up her wrong-headed ideas and agreed to return to the original plan. Divine Endurance was delighted, for the time was ripe. But she could not help wondering how much Cho understood.

'You do realise it is only by joining Wo that you'll help these people, and end their troubles?'

Cho's eyes took on an inward and impenetrable look.

'Yes, I see that,' she said softly, resignedly.

'You're only upsetting yourself now,' said the Cat. 'It'd be better to get on with it.'

'I will see Derveet,' said Cho, and turned to creep back through the roots to Gress's dimple.

Atoon walked through the outskirts of the camp. The red and white merdeka flag was fluttering above the ruins; somehow it had changed sides over the months . . . the allied leaders flew their own banners, under the colours of Gamartha. Behind him scarlet faded to clear, lovely, nameless hues; around him countless little parties huddled around cooking fires. He felt a strange stirring of his spirits. Each little fire was an affirmation. *Yes,* he thought. *We will be brave.*

He saw a treadie arriving in the great square, by the tumbled bulk of the sanctuary of Roh Betina. Who have they brought us today, he wondered. He saw the Dove House boys there. They had arrived in one of the first batches, very distressed because their lady had fled without them. But Atoon was glad: she was

205

safer alone. The garbled stories of how Cho suddenly appeared and escaped had no mention of Derveet: in the other camp this was supposed to be a cover-up – the Rulers were actually holding Garuda in special confinement. But every time a treadie arrived, Atoon's heart lifted defiantly – Derveet and the ocean had always been friends. The crowd seemed excited; there must be someone from Ranganar. Not many of those who had escaped and vanished were still on the loose – 'Handai!' he cried suddenly, and broke into a run.

It was not Handai. The Koperasi said, 'That's your lot, you won't see us again,' and jolted away with grins on their faces, pleased at the joke. The rest of the treadie's load squatted on the ground, trembling and half senseless, and in the midst of them a gaunt dark figure swayed, and was caught in someone's arms. Soon the prince and the causeway people knew the worst, and understood that this was the finishing touch which their enemies had been saving to the last.

When the bad news had been delivered, people began to drift away again. There was nothing anyone could think of to do or say. On one side of the big square was a ruined hall of vast proportions. Around the walls stood stone figures of the heraldic animals; in the middle of the chamber, where the roof had vanished completely, there were trestle tables and benches with a well-used air, under a makeshift thatch shelter – the centre of the camp. Butcher Pao stayed when the crowd had gone, but Garuda did not seem to know her.

'You'll need somewhere to rest,' she muttered. 'I'll – I'll arrange it – '

Now they were alone, Atoon did not know how he would dare speak to her. He thought she didn't know where she was, or what was happening. And then, while he struggled, she raised her face and smiled, the same smile as ever: wry and warm and sane.

'It suits you,' she said. 'You should have done it ages ago.'

A moment of pure relief – but just then there was a sound behind them. Two Samsui women, one small and bent with curly cropped grey hair, stood with a little girl. It was clear they had told Dinah. The Samsui never keep important news from children.

'Aunt?' said Derveet, sounding frightened. 'Don't bring her to me, please – '

206

'It's only fair. Who else is her mother now? She has a right to remember you.'

Derveet stared, wondering perhaps how long Dinah's memories had to live.

'All right,' she said abruptly, 'Don't leave me too long.'

In the hall of the nations the evening grew dark. Derveet lit a lamp. Little Dinah had been crying, but nothing that had happened to her recently seemed very real. She was sleepy now. She rested her cheek on her arms on the table-top and told Derveet helpfully, 'If my mummy was here she would sing to me – ' So, when Atoon came back Derveet was singing a lullaby. He waited in the shadows, listening to her voice: it had been a dark, soft voice for singing; it was cracked and faint now, but still true.

> I know a river
> Where the water runs
> Runs runs ever
> Through the green green trees
> And the sun shines on it
> And the leaves dapple it
> And the rocks and the branches
> Stand still in the water
> But the river runs forever
>
> I know a little girl
> Who ran by the river
> And put flowers in the water
> And the flowers danced away
> Like a disappearing rainbow
> But the river runs forever –

Derveet realised she had lost her audience, stopped singing and drew the child up against her shoulder. Two Butchers appeared; they had been waiting for the right moment. The child opened her eyes.

'Finish?'

'Finish,' said Derveet. 'Go with your people, dear.'

Dinah's hair brushed Derveet's chin, her small body was relaxed and warm and heavy. After a moment she sighed, and got down and trotted away, forgetting to say goodnight.

Atoon stood looking at his friend, sitting alone with the

single lamp beside her. The patience and quiet of her face was intolerable. Something had happened to him, when he first saw Garuda. He stared at her, imprisoned and defeated, everything lost, and suddenly, in a moment, he understood what he had done. The thoughts of a few minutes before filled his mouth like bile. *What am I doing here?* he cried to himself. *Oh God, she told me to keep them safe –*

She glanced up, and saw him.

Atoon said: 'You should have let me kill myself, the time I asked you. It would have been better.'

She had told him to go far, and not come back until he was sent for: to take away the seed of life, and save it. His own family had told him the same. Was that too hard for him to understand? Was simple obedience so difficult?

Derveet smiled. 'No,' she said at last. 'Don't blame yourself Atoon. Sit down. Let me tell you a story.' The lamplight flickered. From the camp outside came muted sounds, of various preparations. 'Once upon a time – ' began Derveet.

'Once upon a time there was a people who lived in a poisoned land. They had to leave it, so they came and became neighbours of the Peninsula. Naturally, they took over the government of this benighted country. But there was always an antipathy; a clash of philosophies. The neighbours had kept hold of a certain kind of civilisation, and it seemed to them the Peninsulans were wilfully throwing away everything of value. So their government was strict and angry. Finally it got to such a pitch that the Peninsulans revolted. We'll never know what really happened. But in the turmoil something came to the Rulers – in the form of a delicate and lovely youth. Perhaps one of them, one of the emissaries they had on our soil then, met this youth one night on the road, and felt his life changed for ever. From then on, the Rulers were not strict or angry anymore. All their resentment ended.

'Now to understand why, you have to realise the Rulers had been dying for a long time. I don't know if the old poison was really, physically, killing them. It seems to me more likely it was because they would not let go of the past, that death had got hold of them. Anyway, by the time of the Rebellion at least, the question was academic. Their population had passed the point of no return. They knew all about this death, they were used to

208

the idea. What filled them with conflict and distress was that our *alien* life would continue.

'I do not know how openly they have admitted to themselves what has been happening. It doesn't matter. Wo works from the longings of the heart. He has certain restrictions; rules built into him that he can bend but not break. But he has found ways around them. For all these years the angel doll, with its great powers, has been helping the Rulers: soothing them so the neglect and abuse of their rule did not seem shocking, and at the same time quietly persuading us, in many ways, towards self destruction.'

Atoon stared. A bitter chill suddenly ran through him, as if his blood had turned to water. He wanted to tell her to stop, but Derveet went on.

'It isn't even their fault, Atoon. *It was written*, as they say. There is nothing that the angel dolls can do but bring chaos and death. They give us our desire, and *desire* is not a little thing. It is one of the powers that hold the universe together – set free it must tear things apart, one way or another. . . . Even, even the desire for hope, to turn the people from despair, will end in destruction – '

Her voice shook, she put a hand up to her face: 'Remember, Atoon, she has always given us what we wanted. She brought me quietness when I was playing Anakmati. She brought you action, when you were pampered and idle and despairing. When I sent you away, her vigour in your heart brought you back. And I, while ruin was plotting, kept my *stillness* in Ranganar. And finally, when they wanted me they took me. It wasn't hard. Like everyone else, I had surrendered already.'

A breath of air from somewhere stirred the darkness, making the lamp-flame shiver and bow. The quiet voice began again, relentlessly:

'When I entered this struggle, I put my faith in the mysterious flower our women found in their garden, who knows how long ago. They used it for what seemed most important: medicine, surveillance – control. They nurtured it and kept it secret at any price, so it could grow, believing it to be the hope of the world. Even I only turned to it in desperation. We were wrong, I believe. I now think the flower is really more like a spark. It needed a wind to make it bloom, not a shelter. Well, the wind came.... But it is no use. Leilah of Gamartha has proved that even the mystery can be corrupted. The Dapur power may approach to God, but it is rooted in our humanity, and our humanity, ours, not the Rulers', is *wormeaten* now. I don't think we have had a chance, since Cho set foot on the Peninsula.'

Silence. Then Atoon said – 'Cho disappeared. We know Leilah of Gamartha stole her, but Leilah never came back to her brother. The Koperasi might have overtaken her in the wilderness. But we wouldn't be waiting here now if the Rulers had Cho....'

He stopped. Derveet was looking at him with a half smile in her eyes, and shaking her head.

After a moment he said in a defeated voice: 'We think Leilah killed herself.'

'Yes.'

She shivered. 'I was very low, up on Bu Awan. The Cat, Cho's cat you know, did a really good job on me ... very professional. I am better now. But things have been different since then. Have you had dreams Atoon? I know they haven't got Cho. She is near this camp. I know it. I don't think it is her fault. I don't think she can stay away. Her brother draws her. They are twins. They act on each other, do you remember I once told you that? He is coming to her, she is going to him. We can't keep them apart. I've been thinking ... but wayang legong can't be destroyed. Oh, Atoon, I couldn't do it anyway. I couldn't do it....'

Her face, by the end of this, was resting on her outstretched arms; the jagged eagle profile and the black long curve of lashes grazing her cheekbone. Atoon asked no more. But at last, as the dead gods listened to the night and the shadows sighed and whispered, he reached out a shaking hand to touch her hair.

210

25   Midnight

Daylight strengthened. Atoon had been watching it grow. He had not slept, but he thought maybe Derveet was sleeping now. He was propped up in a corner of the bed shelf in the cell, the old nun's cell Pao had given Garuda, so she could lie against his shoulder and have some support for her difficult faint breathing. His arm was round her, his hand over her breast. He'd been in starts of terror all night, imagining the dark flesh cooling against his palm, the shallow movement ceased. But now it was morning, and he knew she was still with him, for another day. The last day. Would there be a final embassy, or were all ceremonies over? The camp, he knew, had been preparing for defence as far as possible. And part of his night terror had been to listen for a swift and wild alarm. But he was not afraid now.

The grey dawn was calm and still. What a fool I have made of myself, he thought. Swaggering around the country after Bima Singa, posing in romantic attitudes.... Well, it was all over now. Just a weary wakening from a wild dream, no need for remorse, no place for recriminations. He knew something that Derveet had not told him last night. He knew that he had ignored the visions and portents sent to warn him on that first journey; sent to warn the people from the depths of their own hearts, and he had kept down the mystery, when, if it had flamed, the sparks might have reached Bima's army, making war impossible.... It was hard to believe that nothing would have made any difference. And yet, in the empty silence that filled his heart, he did believe it.... Suddenly – had his eyes closed for a moment? – he realised that he and Derveet were no longer alone.

'How did you get in?' he said, without surprise.

'Through the window,' said Cho. There was a tiny square of pallor, high in the wall, not big enough for a cat –

Derveet awoke and felt Atoon's arm round her. She opened her eyes, and it was like the dreams she had had in prison: a blazing instant of joy, and then the understanding dawning, that if Cho had come back there was no hope left at all. But this time the dream went on. She sat up.

'Please don't be angry,' cried Cho. 'Please – I couldn't help it. I had to see you again.'

Derveet left the couch and went to her. Atoon picked up his blouse and slipped quietly out of the door.

In the centre of the camp of the princedoms was a large space of carefully smoothed earth, guarded by beautiful youths armed with senjata, dressed in white with sashes of the mountain colours; green and purple. Here stood Bima Singa's tent. Beside it, under the steady rain that had begun soon after dawn, hovered a rose-coloured sphere, parked on a cushion of air just above the ground. The dust that was being kept dry under it danced incessantly with a faint hissing sound. Bima had been up all night with the adviser from the shining islands. The youths were yawning. No one was allowed near the prince's quarters while the adviser was on shore, not even to change the watch.

Bima had never liked the connection with the Rulers. His sister had always dealt with them herself; she understood his repugnance. To her strong soul accepting *their* help meant nothing, because she knew she was going to turn on them in the end. But Leilah had disappeared. Since she had left him, a horror had been growing on Bima. He could not take the 'official version' into his heart; he realised there the things she had done, with her strong soul. He had announced her murder, but they had been so close he knew the truth, of course. What could he do now? Not, certainly, abandon responsibility for her rising. He could not give up the terrible venture that he and Leilah had begun together. He must go on. But there was no honour left in this war. It disgusted him.

The adviser from the shining islands had come to offer prince Bima a solution. The suggestion was that Bima should give the renegades one last chance. If that failed, the Rulers were prepared to provide what their ambassador called 'a sort of demonstration'. The prince's sister had wanted decisive

212

weaponry, but the Rulers had given up that sort of thing long ago. What was offered was a relic, left over from the Rebellion.

Bima and the adviser sat opposite each other on the plain canvas floor with a low map table between them. The tent was big but rather bare; Bima liked to live simply. Its walls were tightly closed; a pendulum fan scarcely stirred the air. The prince's visitor was closely encased in a strange sort of coverall garment, but showed no sign of discomfort. Bima found it hard to swallow his revulsion at the smooth, hairless skull and the unreadable bland features, all wrapped in some kind of caul like a newborn animal. He did not want to accept this creature's help. But the Peninsula was in desperate straits. The adviser had been going over with him all the trouble spots – the empty towns; ruffians and criminals harassing Timur Kering; defiant rebels hiding in the Sawah. And *all* the Koperasi had been evacuated.... It was a symbol of good faith, said the adviser. To Bima the causeway people were not a last stand, but a place for a decisive stroke to end the bloodshed.

'I must stress,' said the adviser, through the caul, 'that the offer we are making has *no military value*.'

'But it will impress?'

'Oh yes. It will impress. Please understand we don't want to force anything onto you. This must be of your own free will. But you know, it's only as a last resort. The first suggestion may well succeed, and then everything will be settled.'

Bima passed his hands over his face. He could see, yes, that making them give up the child-in-white would break them.

'What – er – what are you going to do with her?'

The Ruler shook that grotesque head gently. 'Now, now. I told you, you mustn't worry about that.'

'The people won't like it when they realise she is to go to you.'

'These mob fancies pass.'

Silence fell, but for the murmur of the rain, and the sigh of waves breaking somewhere. Bima tried to think. They had been talking for hours, but what exactly had been said? There were times when the Ruler's High Inggris was difficult to follow. Some things didn't make sense. Just what was he being offered?

'Try to make up your mind. It's quite important we get this sorted out now. North-East Wind is coming soon.'

213

Bima was alone, without his family or his sister. How many lives would be lost, in the taking of Pancaragam? If everything could be ended at a stroke did he dare refuse?... And now the Ruler did not look so alien. There was sympathy in that strange face – sympathy and understanding. A moment of intense quietness, then Bima sighed, and the balance dropped. 'So be it,' said the prince.

Somehow people knew that Cho had appeared. When Atoon emerged that morning he found the camp buzzing with the news. Friends and strangers kept coming up to him and congratulating him on his great good fortune, that changed everything. Not long before noon emissaries arrived, to deliver Bima Singa's ultimatum: Forget all other conditions and former terms. Give up the *anak khusus putih*, the child-in-white, or the truce will be ended with all possible force, tomorrow noon. Of course, there was no question of giving up the child. Atoon told the ambassador so, and the Gamarthan nobleman, who did not know he was addressing the so-called former Hanoman in person, looked up and down the trestle table of shabby figures and said something disgusting about monkeys and girl children. And the last embassy broke up in near violence as the representatives of the people all jumped up shouting around Atoon.

All that day, as the rain streamed down, the Pancaragam was alive with purpose, under the red and white freedom flag. The causeway people had been growing quieter and quieter as they realised what was going to happen to them and watched hope trickle away. But now the long awaited moment had come they were suddenly filled with excitement. The return of Cho was being treated as a miracle. It was not clear exactly what was expected – but even victory tomorrow was not impossible. *See,* said Kimlan to Atoon, *we're all volunteers. How many of those masses over there are only here because they're forced, and don't understand what's going on at all? But every one of us few is ready, is willing to die –*

The dishevelled township of tents and shacks was dismantled and brought into close order. The non-combatants were supposed to be packed into the vaults under the ruins, because no one knew what weapons the princes might produce. But there were so many there was not room and shelters were hastily constructed behind the thickest walls.... The *naga* guns – the buried treasure – looked very fine rubbed up and trundled around on wheels quickly made by the smiths. Derveet and Cho walked about together, letting themselves be seen. Atoon pitied them; it seemed a shame they could not have these hours in peace. But the show was necessary.

Derveet and Atoon had fixed on one frail, final plan. They would let the ultimatum run out and the fighting start, and under cover of this send Cho away up the coast by sea. There was a boat available; a smugglers' prahu in which some enterprising Samsui had fled from Ranganar. The Dove House boys would take her, and leave her somewhere to disappear in the desolate lands. The prahu had been well hidden, and sea-going was unknown on the Jagdanan coast because of religious taboos and poor fishing. There was a faint chance that Singa and his advisers would overlook this possibility....

At the meagre night meal people came together. They brought out their last little hoards of achar, beer and spirits and sang and kissed each other and were very emotional. Atoon imagined identical scenes in the other camp; he could not bear it, he hid away. When the night had quietened he came out, and found Derveet sitting alone again in the hall of nations, drinking weak achar tea over a small red brazier, for the rain had made the air quite cool.

'Sit in front of me,' she said. 'Or I can't see you. Haven't been able to see anything out of my bad eye for weeks.'

'I'm sorry.'

Derveet smiled.

'Where's Cho?'

'Gone to fetch Gress, her pony, from where they were hiding. Don't worry, she has an escort.'

'Who?'

'My boys.'

'Derveet,' said Atoon. 'I can't do it. I cannot fight. It is too terrible. It will make no difference, they'll catch Cho anyway, or her brother will pull her back. Why don't we just surrender? We are in God's hands –'

Derveet gazed into her bowl. 'That would be nice, wouldn't it,' she said softly. 'You should have heard Cho's parable, Atoon. I'm afraid it's rather the reverse.' Her words were bitter,

215

but her face was strangely quiet. She looked up: 'No. We can't stop trying. With or without hope, it is never right to give up.'

In the shadows the dead stone animals gathered round: Garuda with the human head lost and crumbling wings, the posturing white ape faceless. A limping stone centipede, token of some long vanished state, seemed to caper weirdly. . . .

Atoon whispered, 'I cannot see any *right* in killing my own kinsmen and making my friends murderers, knowing they are all helpless puppets. . . . I would rather lose heaven –'

'Bima is your brother, Atoon,' said Derveet. 'Don't put yourself above him. . . . Such a mass of contradictions, in the end our only resort is to do what seems to be our duty. Come here.'

When he came she drew him down beside her, and kissed his face, his eyes, his lips.

'There. Have you forgotten? "Thy tears are for those beyond tears, and are your words words of wisdom? The wise grieve not for those who live, and they grieve not for those who die. Life and death will pass away. . . . " Be strong. Arise and fight. Now, go and sleep, my dear. You will find that you can.'

Derveet was dreaming. It was a room in the Samsui house, an inner room with windows into other rooms and courtyards. There was a pleasant low murmuring of other people's lives going on, within the undividing walls. There was a lot of light in the room. Handai was sitting on a square stool with fat claw feet; there was no other furniture. There was a lot of light. She watched Handai feeding her baby – one shoulder bare, the other clothed, the creature fumbling reproachfully at the dark, swollen nipple. It was strange to see Handai's little round breasts so heavy and strained. And yet she was fascinated, all the same.

'You're distracting me,' said Handai.

'But you're not doing anything.'

'Yes I am,' Handai bent her face with a sly smile. 'My uterus is contracting. I can feel it.' She knew Derveet was ridiculously shy about remarks like that. 'It almost hurts,' she said, and laughed at her friend's doubtful expression.

There was a lot of light in the room. As Handai laughed there came a sudden convulsion of that light – no sound. It passed,

216

and Derveet realised there was a storm going on somewhere: a storm of light. She got up and came to stand behind the young mother. The white floor seemed a long way away; another of those soundless invisible spasms, but Handai settled back, accepting Derveet's support. Her body felt warm and solid leaning there, she turned her rough head – you don't trim your hair when you have a newborn baby, for some reason – and looked up.

What had happened to Handai's face? Hollow eyes – from lack of sleep of course, but more. The golden, rosy curves were shrunken in, drawn and drained; only bone and shadow remained under the glowing skin, no substance left. The virtue has gone out of her, thought Derveet. But where to? Not into that purplish, hairless thing with the squirming limbs. . . . Surely not. But where to? . . . . where to? Handai's cheek was pressed against Derveet's bare side where her jacket had fallen open – the touch had such a warmth, of reassurance. The room contracted again in another of those silent convulsions.

'It is the sort of thunder one feels rather than hears,' said Handai.

And Derveet woke up. Her open eyes saw straight away the figure of Cho kneeling beside her but there was something odd – 'Ah,' she thought. 'When I dream I see with two eyes.'

'Have I slept long?'

'Not long.'

The brazier was dying. Derveet thought of pouring herself another bowl of tea, but it was a huge effort to raise her arms, she decided not to bother. Cho, who had been feeding the crumbling fire delicately, as if it was a small animal, looked up and saw that Anakmati had come back; the person she had met by lamplight at Adi's hotel, so long ago it seemed – drab jacket and breeches, and a dark, harsh face alive with vivid energy. But the energy was quenched now. And we did not let them give us a brazier then, thought Cho.

Derveet gazed, on where there was nothing glowing now, only a lingering glimmer under the ashes.

'Derveet,' said Cho softly. 'Do you love me again? Will you always?'

'Dearest, I loved you the first moment I saw you,' said

217

Derveet. 'I never, never stopped. I am so sorry that I hurt you. I will love you till I die.'

'That's what I thought,' said Cho.

A faint sigh, of the grey charcoals settling. Derveet stirred: 'Where are those boys?'

'They are not coming,' said Cho sadly. 'I am not going with them. I am going out to sea, to my brother. Don't be angry with them. I told them it was your orders.'

She stood up.

'Cho! –'

The child trembled. 'Even if you think I am betraying you, I still must go.'

'Cho, what can you do? What power have you – ?'

'I have none now. But I will have.'

'What –'

'Derveet, I knew you didn't want me to do anything about your being ill. So I never did.'

Time seemed to stand still. Then Derveet suddenly moved – to get up, to cry out. But she did not move, nor make a sound. Something had touched her, it was as if her body had turned to stone. Cho stood with her hands pressed to her heart. 'So it's like that is it?' said Derveet, silently. 'Well, goodbye then. I love you.'

Cho darted forward and kissed that mouth – the strong, clever, gentle mouth that had been so sweet, briefly, once, and fled.

Three figures hurried through the ruins. The pony's hoofbeats echoed, the cat bounded dangerously underfoot. No one saw or heard: the whole camp was frozen in a dream. At the last wall the two-legged one stopped, and suddenly turned and flung herself against the stone, her arms before her face. No sound came from her. The pony rubbed her soft mouth against the little one's shoulder.

But the Cat chivvied impatiently: 'Come on, come on. For *that* you will find, one has all the time in the world.'

There was a boat waiting for them on the dark shore, nosing the sand. Not the black prahu, but another smaller vessel, gleaming faintly as it rocked there.

'I'll be waiting,' said Gress. 'Don't forget me –'

'Now you have got your way,' said Cho to the Cat. 'After all this time, how does it feel?'

Divine Endurance looked up at her sharply and said after a moment, 'I believe you have been doing what you shouldn't. I believe you've been prying into things. It won't do you any good, you know, whatever your plan is. It is too late. I promise you.'

Cho did not answer. She knelt gazing at the shore as it fled silently away, and soon the little shining boat was swallowed into the vastness of the sea.

In Pancaragam Butcher Pao, whose watch it was, did not know that a small piece had gone from her night, and neither did her sentries. At dawn she walked into the hall of nations with two of them and they found Derveet apparently asleep at a table. They spoke to her, but she did not answer.

'Fetch Atoon –'

When he came, she was on a stretcher wrapped in coverlets. She was shivering, her skin was burning to the touch.

'Sitting up all night in the chill and the damp – and in her condition –'

Atoon knelt on the ground. She grasped his wrist with hot fingers, the skin scurf and dry as a snake's.

'Atoon you must go out now. Go out *now*.' He could hardly hear the words.

'Don't let her talk –' said Pao.

'It's Cho. I can't tell you why. Not enough – ah, breath. You must take their attention away from what is happening out at sea –'

Her hands fell lax. Her eyes were not quite closed, she murmured but not to him. She would not speak to him again.

'Get her away from here. And come back, quickly. Call all the representatives –'

He turned his back.

'Well, tears won't help,' muttered Pao. 'Now then, you two: lift.'

26   Morning

The shining islands jumped between sea and sky but finally they were visible all the time. They grew enormous. Some had projecting arms reaching down from their flanks. The boat went to one in the middle of the row, and approached a smooth ramp lowered at the end of one of these arms. It was hollow inside: a great, round, climbing tunnel, dimly lit. The ramp sucked the boat to itself, Cho and the Cat climbed out. The seal a little way up the tunnel quietly irided itself, and they stepped through.

The floor cuddled their feet and carried them up into the island world and then, as if sensing they would rather be alone, it left them to walk by themselves. They passed through streets and halls and squares. In some places there were images of trees and flowers built in the air, with convincing blue sky overhead; other places had coloured lights falling and talking like water. There was no one to welcome them. Sometimes Cho heard the murmur of voices, or saw a figure crossing a street in the distance, but no one came near. There was a feeling of peace, long undisturbed. It was a lonely place, but not unhappy.

Without needing to be directed they moved into the centre of the maze. Divine Endurance trotted busily, her tail up and her whiskers pricked forwards. Cho walked with care, her eyes absorbed as if she was concentrating on carrying something precious. It was as if she had a present for her brother, which she held in her heart, and she was afraid it might break and spill over before she could bring it to him.

Finally, in the middle of the island, they came to a private-looking but unassuming hallway. The wall at the end of it unfolded as they approached. They stepped into a small room, very well lit. It contained a table with a chessboard on it, the quivering crystal pieces in disarray, and a sort of string bed; a good imitation of the kind of thing night-watch boys used to use in Ranganar. There were no windows. One of the walls was holding a suit of some elaborate uniform, including a peaked cap with gold braid. On the bed frame, lying on the bare netting, was an old, old man, quite naked. His arms and legs were spread-eagled and tied to the four corners with black ribbons. Kneeling over him was what seemed to be a slim youth, with hair the colour of dust.

The old man turned his head. 'Yes, do come in,' he said. 'I have to admit company does not make much difference nowadays, one way or the other.'

Cho looked at the youth's face and arms, which were covered in blue, whirling, tattooed patterns.

'What happened to them?' she asked. 'The nomads, I mean.'

'Oh, they were taken care of,' said the old man. He frowned slightly, trying hard to raise the spark of pleasure.

'Well, I've come,' said Cho.

Her brother glanced at her sideways, with dark eyes that mirrored her own, and went on with what he was doing.

'He doesn't talk much,' said the old man. 'Never did. You mustn't disturb him at the moment anyway. He's doing something rather hard.'

Divine Endurance jumped up on the chess table, crooning softly in her throat. The pieces fell into the air and were deftly caught and swallowed by it. She began to wash her face.

'Yes. He's managed it at last. He could never have done it without your help and your friends', especially the coloured lady. You see just now everybody, all at once, is longing for an end of some kind. So now it can be done, and none of us will feel bad at all. Of course, he's had to cut through a bit of red tape. He's not *breaking* the rules, but it is a rather delicate piece of interpretation, and on top of all his usual load it's a bit of a burden. That's why you mustn't bother him. He is only doing this for me because I'm the king you know, and I ought to have special attention.'

On the Pancaragam, Cho thought, it was morning now, and the battle had begun.

'Is it true then?' she said slowly. 'Have I really come too late?'

The king said kindly, 'Never mind. I'm sure he'll be glad to meet you anyway.'

Divine Endurance tucked up her back leg, and began to lick inside it contentedly.

On the morning of that day, a party of riders came galloping out of the south. They pressed urgently westward down the old road to the holy city, through stripped fields and deserted villages. In sight of the ruins they reined in and stared. They were in a grove of coconut palms; some hacked and seared, some still standing in tall, graceful curves. There was a smell of brine in the air, but it was mixed with acrid smoke. The horses fretted, frightened by the noises carried on the sea breeze, the riders hesitated. Then one figure broke away, urging her horse onward, her black veils flying, not looking to see whether her companions followed.

She rode blindly, until the battle was all around her: screaming faces and blundering bodies flashing out of the turmoil and vanishing. Once someone grabbed at her bridle and yelled at her, 'Get that horse back behind the lines! This is no place to bring a poor dumb animal –' She saw a woman's face, haggard and furious, topped with thick greying hair – The face fell back and she rode on. She was aiming for the red and white banner she had seen, flying high above the battlefield.

When she reached the spot she got down and stood uncertainly. The uproar was all behind her. She found herself in a courtyard paved in stone, quiet and hushed, surrounded by mouldering carved walls. The white flag with the red dagger, which she knew was freedom's banner, hung on a bamboo pole looking like something forgotten. Old women and boys came in and out of dark doorways carrying linen and trays. They glanced at her and ignored her. She could hear children chanting a lesson, somewhere close. She had been told by the women at the derelict farm that she must reach this place today; that she was needed for an important duty. Her back still tired easily, she wanted to lie down.

At last a woman went past, younger than the others, and looked at her brightly.

'Excuse me –' she said. 'I'm Annet.'

'Ah,' said the woman. 'Who? I don't know all your names. Come to sit with her? What are you – convalescent? Is that why

222

you're not fighting? Come on then. That other girl's worse than useless.'

She was a Baker. She wasn't political at all; the troubles had just thrown her in with 'this lot' by accident. But she'd always been good at sick-people duties, which was lucky. So she told Annet, leading her along a passageway and up a little stair.

'It's the fluid on the lungs now, and the fever, that will settle it,' she said. 'I daresay she could have had a few more months, living quietly, but I can't be sure. When this disease turns nasty, it is pretty quick –'

Annet was bewildered. In the door of the room they were entering was a very young woman, with reddish skin. She was sobbing. Someone murmured – 'Jhonni –' and she ran and crouched beside a mat on the floor. The person lying on the mat stroked the girl's hair with a weak, awkward hand, and said something to Annet's guide.

'Don't worry,' said the Baker. 'I'll find her plenty to do.'

Then Annet was left alone, looking down at the dying woman.

'*Garuda* –' she whispered.

Derveet had closed her eyes for a moment. She opened them and saw the leader of Bu Awan, wearing the black and indigo robes of the garden. She was splashed with mud and dust, her startling hair was tumbling out of the veil in a flood of gold.

'Annet,' she said, as if they had parted yesterday. 'Annet, I'm so glad to see you. Do you think you could call me by my own name? I'd prefer that.'

Annet knelt down, biting at her lips. She put her arm gently under Derveet's burning, wasted shoulders and turned the sweat-soaked bolsters, propping them up higher. She saw fresh sheets lying on the floor, abandoned by the weeping girl presumably. As gently as she could she stripped off the stained and clammy bedding, and replaced it.

'Ah,' said Derveet. 'Thank you.'

'They would not let me lie with other people. Bad for morale, I suppose.'

The room had a floor of boards and a roof of tiles: at some recent time people had lived in this part of the ruins. It was very still. There was nothing in it but Derveet's mat, and a tin

223

bowl placed under a hole in the roof. Through a long arched window in the thick wall came a distant threatening murmur.

'Derveet, what is happening?'

Derveet looked up. Her mouth quivered. 'They are fighting,' she said gravely. 'Didn't you notice, as you came in?' Then she repented. 'Annet, please. I'm sure someone will explain. But not me. I really can't.'

Then she could not speak anymore. She lay listening to the ragged, careful noise of her own breathing. Annet moved closer, and offered her hand. Skeletal dark fingers closed over it gratefully.

'Think I'll sleep for a bit now. You'll stay?'

'Oh yes.'

'Dreadfully hot, isn't it. . . . '

It was midmorning. The heat of the day had begun. The air around the Pancaragam was full of the smell of blood and black powder, and horrible confused sounds. Atoon, once prince Hanoman, rode the black horse, Bejak, along a ridge of higher ground above what had been the Timur Kering lines, and looked down on the battle. The few thousands of the causeway people were still holding ground. The fierceness of their reckless sortie had thrust them into their enemies' ranks, sending great masses of the immaculate warriors reeling. Now the two parties were locked together in an inextricable embrace. The princely armies did not see how pitifully small the forces of the renegades were. The causeway people took no account of the vast numbers against them. They would all of them slash and blast and kill as long as they could stand.

Atoon could not see the banner of sunlight and blue sky anymore. He wondered if his heir, the young prince of Jagdana, was alive or dead. Perhaps I killed him myself, he thought. He had been deep in that chaos, he had only left it briefly to make this survey. He did not remember much of what he had done there. Suddenly, as he sat Bejak's trembling shoulders, staring at the butchery, it seemed to him that his mind was cleared of madness. He knew what he must do. He called someone to come and take Bejak: he was going back to the field.

The rosy sphere had been forced to move a little out of the way of the fighting. Now it rested lightly in the feathery shade

224

of a grove of casuerina trees on the edge of the battlefield, and just above the seashore. Bima was there, with the adviser, when his bodyguard brought the renegades to him. There were three of them: a big, red, brutal-looking Koperasi, one of the Samsui women and a third; small, with cropped hair. They were all dressed in shabby blouse and trousers, smoke stained and bloodied. The woman and the deformity seemed puzzled, almost angry. The small person looked resolute. Bima had difficulty recognising prince Atoon. But when he did he rushed forward and grasped his brother's hands.

'I prayed you would come,' he cried. 'There must be a way to end this. We must find a way. God will not forgive us if we fail –'

'You don't understand,' said Atoon, 'I have come to surrender.'

A few paces away the warriors of the princedoms were still thrusting against the renegades. The bubble's inner and outer apertures were open: glimpses and sounds of the battle came in by the connecting passage, through the smooth opening in the outer sphere. But within all was calm. The adviser was sitting before a bank of instruments, gazing with mild interest at some dancing dots on a screen. Bima dropped Atoon's hands. He turned round sharply.

'Call it off,' he said.

'I'm terribly sorry,' said the creature. 'But I can't do that.'

'It's not noon. Call it off, damn you –'

The large figure in its sleek, alien clothing turned with a tired smile. 'Ah, but I'm not controlling it. Our young friend, who does everything for us, is in charge. I don't know a thing about it. I certainly wouldn't know how to stop it now, or from here.'

For the benefit of the three newcomers the Ruler began to explain. 'The princes wanted something that would bring all the disturbance to an end. Now this has never been made public, but we've had some – ah, devices, in site on shore for a long while. They were put in place just before the Rebellion, up along the edge of the landmass. We never used them: we realised in time we would never have forgiven ourselves – we are not monsters after all. But the situation is different now, isn't it, and prince Bima freely consented. Don't worry. The blast area is, so far as we can find out, quite unpopulated, and

225

the explosion will be in the air, so there's not much risk of triggering earthquakes. Of course, you won't believe what has happened at first, but you'll soon understand, when North-East Wind sets in. And then you'll join us on the islands. . . . Life will be so much more pleasant when we're "all in the same boat".

'Our agents, the – er "Koperasi" have already had all this explained to them. Likewise the "Samsui". There's a medical examination: those who need it, probably not too many if I've followed your recent history, will have treatment to make them suitable for a contained environment. And that's all there is to it.'

Prince Bima stared. The blood had fled from his face. The bones stood out of his handsome flesh as if he were already dead.

'Didn't you understand?' said the adviser, with a worried look. 'Oh dear. It can't be helped you know. Even from here the event will be extremely impressive, just as I promised. It will stop people in their tracks all right. But I'm afraid it is going to be *rather* dirty –'

Prince Bima stood for a moment, as if puzzling what this strange term 'dirty' might mean. Then he said to Atoon, calmly, 'Brother, we are betrayed.' He was carrying no weapon but a knife in his sash. He threw this on the floor and ran out of the bubble's side, unarmed into the mêlèe. His bodyguard ran after him, and Breus, and Pao. The Ruler turned back to the screens, smiling tolerantly. One of the instruments counted out numbers.

'Ah – we're leaving in a minute.'

But Atoon stood transfixed. His hands hung empty at his sides. He could neither move nor speak.

The courtyard underneath Derveet's room had been very busy: full of running footsteps and urgent voices and sobs and cries as the injured were brought in. But to Annet all these sounds seemed far away. She knelt at her friend's side, waiting and watching. Someone had brought a bowl of water, she soaked a cloth and cooled Derveet's face and hands with it every few minutes. Slowly, the morning passed by. Several times Annet thought she found herself alone. But not quite yet.

At last, Derveet stirred and opened her eyes again. 'Hallo,' she murmured.

'Hallo. There's some water here. Do you want to drink?'

Derveet moved her head a little: No. She was silent for a while, then she whispered: 'Is the fighting still going on?'

'Yes.'

'Not much longer –'

Annet saw she was smiling, faintly and sweetly. But her eyes were very sad. A few minutes later she spoke again; Annet bent close, she could barely make out the words.

'Dear, I have not said. I'm sorry – forgive me?'

'What? what?'

'Bu Awan –' breathed Derveet.

Annet could not speak. Her eyes filled, her throat was closed with tears. When she found her voice she cried, 'Ah no, no blame –'

Too late.

In the small bright room, far away out at sea, Cho stood waiting for her moment, a look of listening concentration on her face. The moment came. For an instant she felt as if great wings were beating round her, holding her in love and sweetness and strength. The eagle rose shining into the light of the sun. Cho was alone, forever.

She said to her brother, 'You help people don't you?'

The youth with the dust-coloured hair raised his strange face.

'Well then, help me.'

Wo felt pain. It was not like the crying of the world, which he had learned so well how to soothe. It seemed to belong to him; it seemed to be inside him. When he tried to help, in his usual way, he found himself in peculiar difficulties. The mind was like his own: it was his own. It couldn't deceive itself, it couldn't forget, it couldn't die, it couldn't be offered the prospect of a meeting in another world. It couldn't destroy itself either: *that's not allowed*. The youth frowned. A ripple of dissatisfaction, even uneasiness, passed over the blue whirling lines of his face, for the first time in many years. All the other things that he was doing, and people he was looking after, were like juggler's eggs forgotten in the air. He made one more determined effort....

227

There was a sudden, palpable change in the air of the bright room.

'Now look what you've done,' said Divine Endurance. 'You've broken him, you naughty girl.'

Annet in the upper room dropped the lifeless hand and stared wildly around her – 'What's happening!' she cried. . . . And on the battlefield above the seashore spitting firearms were dumb, long knives fell from lax hands. The warriors and the renegades stood in dazed attitudes, gazing about them in bewilderment.

Cho went to look at the youth's body, which had fallen from the bed and lay on the floor.

'He is gone.'

The king, who had been woken from a peaceful little doze by the bump, twisted round to have a look.

'Why so he is,' he said. 'My goodness, isn't that clever.'

Cho stared.

'Well, he isn't just dead you know,' he told her. 'He couldn't die, you know that. He's ceased to exist. He has left the Wheel. It is called Nirbhana. It's held to be quite an achievement.'

'For human beings,' said Cho. Then she said, 'But I am still here. I wasn't sure about that. I wonder what happened in the olden days. I hope there was some humane arrangement.'

Divine Endurance had got down from the table and now stood looking up at Cho. Her scheming was all over, and nothing had turned out as she had planned. Not even her curiosity had been satisfied: now no one would ever know what happened when you fastened the bad babies together again. But to her surprise none of this seemed to matter, beside the desolation in the child's face.

She said, 'We'll go away. We'll go somewhere nice. And anyway, you can't tell. For ever's a long, long time. There might always be a big earthquake. Or we might wear out –'

Cho was not comforted. 'Divine Endurance,' she said, 'How old are you?'

The king, getting restless, coughed to attract their attention and plaintively requested that he be untied.

The sky had cleared over the battlefield. The sun stood at noon and then moved on serenely westward in its usual course. Some people tended the dead and wounded, making no distinction between friend and enemy. Large groups stood looking out to sea. A little pale disc had appeared, between the shore and the shining arcs on the horizon. It was a kind of bubble. It approached very quickly and stopped suddenly a little way down the beach, hovering above the gently breaking waves. Cho got out, carrying Divine Endurance. The king followed with dignified care, dressed in his uniform, holding his braided cap under one arm. But at that moment someone came pushing through the crowd: a woman in dishevelled Dapur robes. She ran to prince Atoon, spoke to him; bowed her head and wept. And then a wave of grief, shot through with glory, broke from those two and swept through all the people.

The king had wanted to give his hat to someone; he thought this would be the correct thing. But he could not see anyone who looked interested. So he left it in the water, rolled up his trousers and pottered off by himself along the sand.

But later he came looking for Cho again. He found her crouched with Divine Endurance under the casuerina trees behind the empty bubble.

'Ah, there you are. I wanted someone to help me off with these things. And I thought I'd like to say goodbye too.'

'Where are you going?'

'Oh, anywhere.'

She helped him to shuffle off the heavy clothes and watched him wind a long swathe of saffron cotton around his shrivelled body. He did not seem sure how to handle this garment and ended up with some odd patches of nakedness. The peace celebrations were a background presence.

'Well, well,' remarked the king. 'So it is all over. I am not sorry you know. We only wanted this, really – for it to be all over. So you see, you two angels did manage to make everybody happy, after all.'

Cho said nothing.

The king smiled at her. Behind an irrepressible look of utter carelessness his old eyes were compassionate. 'Wo taught me a lot,' he said. 'And not all of it bad, whatever they may say. In this game of ours your achievement is great, greater than his, even. For you turned back, with your foot on the threshold of heaven, because you heard the cry of the world.'

'I am a wayang. I had no choice.'

'No? Ah well.' He had produced a small wooden bowl from a pocket of his discarded finery and was examining it fondly. A moment later he was gone, the pat-pat of his bare feet fading into the sound of the murmuring sea. Gress came out of the trees, and stood close to her friends.

'Shall we go away soon, child?' said Divine Endurance.

That night the victorious army spread themselves generously to entertain those who had surrendered. No campfire or outside kitchen of the princes' forces was complete without at least one renegade to fete. It was like a great banquet, spreading all over the shore and spilling into the ruins. Distinctions were blurred: the warriors and the causeway people were so mingled, so light hearted it was as if they had known all along that the battle was just a game.

Atoon walked alone in the darkness that surrounded the flowers of light. He had excused himself from the company of the other princes. Bima, of course, had tried to disclaim the victory, saying that it belonged to the causeway people, and the part that he and his armies had played was simply shameful. But Atoon had no desire to share this triumph. Today life had been saved from the terrible gifts of the wayang legong. One of them was destroyed; the other harmless because her motive force was gone. All around him were women mingling freely with men and youths: fastidious gentlemen and bigoted peasants eating from the same dishes as outcasts and Koperasi. The new world was beginning. But his heart ached. It seemed so little to gain: '*merdeka*', and a new social order. He knew the people were making legends already: Anakmati who feared nothing and despised no one, not even the most degraded. . . . Garuda weeping upon Bu Awan. . . . It is not enough! he cried out silently. Nothing, nothing could make up for Derveet, alive and human as she would never be again, never again –

Then suddenly he noticed something. In his blind grief he had walked past, already, fires where a strange quietness reigned. There were not many. They were scattered all over the shore. He did not know how he could pick them out, but he could. Stillness, silence; eyes moving like stars – mind to mind and heart to heart, just as Kimlan had said . . . (Ah, where was Kimlan now?) Atoon stood. In the morning they might forget; they might hold on to the old ways for a while. But the spark was leaping now with nothing to hold it back. He had a vision of that fire: spreading, spreading, until it overwhelmed the world and swallowed up everything he had ever known, ever loved. . . . His loss was greater far than he had imagined. It was so great that, after all, he was satisfied.

Derveet's boys brought out the black prahu, which was meant to carry Cho away. They draped it with silks abstracted from the tent of a rich nobleman and all night it lay on the sands, bearing its slight freight. They had dressed her in the plain breeches and jacket of Anakmati. They had combed her hair on her shoulders and folded her dark beautiful hands on her breast. Just before dawn the tide turned, and Garuda was sent out on her last sailing, the way the dead used to be sent by the diving people, on the islands where she spent her childhood. The sail was set; the breeze caught it, Garuda flew away. And up behind the watching crowds rose the white rim of the morning.

When it was over, Atoon and Annet rode down the shore with Cho.

'Stay with us,' said Annet. 'At least for a while. You can't do us any harm now. I'm sure of it.'

Cho shook her head. 'It's time I was going.'

'Where will you go?' asked Atoon.

'I will go north,' said the child. 'If you go far enough north, the ice and snow I saw once in the distance on the glass plateau comes down from the peaks and covers everything – all the land and sea. I've never been very cold. It might work.'

Atoon looked into her eyes. He said softly, 'Well, there is a new prince in Jagdana. I don't feel like disturbing him. Perhaps I'll follow you one day.'

Someone came running up breathlessly; she had been following them, not sure if she dared approach.

'Here –' said Cycler Jhonni, shamefaced and awkward. 'I thought you might like to have this.'

She had been crying again. The package she held out fell open, revealing a lock of glossy black hair. Cho looked at it. She could

231

feel the harsh silk on her palm. Her hands, not wanting to be rude, tried to reach out – but they could not.

'Thank you,' she said politely. 'It was nice of you. But please keep it. Come on Gress.'

She scrambled up, and Divine Endurance came lightly after and settled in the crook of her arm. The little waves sighed, the sea breeze whispered in the casuerina trees. Cho left the people behind and began her travels again, with the pony Gress and the Cat, Divine Endurance.

Acknowledgements

My thanks to Maud Casey, Bryan Loughrey, Chris Magness, Anne and Graham Holderness and Shantini Sockanathan. I must also acknowledge my debt to Bill (the bible) Dalton's *Indonesian Handbook* (Moon Publications, Michigan, USA, 1977), the best traveller's book in the world. The poem by Bettina Pfoestech appeared in *Emphasis*, the college magazine of UWCSEA, Singapore, 1978. The Mao Tsedung poem comes from *Mao Tse-Tung Poems*, Foreign Language Press, Peking, 1976.